THE CITY OF ONE-NIGHT STANDS

Stanley Carten

First published in Great Britain in 1992 by
Nexus
338 Ladbroke Grove
London W10 5AH

Copyright © Stanley Carten 1992
ISBN 0 352 32822 3
A catalogue record for this title is available from the
British Library

Typeset by TW Typesetting, Plymouth
Printed and bound in Great Britain by
Cox & Wyman Ltd, Reading, Berks.

CONTENTS

6 p.m.

AN APARTMENT ON HOLLYWOOD BOULEVARD

'Leave the panties on. You must not remove them – absolutely not – remember what I told you just a few minutes ago. Don't take them off, it will only spoil the effect, but yes, remove the bra – slowly, that's better – with your back towards me. Turn slightly, very slowly – I want Emilio to feast on your superb body for just a small moment.'

At twenty-seven Julia Majors was gratified to hear that she had a superb body. By any objective standard she did, but it never hurt to hear it verified. Unlike most of her competitors, Julia didn't have to spend hours in trendy west LA health clubs to maintain her figure. She was one of the lucky ones. Or was it really unlucky? She was never quite sure whether being beautiful in this land of plenty was a benefit or a detriment. Her good looks just always seemed to bring her as much trouble as they did good fortune. Julia Majors was the stereotypical Los Angeles beauty. Tanned, petite at just one hundred and five pounds and a slight five feet three inches tall, with shoulder-length strawberry blonde hair and a body that justifiably seemed to belong to somebody bigger, Julia defined sensuality. Her breasts jutted proudly from her small form, amply supported by what seemed like the longest legs in existence. Larger than life and effervescent to boot, Julia could easily pass for a much younger woman if she wished, and she'd learned that such perpetual youthfulness could be helpful in climbing the Holly-wood ladder.

And yet Julia was caught in a holding pattern by the very beauty that helped her open doors and melt hearts. Men wanted to possess her like some fragile china doll and were willing to promise her the moon in return for soon-to-be-revealed, undisclosed favours. Desperately desiring to be an actress, Julia was forever trapped on the casting couch, locked in the chains of her own good looks. And she was convinced it was time to break those bonds. And if it took drastic actions, so what? Hollywood thrived on headlines and scandal.

Just contemplating what she was about to do Julia Majors was sweating profusely in all of the places gorgeous Los Angeles women weren't supposed to sweat. She had rehearsed her fateful actions a thousand times, but it didn't seem to lessen the sickening sense of apprehension she felt now that The Moment was at hand. For the last few weeks she had thought about nothing but The Moment. In the shower, stuck in traffic, at slow times at the restaurant – even whilst making love – she had deliberated every action, practised every nuance. She knew what she must say and what she must do if she were ever to break free of the rut in which she was trapped. She kept telling herself it was now or never.

As instructed, Julia let the bra fall from her tanned shoulders whilst tantalisingly keeping her back to the rather overweight Emilio, who reclined, obscenely naked, on the undulating waterbed. In the shadows behind the bed stood the mysteriously slim figure who uttered commands and acted like he owned every aspect of Julia's being at this pivotal moment. She tried not to think of the two men gazing at her nearly nude beauty, but concentrated instead on extracting a relatively small object from her black leather purse. For what seemed like an eternity she rummaged through the 1990s flotsam and jetsam of her private necessities until her hands gave up the dance and gripped what she had been studiously trying to avoid finding.

As if anticipating the act she was about to commit, early evening sirens punctuated the Los Angeles sultry heat. Her fingers gripped the shiny steel object around its mother-of-pearl handle. She pivoted quickly, pointing the small Derringer pistol at the apparently surprised figure on the bed. Her deliciously full breasts swung to and fro in slow motion as she caught her breath. Like the point of a pendulum counting down the moments remaining in a man's life, her nipples inscribed condemning arcs in the stifling heat of the room. Julia's full camisole panties fluttered in the heavy air, stirred by an overworked electric fan that had long since given in to the oppressive Southern California summertime heat. Mesmerised by the hollow beating sound of her heart, she silently gasped as she felt moisture building between her thighs. Of all the feelings she had expected to experience at this moment, getting randy wasn't one of them.

She told herself her sexual excitement must be due to the shock of what she was about to do. Thoughts ran through her mind – perhaps this was the executioner's exhilaration? – a final salute – the ultimate kiss of death or something equally poetically cliché-ridden – to the hated figure before her. But more than thoughts coursed through her being as Julia tried desperately to ignore the slippery sound of her cuntlips separating as she stood, legs apart, aiming with accusingly rigid arms the small pistol at the startled figure struggling to extricate himself from the waves of the waterbed. Julia spoke clearly, trying not to let her nerves master her vocal cords.

'Never again you bastard. Never again. I'll never let you touch me. I'll never let you use me. I'll never let you fuck me – never – never.'

In the space of time it had taken her to utter those few phrases Julia had started screaming her words at fever pitch. Like some tragic opera soundtrack in concert with her aria, the sirens grew louder but they were not loud enough and close enough for the nude man whose erection was rapidly disappearing. He tried to speak and at the same time valiantly cover his dwindling manhood, as if his hands might fend off the projectile that the Derringer would soon emit. Julia knew she mustn't let Emilio utter a word. She did not want him to beg – this was not about humbling, it was about revenge. She could not let him use his well-worn phrases on her, for her resolve might too quickly break under the spell of his velvet tongue, as it had so many times before. She might never get another chance. She kept telling herself, no more chances – for him, nor for me.

'You've used me for your little games once too often. Your fucking days are over. This is for all the women you've fucked, and for all the good men you've screwed.'

'No – no – no . . .'

Several loud explosions shattered the room. Julia's ears rang with the blasts of the small gun and her vision was obscured by

3

smoke from the barrel. She'd had no idea that the gunshots would be so loud and that there would be so much smoke. It made her cough. As the blue smoke cleared she realised she was shaking and her knuckles were white with tension. Her nipples were as hard and as cold as the bullets she had loaded into the gun just a few moments ago. Small droplets of sweat and cunt moisture mingled and trickled past the delicate cream silk of her panties, making the long and exquisite journey down her tauntingly desirable thighs.

The sirens continued to grow louder. Closer.

The tall thin man wrapped the exhausted Julia in a light silk kimono decorated with extremely naughty hieroglyphics.

'You were *magnificent*, truly.'

'Really? You think so?'

'Yeah – the best we've seen yet. Ask Emilio.'

'Yeah – I thought I was a goner.'

Emilio lay on the waterbed drinking a beer. He was still naked, and he still looked obscene. Even more so because his erection had started to return now that he'd been granted his reprieve for the fourth time today. Julia pretended not to notice, assuming that the sexual reaction she'd experienced must also be felt by the victim, but somewhat delayed.

The tall thin man broke the silence.

'Well, just one more scene and I think we can call the audition a very successful wrap.'

Julia hesitated. She had to be at Ciao Baby to start waiting on tables by seven-thirty. It was already six-fifteen, and it was at least ten minutes to the restaurant at the best of times.

'No problems are there?'

'Well, I have to – no, no. Let's do it. Which scene do you want to see?'

Julia had quickly decided that she could afford to be a little late, especially if it meant landing her long-sought-after movie role. And she had a good feeling about how things were progressing. It quickly started to evaporate.

'Let's see – I think something difficult. You're obviously better than most of the girls we've had today, so let's go for scene six. You up for that, Emilio?'

'Six! Always.'

Emilio stroked his fat cock and chuckled.

Scene six was a particularly degrading one for the female lead. It was the scene that explained the origin of the woman's hatred for the man she would eventually shoot. Julia had hoped they wouldn't include it in the audition. A part of her knew they would. She toyed with the idea of walking out. Xavier, the tall thin man, sensed her hesitation, put a well-practised arm around her and shepherded her to a corner of the room. He spoke in staccato phrases, seemingly unable to finish a sentence, so typical of the lingua franca of the Los Angeles movie industry.

'Look, Julia babe, I know you're hesitant about doing six, but trust me – I gotta know if you're that good. *Avenging Beauty* is a tough movie, and I need a tough babe to play that lead. I think it could be you, but I can't take a chance with my backers. If I sign you – a relative unknown, who I happened to meet when she served me dinner at Ciao Baby – and we could sign tonight, really – I mean it – I'll even come by the restaurant and let you know our decision in person. That's how confident I am that they'll like what they see – but put yourself in my shoes. If I sign you up and you go cold on us when it comes to the real thing – well, my ass is grass, babe. I just gotta know.'

The references to her job had the desired effect of letting Julia know just where she stood in the grand scheme of things. She needed them more than they needed her. Or at least that's what they wanted her to think. Julia decided to be more agreeable.

'You think I'm that close?'

'Trust me. Union rules won't let me show you the tapes of the other girls, but you are miles above them. If you can put everything you've got into scene six, and I mean everything – well, it's showtime for you, babe.'

Julia smiled and nodded with a delightful shrug of her shoulders.

'OK. Let's do it.'

'That's my girl. Now why don't you go and get changed into your gear, and I'll set the lights and the room ready for the scene.'

'OK.'

* * *

'*Aaand* – action!'

Xavier knocked on a wall to simulate the tapping on a door. Emilio, sitting at a typical office desk, responded without looking up from his papers.

'Yes?'

Even though Emilio was now dressed in a slick $1200 Hugo Boss charcoal grey double-breasted suit, he was still overweight, and he was still obscene. As she walked passed the camera, simulating her entrance into the room, Julia fought keenly to put all of her personal distaste for this grotesque man out of her mind. She kept telling herself that this was acting, playing a role. Famous movie stars did it all the time. Not to worry – it was just acting, a job. Be professional.

'Mr Waxman – I was quite surprised that you wanted to see me and not my husband. He is much more knowledgeable about our finances . . .'

'Well, yes – that's the point. In transactions of this kind where the husband mortgages everything that he and his wife own to save a business, we – I – like to be sure that it is indeed a joint decision, and that you are not being pressured into risking all that you've worked for.'

'That's very considerate of you, Mr Waxman.'

'Call me Bill.'

'Bill.'

'I need to be sure that you are behind your husband all the way.'

'Well, rest assured I am. All the way as you say. This loan means everything to him, and so many banks have turned him down. You are his last chance, and I'm very grateful that you are going to help us. He's been a new man since you told him that you'd go ahead with the loan.'

'A new man?'

'Yes. So much more carefree – so much more loving.'

'I'm so glad. He is a lucky man to have such a nice, young, beautiful and willing wife to support him.'

'There's isn't anything I wouldn't do for Roger. We are so much in love.'

'Really. Well, if this loan means that much to you, I'm going to have to ask for a little more collateral.'

'But – but we don't have anything else. Just the house.'

'I was thinking of something more intangible.' The look on Emilio/Bill Waxman's face left nothing to the imagination of the viewer. Emilio played a good pervert.

Julia Majors, aka Mrs Lynn Wordley, loving and faithful wife of Mr Roger Wordley, stared at Mr Bill Waxman in disbelief. Julia had practised the look for weeks. She was proud of it. As required by the script she stood up in a huff and turned to leave. With Waxman slightly out of focus in the background the camera close-focused on her lovely blue eyes. Waxman's voice echoed in the room.

'Your husband tried to commit suicide, didn't he, after the last loan rejection?'

'You bastard. You absolute bastard.'

'Come, come, Mrs Wordley. You are in no position to call me names. Beggars cannot be choosers. Now just come over here and drop your knickers while I fix me a drink, and we'll consummate the deal. Or walk out of here and start making the funeral arrangements for Roger. What's it going to be, Mrs Wordley?'

Waxman's last few words weren't a question. He knew he had her. He knew he would have her.

The camera focused on the tears forming at the corners of Julia's deep blue eyes. They were real. She wasn't acting any more. The scene had become real. All too real.

Julia/Lynn walked back to the desk and placed her purse on the chair. She didn't sit down. Emilio/Bill fixed himself a large scotch on the rocks and sat down in his executive chair.

'Now don't be a stranger, Mrs Wordley. Come here.'

Julia made her way behind the desk and stood next to Emilio's rotund form. He started to sip his drink from the glass in his right hand, and with his left hand he reached around and pulled Julia towards him. Her body went rigid as his hand squeezed her firm pantyhose-covered bottom through the thin fabric of her light summer dress. He marvelled at the delicious feel of her tight ass under the tautness of the nylon. He could tell he was going to enjoy this one.

'You certainly have a nice ass, Mrs Wordley. But I think it is a little overdressed. Didn't I tell you to take your knickers off?'

Again, the Waxman character wasn't asking a question. The Lynn Wordley character wasn't supposed to respond.

'I said get your knickers down. Or would you like me to tear up these loan papers?'

'No! No – I will. I'll take my panties off for you.'

Julia's words were barely audible. She was lost in the role. This was no longer acting. She had become Lynn Wordley. Julia's plight was Lynn's and vice versa. For Lynn it was the saving of her husband's business and perhaps his life – for Julia it was the chance of her big break and the saving of her own career. She thoroughly identified with Lynn Wordley's predicament. She wanted the movie role as bad as Mrs Lynn Wordley wanted to save her husband's business, and had resigned herself to doing whatever she had to to get her big break in the movies.

'Well, the moment I see your bush I'll start signing these papers.'

Reluctantly Julia lifted underneath the hem of her dress and hooked her fingers into the taut band of her flesh-coloured tights. Gripping her camisole knickers at the same time as she pulled her pantyhose down, the script called for Bill Waxman's interruption. Emilio didn't miss the cue.

'Don't take them all the way off. Leave on those nice high heels – spread your legs a little and leave your knickers and your pantyhose around your ankles. It'll stop you from running away, although I don't think you will. I've never had any complaints, you know. Now why don't you show me what a nice little bush Roger gets to fuck.'

Julia slapped Emilio's face with all the force she could muster. She meant to hurt him, but the fat of his cheeks easily absorbed the blow.

'Temper, temper. That'll cost you at least an extra point on the closing costs. Now lift up your dress, Mrs Wordley.'

Obviously beaten, realising the futility of her protests, Julia complied with Emilio's commands, lifting the hem to her waist. She felt degraded beyond her wildest fears. It's only acting, she kept telling herself – only acting.

'Hmmmm.'

Emilio sipped his scotch and continued his appraisal of Julia's fine body.

'This is good scotch, you know – the best money can buy. And by the looks of that pretty little blonde bush, so are you. Roger sure is a lucky fellow.'

This time Julia didn't slap Emilio.

'Good, good – now you are learning. I think I'll start looking over the fine print of this loan agreement if you don't mind. Just stand there looking sexy. Try and get a little juicy if you could.'

Emilio began to read aloud word by word the thick bundle of legal papers. Every few sentences he'd pause and take a long look at Julia's pussy as he casually sipped the scotch that was rapidly diluting under the clammy heat of his sweaty hand. By the end of the first paragraph he'd let his left hand slip from the desk to stroke the inner flesh of Julia's warm thigh. As Emilio made his way down the first page of the document he inched closer to that lovely spot between her trembling legs. She could not watch his progress – she stared out through the dusty window into the smog of the Los Angeles basin and choked back her emotions. She felt as if that hazy brown atmospheric mud on the horizon was swallowing her body and soul. She felt as if she was drowning and there was no one to throw her a life preserver. The script said that at this point Lynn Wordley was to look as if she was thinking of the sacrifice she was making for her husband. Julia had no difficulty in creating that impression. She simply focused on the sacrifice she was making for her career. No one could have told the difference.

As Emilio turned the first page of the document he moved his pudgy fingers in one deliberate and forceful movement from stroking the upper part of Julia's soft thigh to up between the flesh of her pussy lips, past her clitoris where he began to tease her tawny blonde pubic hair, creating the impression that perhaps he wasn't interested in Julia's tender flesh. She fought her body's natural tendency to lubricate, trying not to let Emilio know that his toying was having any effect. She tried to pretend it was just like visiting the doctor, but her concentrations were to little effect. Slowly and surely, Julia felt her cunt begin to release its telltale musky signature.

Emilio continued the teasing of Julia's pubic hair for a few more moments. Balanced precariously on her high heels, legs locked at the ankles by the taut constrictions of her pantyhose and camisole knickers, she teetered backwards and forwards as Emilio pushed and pulled at her pubic mound. Once Julia almost fell backwards until Emilio's fat hand reached behind her and stopped her rocking by grasping tightly at her ass. He pulled Julia closely towards him and breathed his hot, scotch-tainted breath on her tanned skin, rustling her soft pubic hairs in the process.

'You have the tightest butt. Does Roger fuck you there? You know, right here?'

He'd slid his thumb from Julia's buttocks and was letting the digit dance around the sensitive skin of her puckered sphincter. It wasn't hard for Julia to recite her lines.

'No, no – he doesn't.'

'Doesn't surprise me – I bet he likes it here, though.'

Emilio rapidly cocked his thumb and like a released coiled spring it shot past Julia's asshole and penetrated her cunt. He burrowed his thumb into her pussy as far as her body would allow so that the top of his clenched hand was grinding against her clitoris. Julia gasped like a burst balloon at the sudden penetration of her sensitised pussy.

'Now, where was I? You sure are some distraction, Mrs Wordley.'

Emilio turned from the seductive sight of Julia impaled upon his thumb and went back to the reading of the loan agreement. Never once did he give her any relief, all the while keeping his thumb firmly imbedded in her cunt. As called out by the script he mumbled parts of the contract out loud, intermingled with lewd comments designed to infuriate and degrade the black-mailed woman. The script called for Julia to close her eyes and act almost zombielike whilst gradually displaying a sense of sexual enjoyment from the fat man's stimulations. It wasn't difficult for Julia to comply. It came naturally. She was disgusted with her actions but excused them under the banner of the potential gains she would reap once she hit the big time. And besides, she kept telling herself, it's only acting.

'Payments shall be due on . . . Isn't this the best hand job you've ever had?

'This agreement supersedes all oral . . .

'Do you clit yourself like this when Roger is away on business getting a bit of cunny?

'The term of the loan shall be . . .

'Have you ever thought of whoring, Mrs Wordley? You'd be real good – you'd earn a pretty penny with a cunt as tight as this.

'Insurance shall be the responsibility . . .'

Julia didn't answer any of his jibes – she just stood there rocking backwards and forwards trying hard to act disinterested. Finally, after a few more pages of contract talk, right on cue, she broke down.

'Can't you get it over with? Why must you do this to me – this way?'

'Because you'll like it so much better when I finally do stick my dick inside of you – and I'm in no rush. I've still got at least six more pages to go. Don't you like foreplay? Don't tell me Roger just sticks it right in without warming up the old honeypot.'

Julia rolled back her head and closed her eyes in submission. The script called for her to look as though she realised that she'd made a mistake by protesting, and that the helplessness of her situation was taking charge of her body's actions. Julia achieved this impression by quietly moaning a catlike purr as her bottom slowly gyrated on Emilio's hand. Her cunt gripped his thumb tightly as she let her juices flow over his cocklike digit. His thumb was large and fat with many ridges, and as she ground her pussy against his hand she could feel his thumb flex at the joint as it probed deep inside.

'I do believe you're enjoying this, you naughty woman. What would Roger say?'

Julia just let out a louder, deeper moan. Her head rolled back and her shoulder-length blonde hair tickled her back, damp with sweat.

'I think Roger would want you to learn a few new tricks – like how to take it in the ass.'

Emilio slipped his largest finger straight into Julia's tight bottom. The juice from her cunt had liberally lubricated his hand making entry into the constrictive opening relatively easy. At the shock of such unexpected entry Julia collapsed her weight on to Emilio's arm. He used the corner of the desk to support her. Grinding his thumb and finger together between the thin no-man's-land of flesh between her two openings, Emilio toyed with Julia as if she were a hand puppet and he the puppetmaster.

With his free hand he finished the last of his scotch and went back to the loan agreement. His fingers masturbated Julia as if he were some automatic finger-fucking machine. He paid her little attention other than the physical abuse his hand doled out. Julia repaid the courtesy admirably, acting as if she were spending an intimate session with her favourite dildo. She lifted the hem of her dress higher so that her hands could touch the points of her nipples through the soft cotton of the dress. The lace of her bra was soaked in sweat, causing the two little points to peak through the dampness and stand out under the stark glare of the video lights. This movement hadn't been called for in the script but Julia had heard that all great actresses improvised – and her body was at the point of losing complete control, on a sexual autopilot all of its own creating. This is how Lynn Wordley would have acted, she kept telling herself. She would have played with her nipples. Julia was sure of it.

'The reason you're enjoying this so much is that being frigged standing up is the best way for a woman to get off.'

Julia just rubbed her mound harder on Emilio's thumb and nodded her assent. The sensations were more intense. She increased the pressure on her nipples by pinching them between her fingers. Her lips puckered with the painful feelings the action caused.

'Yeah. All your weight is concentrated on your little clit and when you come your legs will melt. The last bit of support you have will give way and your come-drenched cunt will be forced by all your weight on to my hand. You'll come like it was the first and last time you were fucked. I bet you'll make Roger do it standing up tonight. You'll be so randy after I've finished with you that you'll fuck the doorknob if Roger can't get it up.'

Julia's cunt was flowing heavily with her juices. Emilio's hand was soaked and wrinkled from the torrent. It made his skin all that more pleasurable to rub against. Every ridge and wrinkle flicked her clitoris to and fro in a crazy roller coaster ride over the titillating terrain of his hand. Almost without noticing her resistance crumble, Julia began to enjoy the feeling of being touched this way.

Emilio was a master at manipulation. He knew he'd won the battle. It was now time to win the war. He turned back to the contract.

'Now where was I? Oh, yes – the last page. And the parties do hereby consent and agree . . .'

To Julia these words were lost in a general buzzing that bounced around the room uncontrollably. Her head spun as her cunt ground into Emilio's hand. Her pussy splayed open, completely baring the raw pinkness of her inner lips. His finger, deep inside her ass, pulsed within the dark canal, sending lightninglike shafts of pain and pleasure up her spine. She could feel herself closing in on orgasm.

'Signed this day, Bill Waxman, President of Waxman Financials. Looks OK to me – what do you think, Mrs Wordley? Anything you'd like to change? Are all the i's dotted and the t's crossed? Hmmm? I don't think you're listening to me, Mrs Wordley.'

Julia was bucking violently as her body shook to and fro. Her legs were bouncing off of the floor as her orgasm racked through her. Without any real warning her splendid gams collapsed, focusing all of her one hundred and five pounds on to one small spot of flesh that at the present moment seemed to contain her whole being. The rapidly changing sensations were like electric shocks that tossed her body skyward, almost at once to be pulled roughly back down hard on to Emilio's clenched hand by the finger that was up her bottom. The repeated vibrations further taunting her sensitive clitoris to heights of ecstasy Julia had before only imagined. Like the inner mechanisms of an electric buzzer, Julia was repelled and attracted in rapid fashion, banging her cunt on Emilio's fist. It was as good as he'd promised.

'I'd better sign this thing. Oh my goodness, is that the time? I have another appointment. My – how time flies when you're having fun.'

Emilio pulled his hand away and Julia collapsed on the floor. Breathing heavily she could hear the scratch of his fountain pen on the crisp legal paper of the loan agreement. From the depths of her orgasm-drained body she couldn't help but feel that she'd won.

It was a Pyrrhic victory.

'Get up, Mrs Wordley – get up! Pull up your panties and your pantyhose and get up. I have another appointment, and there is no other door for you to leave by, so you'll have to hide here, under my desk. Quickly – he'll be here any minute.'

Grabbing at her purse and half-heartedly pulling up her undergarments, Julia/Lynn Wordley practically fell under the executive desk. Luckily it was completely enclosed so the appointment wouldn't be able to see her slouched form. Her mind wandered over the times that she'd read the script over and over again, gradually realising how intense an erotic thriller *Avenging Beauty* would be, going much farther than the accepted standards of the day. She'd recalled that a lot of what was done sexually in the script wouldn't make it on to camera. There would be a lot of close-ups of carefully cropped body parts and a lot of moaning and heavy breathing. All of the tantilising editing would be to prevent the movie from receiving an X rating, something that would be fatal to its commercial success. So, since most of the sex was going to be implied, Julia didn't quite see why she had to go all the way in this audition. She'd thought to bring this point up with Xavier when he'd suggested doing scene six but thought better of it. They wanted to see if she'd got what it took to do the job, that was it. She was sure she'd more than convinced them of her capabilities as an actress, but perhaps this was some sort of test of her professionalism? Emilio and his alter ego Bill Waxman disturbed her musings with something that she was sure wasn't in the original script. She had reached the point where it was easier to say 'yes' than 'no'.

'Now, Mrs Wordley, I want you to suck on my dick while I conduct this next appointment. Don't make too much noise while you're doing it either. I'm sure you wouldn't want to give yourself away. Roger wouldn't like that, would he? I'm sure he wouldn't want to know that his pretty little wife let herself be frigged by, fucked by and sucked off the kind Mr Waxman just to obtain Roger's precious loan. And to think she enjoyed it as well. He wouldn't want to know, would he? He might go over the edge and do something silly. You never know, do you, Mrs Wordley? And I still could tear up these papers. So wrap your lovely pink lips around this and be nice. Suck it as good as you suck Roger's penis. OK?'

The last few words were mixed with a truly diabolical laugh that left Julia in no doubt as to her options. Emilio unzipped the trousers of his Hugo Boss suit and let a fat dick fall out. It was stubby, but large in circumference. The foreskin was tacky with a foul stickiness. The slit in the top seemed to be leering at Julia.

'Well, what you are waiting for? Suck my dick, Mrs Wordley. Slowly, please.'

As soon as Julia had put her lips to the tip of Emilio's cock, she heard the simulated knocking on the door. As much as she knew it was fake she jumped and pulled away from her ministrations. Emilio's hand cradled her head and forced her back to his cock.

'Come in – enter.'

'Ah, good day, Mr Waxman.'

The voice belonger to Xavier. Julia surmised he must have put the camera on automatic and decided to play this part. Slowly the script that she'd learned so well came back to her. Even so, she still wasn't mentally prepared for what came next. So well had she immersed herself in the role that the next declaration hit her like a low punch to the solar plexus.

'Good day, Mr Wordley. Forgive me if I don't get up but I pulled a muscle exercising and it is a little painful to move.'

Julia tried to pull her head back, but Emilio's grip was like a vice. He squeezed her temples until she complied and kept sucking his throbbing dick as quietly as a mouse.

'Well, let me shake the hand of a soon-to-be-very successful businessman, Mr Wordley.'

'Why, thank you. You won't regret it.'

'I'm sure I won't.'

Emilio shook hands with Roger Wordley with the same hand that moments earlier had been up Mrs Wordley's cunt and ass. Julia was horrified. Too horrified to stop. She thought how Mrs Wordley would feel. Desperate not to be found out by her husband, she would suck away like the expert cocksucker she was. She would not give Waxman the luxury of seeing her crumble.

'Now, why don't you look over the contract word for word? Take your time. I don't want there to be any surprises for you or Mrs Wordley.'

Julia started at the mention of her character's name. It made her try to ignore the predicament she was in. She resolved to concentrate solely on the fat hard cock between her lips and shut out all other comments. Julia pressed her lips tightly against the shaft and moved her head up and down its stubby length. She used her tongue to probe the cock's head, toying with the foreskin. Emilio squirmed in his executive chair as Julia's hands cradled his balls. She pulled individual hairs on his scrotum almost to breaking point. Once more Emilio shifted. This time he forced her head down into his furry nest of sweaty hairs and held her immobilised there. With his stubby cock fully down her throat, Julia fought to stop from gagging on the obstacle. She swallowed deeply, compressing the cock with her mouth. After several pulsations, Emilio released her head. With long strokes of her hand she continued her onslaught, combined with liberal lashes of her tongue, she was attempting to bring Emilio off with her character's husband still in the room. Call it vengeance, call it perverted, call it whatever – Julia was sure that Mrs Wordley would have done the same.

'Is everything in order?'

'Yes, yes – everything seems to be as it should be. Do I sign here?'

'Yes, please.'

At the sound of the imminent loan agreement signing Julia increased her throaty pressure on Emilio's cock. Her thumb and index finger barely wrapped around the turgid shaft making a constricting opening with which she wanked Emilio's dick. Emilio was shifting his weight every few seconds as Julia sucked the life from his cock.

'It is a pleasure doing business with you, Mr Waxman.'

'Oh, the pleasure – the pleasure – is all mine.'

It was clear to the Mr Wordley character that the Waxman character was being distracted by something. The script called for Roger Wordley to assume it was the muscle pull contracting painfully.

'Well, I can see that you'll want to get some attention to that pulled muscle of yours, so I'll be on my way.'

'Here's the ccchhheeccck.'

Emilio coughed loudly as he emptied his balls into Julia's

16

throat. She sucked tighter and tighter, swallowing the load and further sensitising his swollen head.

'You won't regret this, Mr Waxman. My wife and I are forever in your debt.'

'Ah, my pleasure – and give my best to your lovely wife next time you see her.'

'Oh, I certainly will. We'll have some celebrating to do tonight.'

'I'm sure you will. Good day, Mr Wordley.'

'Good day, Mr Waxman.'

Julia finally released the still swollen cock from her mouth's vicelike grip. At this point the script called for a fade to black and a change of scene, only it seemed that Julia wasn't the only one in an improvisational mood.

'OK, Mrs Wordley, the foreplay is over. Now I want that pussy of yours.'

Emilio offered his pudgy hand to Julia, who refused his offer with a shrug of disgust. She wrestled herself out from under the desk just to be quickly thrown on top of the walnut desk like some child's rag doll. Emilio pinioned Julia on the polished wood of his desk with his bulging form. Papers, pens and other business items flew all over the room. Julia was breathing hard. Emilio was snarling in her ear. She wasn't the only one lost in the intensity of the script.

'Thought you could get the upper hand, did you, Mrs Wordley? Well, I admire your spunk – but I've got more than you and I'm going to give you a fucking you'll never forget. There's a lot of interest on your husband's loan, and I find you very interesting, Mrs Wordley. Think of this as your first payment. And I'm very interested in fucking you a lot. How shall we compound the interest? Monthly? Weekly? Or perhaps daily?'

Julia just started laughing. It seemed like the exact thing that Lynn Wordley would do in the same situation. The carefree taunting enraged Emilio further. He wasted no time in hoisting Julia's legs on to his shoulders and tearing open the front of her cotton summer dress. The material gave way like tissue paper under his forceful grip. The fancy lace of Julia's bra provided a similarly weak barrier to Emilio's lustful attentions. He eagerly foisted his hands on her titties, twirling the nipples in agonising circles of twisted flesh. Julia seemed not to notice. She just kept laughing and rolling her head from side to side. Emilio's cock was still hard from the vampirelike sucking Julia had administered. Her cunt was still soaked from the hand job he had wrought upon her. Grabbing Julia by the thighs he slid her whole body on to his cock. The desk was the perfect height for someone of Emilio's stature to be fucking Julia. A taller man would have had to crouch to insert his cock into her soaked cunt.

Such details mattered little to Julia as she locked her legs behind Emilio's neck and used the leverage they gave her to twist from side to side. As Emilio's engorged dick slammed into her mound her twisting allowed her to rotate her cunt around his cock delivering a delightful swirling feeling to Emilio's penis. The tightness of her wet cunt pulled at his fat cockflesh like a wine bottle refusing to release its cork. Emilio would thrust in as hard as he could, and Julia's cunt would hold on to the shaft as long as her muscles could remain tense. And still she laughed.

'So you think it's funny do you, Mrs Wordley? How funny is it going to be when Roger smells my come in your cunt when he tries to eat your muff tonight? Will you be laughing when he calls you a slag-bitch-whore?'

Emilio's taunts had little effect on the lust ravaged Julia who was in a world of sex-induced delirium. Laughing was the perfect defence that told the man fucking her that it was all in good fun. You can't hurt me her laughs shouted. I'm enjoying this – keep it up.

The fullness of Julia's tits shuddered as she lay on her back on the desk, her luscious body being pummelled by Emilio's hefty bulk. From side to side and in hypnotic swirling motions her breasts gyrated as her cunt was pounded. She kept her long tanned legs wrapped around Emilio's neck affording her the extra purchase to squeeze her pussy that much tighter around his dick. In doing so she would prick Emilio's neck with the pointy heels of her shoes, like some pony-express rider desperate for every ounce of speed out of her mount.

Emilio never really noticed the pain of Julia's heels, so much was he captivated by the sight of his penis forcing its juicy way into Julia's cunt. With her legs hooked around his neck, he had a perfect view of her pouting cuntlips being pried apart with each urgent thrust by his fat cockhead. His fat pudgy hands tightly gripped Julia's thighs as he attempted to fight her twisting motions. Emilio wanted to plunge in and out as fast as his cock could stand the intensity, but Julia's wrestling body held his cock firmly deep inside her, refusing to let it escape so easily. And still she laughed as though Emilio's cock was a feather duster tickling her most sensitive of spots.

Deep within his balls Emilio felt the first surgings of his second orgasm willingly building to release. The writhing cunt on the desk was good – very good – even if she was a little bit crazy. She was easily the best of the girls he'd fucked today. None of them had lasted this far.

From deep within her Julia felt Emilio's cock building for orgasm too. Her sensitive insides detected the minute twitching and rhythmic throbbing of Emilio's shaft that betrayed the explosion of sperm soon to erupt from the bubbling slit at the top of his cock. With every ounce of strength her body could muster she gripped Emilio's penis tighter than she would normally have done to her nastiest of dildos. Her sex-pounded brain actually visualised snapping off the stubby member. She laughed harder as she imagined her cunt spitting out the shaft, and the look of absolute horror on Emilio's face at the sight of his proud maleness rolling and flapping on the floor like a dying fish out of water.

The extra tightness around his cock was not unnoticeable to Emilio, who actually enjoyed the sensation. It was rather like masturbating, he thought – the way her cunt gripped the lower portion of his shaft was almost as good as the way his hand would strangle his penis just as he was about to come when he'd jack off to a really good porn movie.

With one almighty thrust Emilio pushed his cock as far as it would go inside Julia's writhing cunt. She responded by twisting her whole body almost totally off the desk. From side to side she rolled, desperate not to let go of the pulsating member. She could hear the deep moanings of Emilio's orgasm cry building in his chest. She felt like coaxing him to release.

Amidst her laughing Julia improvised a few lines that she thought Mrs Wordley would most probably have uttered at a time like this.

19

'Fill me with your spunk, Bill. Show me you can fuck better than Roger. He can do it two, three, sometimes four times. He knows just . . .'

Julia was interrupted by Emilio's bellowing. He didn't moan so much as scream. He stood fully on his tiptoes and pulled Julia off the desk by her tits. Impaled on his turgid cock she wrapped her arms around his neck to take the strain off of her breasts as the orgasming brute staggered around the room. Bumping against walls and stumbling into furniture they resembled some crazed wounded animal, resiliently refusing to give way to its desperate death throes.

Held firmly on his cock, Julia kept bucking into Emilio's flabby abdomen, slapping her ass against his stomach, draining every last drop of come she could out of his cock. As if Emilio's will to continue evaporated with the last drop of his orgasm, his eyes rolled skyward and he collapsed backward with a resounding slap onto the wood floor of the apartment. Julia sat on top of him, like some conquering fighter, proud of her accomplishment.

'*Aaand* – cut.'

Julia was startled – she'd completely forgotten about the erstwhile director Xavier. His clinical announcement brought her immediately back to earth and the grim realisation that all along she had been supposedly acting. She stood quickly up letting Emilio's cock slip out of her cunt and slap against his flab. It was a rude and fitting fanfare to the fucking that had just taken place.

'Words can't describe how brilliant you were. You are a natural – you're gonna go far just the way you are, baby.'

Xavier was positively gushing with clichéd superlatives. Julia noticed that the bulge in his designer jeans clearly indicated that he'd enjoyed her improvising.

'So you think I'll get the part?'

His response was almost too gratuitous.

'Of course, of course. You will most certainly with a performance like that. Words – they just fail me.'

'When will we sign a contract?'

It mattered little to Julia that she was half naked talking business with a sleazy director with a hard-on in too-tight designer jeans. She wanted to strike while the iron was literally hot.

'I'll meet with the backers in a little over an hour. We should be able to finalise everything this evening. Contracts should be ready by early next week. I'll come by Ciao Baby tonight to give you the good news.'

The mention of the restaurant brought Julia back to the necessities of earning her living. It was already seven – she just had enough time to get changed and fight the early evening traffic. With any luck she'd make it to work on time and avoid a leering lecture from the lascivious manager who relished every opportunity to order her into his office for a 'reprimand'.

'Great – well, I'll get changed and see you later. Tell Emilio I'm sorry I got a little caught up in the part.'

'Oh, you weren't the only one – I'm sure he didn't mind.'

The snoring obscene blob on the floor snorted its compliance.

The gods of LA traffic smiled on Julia Majors' old VW. With just a few evasive turns here and there she was able to miss the stalled automobiles and get to the restaurant with at least three minutes to spare. Not bad, she thought. Not bad indeed. As Julia clocked in and donned the 'cute' tuxedolike waitress uniform, she daydreamed longingly of the day when she wouldn't have to wait on tables ever again. She looked forward to the day when she wouldn't be half lying when she told people she was an actress. Maybe today's audition would be the big break she'd so desperately thought she deserved? With every order that she took she kept her eye on the door hoping to see Xavier brimming over with good news.

They had planned it well, even down to having a 'legitimate' script for *Avenging Beauty* printed on a major studio's stationery. Xavier and Emilio had even gone so far as to rent one of those movie equipment rental trucks and park it outside the apartment to create the impression that a professional crew was on hand. And the five girls that had fallen for the audition story had all been real good lookers and all too eager to get the part to read the fine print of their audition agreements. Tucked between paragraphs about rights of first refusal and force majeure was a paragraph that said that the producers had the rights to use the audition footage however they pleased in whatever form they pleased without any further consent from the auditionee.

There would be no visit by Xavier (not his real name) to Ciao Baby to bring Julia the happy news of her big break, tonight or any other night. If the five girls who'd literally given their all for the promise of a major movie role were lucky, they'd just forget the whole experience and chalk it up to another one-night stand. A matter best forgotten. Nothing ventured, nothing gained and all that stuff.

And if they were unlucky enough, sometime in the next few months, Julia Majors and the other four girls might hear of a cheaply produced extremely sleazy porno movie, featuring women that looked a lot like themselves. It would be no small consolation to Julia that out of the five women duped that hot Hollywood afternoon, Xavier had had three of them and Emilio two, although they both agreed that the last one was by far the best.

They had at least been honest with Julia about that.

7 p.m.

A Downtown Penthouse

The tanned muscular body sprawled underneath Marlene Neumann reminded her of the city some thirty floors below her penthouse suite. Seemingly without end, as far as the eye could see, Los Angeles teemed from ocean to desert. Subtle and crude at the same time, the city and its environs always held some surprise for even its most jaded of residents. But it was so easy to get tired of its plenitude.

Just like this young male body I'm riding, mused Marlene as she rocked backwards and forwards on his statuesque penis. He lay back on her gigantic king-size bed, arms stretched towards the San Gabriel Mountains, legs spread wide to the beckoning Pacific. Through the floor-to-ceiling windows the gradually setting sun illuminated his Adonis-like form in a warm orange glow. As Marlene slid up and down upon the immense length of his dick, the sun, shining through her open thighs, cast an intriguingly tall shadow of the young stud's shaft all the way up from his pubic hairs to his chest. In that frozen moment of time in which Marlene reversed her motion she found herself hanging in space, her breasts swaying pendulously, her body poised on the pinnacle of his cock, all in an effort to prolong the startling visual effect created by the unique alignment of his erect dick, the setting sun and her own open and moist thighs. Marlene's mind wandered from fucking to thinking of ancient druids building unfathomable monuments whose sole purpose seemed to be to cast a shadow of some erected stone through an archway of similar stones at one equinox or another. At precisely the right moment some ancient old man with a beard and flowing robes would sacrifice a virgin and there would be a lot of blood and a lot of fucking, and then . . .

'What are you thinking about?'

Amazingly, the muscular hulk on the bed had noticed that Marlene seemed to be in another universe that didn't have him at the centre. She toyed with the idea of telling him exactly what she'd been thinking, but thought that talk of ancient druids might confuse him. She decided it would be best to flatter his immense ego.

'Oh, I was thinking what a great fuck you are. How I haven't had a dick as good as yours for – for ages.'

'Yeah – I like to keep in shape.'

He was so predictable. Marlene closed her eyes and let the sun warm her back as she continued to work his throbbing boner for all it was worth. She fought the little nagging demons in the back of her mind that told her that this early evening one night stand was all a very big mistake that she might soon deeply regret. As she happily satisfied her primal urges in a most whorish fashion she primly chastised herself for taking the real-life equivalent of the Incredible Hulk to bed. A few hours ago it seemed like the right thing to do. Now she wasn't so sure.

He worked in the law office's mail room and had been assigned to help Marlene move several heavy boxes of case files from a client's office to her office. There was a certain urgency in accomplishing the transfer so Marlene readily agreed to take care of the business on Saturday. They'd met at the law office at noon. For the life of her she couldn't remember his name. It was one of those names like Scott or Brent or Troy, but he seemed to answer quite well to 'hey you', so Marlene didn't try too hard to get his moniker down.

Marlene had dressed for business as she would normally do on a weekday. The clients were important to the firm, so she thought it best to look the slick $300-per-hour lawyer she was. Shane (that was his real name) had dressed for moving heavy boxes on a hot summer day. He wore skimpy running shorts that flared open at mid-thigh and a very brief muscle-revealing tank top. Marlene and Shane were a study in the contrasts so typical of life in Los Angeles. He had sun-bleached curly blond short hair and every inch of his two-hundred pound, six-foot-four hard body was tanned. She had straight shoulder-length auburn hair and was porcelainlike fair all over her slender five-foot-six, one-hundred-and-ten-pound figure. Against Marlene's primly conservative blue silk suit, charcoal grey stockings and properly low blue-suede Via Spiga designer shoes, Shane looked almost like an overgrown little schoolboy being taken to play with his friends by his very proper mother. Only Shane wasn't so little, Marlene noticed as he stepped into her BMW 325i convertible, 'accidentally' revealing quite an expanse of cockflesh peeking out from underneath his shiny black running shorts. And Marlene, successfully single and always on the lookout for a new dick to try, wasn't thinking like a very proper mother as she put the car in gear and headed out to the client's offices in Burbank.

It took the better part of three hours for Marlene to go through all the files and tag the items she needed transferred. Due to his rather casual appearance, Marlene thought it better to have Shane wait outside by the car until she needed his muscles. As she boxed manila folder after manila folder of contracts and agreements that probably weren't worth the paper they were printed on, she kept glancing out of the window at Shane's provocative sunbathing. He'd taken off his next-to-nothing tank top and was lying face down on the grass listening to exercise disco music on his personal stereo. Every so often he'd thrust his pelvis off of the ground and wiggle it in the air quite suggestively. Marlene found herself staring through her studious glasses at his gyrations and thinking what it would be like to be under his thrusting hulk. The thought shocked her – he wasn't her type at all. Marlene found herself wondering what the brutal attraction of this dolt was. She always went for the more sophisticated men – usually older and worldly, not rough-trade-raw-meat like Scott or whatever his name was.

It must be the heat, she told herself, and resolved to go for a cooling swim in the rooftop pool the moment she got back to her penthouse apartment.

It was thus quite a surprise to her to hear the following words come out of her mouth once Shane had finished unloading the mountain of boxes she'd crammed into the BMW.

'I wonder if you wouldn't mind help me moving some of my furniture. I've only been in my apartment a month, and I'm just finding out how wrong the movers were when they placed things . . .?'

'Sure. Lead the way,' had been Shane's innocent reply. The look on his face had been anything but innocent as the car pulled out of the underground garage and into the bright sunlight for the few blocks journey to DownTown Towers. Little was said as they rode up the thirty floors in the elevator to Marlene's penthouse apartment, both imaginations being too busy to bother with words.

'Let's see. Do you think you could move that table more into the centre of the room?'

'No problem.' And indeed it wasn't. Shane hardly broke a sweat.

'That's much better. Now do you think you could come here in the bedroom and help me move the bed?'

'I'd love to come in your bedroom.'

Marlene gave Shane a mock reprimanding look as he smiled smugly at his ability to dish out double entendres.

'I'd like to move the bed over to that wall so that I can see the sun rise and set from it.'

'Planning on spending a lot of time in bed?'

Again there was the smug smile. Marlene couldn't help but feel like a child molester. Shane must have been all of eighteen or nineteen – and here she was, a thirty-year-old lawyer, soon to be partner in one of Los Angeles' most prestigious law firms. It was obvious that he knew what she had in mind, and he seemed more than willing to oblige.

Marlene took one corner of the bed and Shane the rest. He was capable of moving it on his own, but Marlene felt obliged to do some of the positioning. She was bent over the corner of the bed, facing Shane, when a seemingly innocent comment he made caught her unawares.

'Nice view.'

Marlene looked over her shoulder at the sprawling landscape of downtown Los Angeles, resplendent through the floor-to-ceiling windows of her bedroom. She'd wondered when he would show some signs of being impressed with her rather exclusive location. It had taken a while for Shane to show his appreciation of her wealth. Most people usually gushed superlatives upon walking through the door. Satisfied that she was starting to get the upper hand, Marlene went back to tucking in the bed covers.

'I didn't mean the city. I meant your breasts.'

'What? Oh – I – I don't know what you mean.'

Marlene stood bolt upright and took a few steps backwards away from Shane and the smug smile he wore as a badge – her hand held in surprised fashion against the soft pale silk of her blouse. He must have been able to see down her cleavage when she was bending over. Marlene's breasts were large for her size. Shane must have gotten a spectacularly revealing look, considering she'd worn a low-cut ivory lace bra that barely covered her nipples.

'I – I'll get us something to drink. All that moving must have made you hot. Wine OK?'

Marlene felt like escaping from the bedroom to collect her thoughts. Did she really want to do this? Too late now, her flustered mind threw in for good measure.

'Sure. Whatever you want is fine with me.'

Again, there was that smug smile. Marlene scurried past the huge form to the sanctity of the kitchen where she took her time opening a nicely cool Pinot Grigio. Calmness returned. They'd have a drink and she'd thank him for his help and apologise for any misunderstandings, and so sorry but I have to be somewhere soon so could he make his way back to the office and his car . . .

Yes, that's what she'd do. It would be for the best . . .

She knew it was the kind of empty reasoning that went under the general heading of rationalising. Her good intentions totally disappeared when she walked back into the bedroom carrying the wine, two frosty goblets and a bucket of ice on an elegant sterling silver tray. Her eyes immediately fell to the floor where a small pile of carelessly tossed running shorts and tank top adorned her polished wood floor.

'Oh my.'

Shane didn't say anything. He let his body do the talking. He lay on the bed, semireclining, legs spread. He still wore that smug smile. Perhaps the reason for his cockiness had something to do with the foot-long penis he was stroking so matter-of-factly.

Marlene was determined to not act in the slightest bit shocked or impressed.

'Wine?'

'Please.'

'Don't get up – I'll pour.'

It was the largest dick she'd ever seen, and in a few minutes that monster would be inside her. She'd never get it all in. And how did he get it that hard without passing out from loss of blood to the brain? No wonder he had big muscles. He had to just to lift that thing.

'Your wine.'

'Thanks.'

Marlene sat on the edge of the bed facing Shane. He stopped stroking his cock and took the wine goblet. His cock stood proudly, defying gravity in a most amazing manner. Marlene raised her glass in a toast.

'Thank you for helping me this afternoon.'

'You're very welcome, Ms Neumann.'

'You can call me Marlene.'

'And I'm Shane.'

'Well, Shane, here we are.'

'Yes, here we are.'

'Tell me, Shane,' Marlene inquired, sipping wine delicately, 'are you always so cocksure of yourself that you strip off in a lady's bedroom and play with that unit of yours? What makes you so sure that I'm not going to call the police and have you arrested?'

'And miss a chance to sit on this? I think not,' Shane smugly replied, gulping wine fervently. 'You've been giving me the eye all day. And that excuse to move furniture – give me a break. With a place like this you don't need any favours like moving furniture. That was just a ploy to get me up here so you could see me naked and have sex with me.'

'Direct, aren't we?' Now Marlene was gulping wine fervently.

'I've found it is best. Could I have some more wine while you undress?'

'Certainly, help yourself, Shane, while I take off my clothes. I don't want to ruin my stockings on that prick of yours.'

Marlene was feeling more comfortable with the situation. Perhaps it was the wine, but the butterflies in her stomach had metamorphosed into sex-starved vultures. If Shane can flaunt his body so can I, thought Marlene. She waited for him to return to the bed with his goblet of wine and then began her striptease show. She decided to be nonchalant, removing her clothes as if the well-hung stud on the bed wasn't even there.

The skirt was first. Marlene turned to face the windows, her back to Shane. She reached behind her with her perfectly manicured ivory-coloured fingernails and slid the zipper down to the beginning of her bottom. Her hands slid from the zipper and cupped her ass cheeks ever so carefully, placing enough pressure on her skirt to slide the tightness of the blue silk over her hips. As it fell to the ground she bent carefully over to pick up the garment, stepping ballerinalike out of its confines. Shane was treated to a perfectly unobstructed view of Marlene's ass, save for the few microns of diaphanous ivory lace panties that cradled her delectable cheeks. She knew she had his undivided attention, so Marlene strutted to her closet where she took all the time in the world to hang up her skirt. Directing her attention to the grinning stud on the bed she added nonchalantly, 'I didn't want to wrinkle it.'

Shane just smiled and slowly stroked the full twelve straining inches of his cock while sipping at the wine. As she walked from her closet to her position at the foot of the bed, Marlene couldn't help imagining that the bulbous head of Shane's dick seemed to rotate and follow her stately progress like some predatory animal about to pounce or a submarine's periscope searching for ships to sink.

Next it was time to lose the blouse that Shane had already had the pleasure of seeing under. Marlene rotated to face the windows giving Shane another excellent view of her bottom resplendent in ivory lace framed by her charcoal grey suspender belt and matching stockings. Marlene was sure she could feel the slit eye of the throbbing penis probing every inch of her skin, raising goosebumps on her warm flesh.

Marlene crossed her arms behind her head, latching on to the shoulder straps of her pale silk top and extended her limbs to extricate her body from the soft covering with a teasing shake of her auburn hair. In one sweeping motion reminiscent of the naughtiest of strippers, she clutched the silk top with her outstretched right hand and let it flutter down to the top of her dresser, keeping her arm extended, casting a most erotic profile to the enthralled viewer on the bed.

Marlene decided upon a profile shot for the removal of her half-cup bra. Swiveling on her heels she arched her back to cause her more than ample breasts to jut suggestively outward. Her freedom-minded nipples chose the opportunity to poke mischievously out of their marginal confines adding just that extra touch of sauciness to her lusty profile. The bra was fastened right in the middle of her cleavage by a little clasp that Marlene pretended to have difficulty with, causing her tits to jiggle under her touch. Finally, they broke free as the lace cups cascaded aside under the tension of Marlene's arched back, her tits swinging with their once-contained momentum, gradually relaxing into a supremely suggestive equilibrium. Marlene's breasts were full enough that once free of the support of the bra they drooped ever so slightly under their own weight. It gave them that extremely sexy jiggle that women with smaller or firmer tits don't have. Marlene knew this and sent ripples of energy through them as she walked from the foot of the bed to her dresser.

Her Via Spiga heels clicked on the wood like the ticking of a clock counting down the instants to her most erotic act of undressing yet: the unsheathing of her legs from her extremely sheer charcoal grey French heel stockings. Turning sideways she raised one leg, cocking it at the knee, and ran her fingers all the way up from her ankle, past her tensioned calf muscle, along her thigh, finally coming to rest on the front clasp of the suspender. She paused as if admiring the shapely profile of her leg, letting her hanging breasts sway slightly as she toyed with the clasp. With an innocent flick of her middle finger the clasp released and she let her hand trace a sweeping curve around her buttock to the rear clasp. Again she paused momentarily, acting as if she couldn't find the fastener. She retreated along her bottom and found the suspender strap. Inch by inch she traced the line down the curve of her ass and flicked free the restraint. The dark band of the stocking top lost some of its tension sending sensual ripples through the sheerness of the nylon. Marlene gripped the top band of the stocking and slowly rolled the sheath agonisingly down her cocked leg, leaving it bunched into a delicate band around her ankle.

It was time to remove one of her shoes. Her hand gripped the ankle strap of the Via Spiga and pulled it to release the snap. It popped free and Marlene arched her foot skyward letting the shoe fall with a clatter on to the hardwood floor. She kept her foot in the arched position, making sure that Shane could see her tensioned muscles and the erotically contrasting heel reinforcement of the stocking. Sweeping her fingers down her legs, Marlene continued rolling her stocking down to her toes until it came completely free from her foot. Outstretching her arm, she let the stocking dangle its full length and delicately placed it on the back of the chair.

It was time for the other leg. With deft precision she repeated the process, careful not to look directly at Shane. Out of the corner of her eye she could see he was still slowly pumping his massive unit, obviously enjoying the show. So too was Marlene who could feel her juices begin to flow. She'd undressed before for many men and had learned the power of her casual eroticism, but this situation was different somehow. She viewed Shane as more of a challenge. He apparently viewed himself as some sort of sexual athlete whom women craved. A gigantic gigolo with a dick and an ego to match, he had most probably never wanted for female company, but Marlene was determined not to become just another score. She was steadfast in her desire to teach the boy a little humility. The prospects of the lesson caused her cunt juices to flow with torrential abandon. As she turned to face the masturbating tanned body on the bed she had but one garment to remove – her ivory lace panties – which, as she straightened her body from removing her stockings, she could feel were soaked through with her moisture.

She hooked her fingers on the thin lace sides and bent slightly forward to take the drenched garment off. Her tits dangled playfully forward, rocking from side to side as she teetered while removing the panties. She thought it about time she broke the silence that had electrified the room.

'Nice view, uh?'

Marlene thought she'd use Shane's playful words back against him. His response was perhaps typical of his desire not to be one-upped.

'Yeah. I bet you can see Catalina on a clear day.'

'I didn't mean Los Angeles, you asshole.'

Marlene made a face and hurled the panties at Shane along

with the joking rebuke. The lace almost-nothings were intercepted by the obstacle of his penis, the stickiness of the panties causing them to wrap tightly around the bulky shaft. Marlene chose the accident as the basis for her first contact.

'Your hand must be getting tired. Here, let me take over.'

Instead of removing the panties from Shane's monolithic cock, she wrapped the soaked lace tightly around the pulsing girth of the shaft and began to masturbate Shane's dick with both of her hands. Slowly and deliberately, Marlene moved her pretty hands up and down the foot-long cock, making sure to slip the lace of her panties against every glistening ridge and feature of the monster. She felt like some ancient priestess praying at an altar during a secret sexual initiation ceremony. Through the lace her long fingers marvelled at the supple texture of Shane's almighty dick. She wasn't sure what she'd expected, but she was pleasantly surprised by the cock's responsiveness to her touch. It was fascinating the way his balls rose as she pulled at his shaft and then hung there in space, gradually descending back down to the satin sheets of the bed.

The sun cast amazingly intricate rainbowlike patterns through the lace and on to the pulsing colours of Shane's blood-engorged member. The fine veins of his penis seemed to change colour with every touch of Marlene's skilled hands, contrasting deeply with the pale ivory of her fingernails. And where the mushroom-shaped cockhead blossomed proudly from its stem, Marlene concentrated the most pressure, almost strangling Shane's cock with the twisting of her soaked lace panties.

All this was a bit of a new sensation to Shane. Most women, when confronted with the sight of his admirable boner, just leapt right on top of it out of intense sexual curiosity. And he'd never had a woman wrap her soaked panties around his prize unit and wank him off, but then again his average girlfriend had nowhere near the experience and sophistication of Marlene Neumann. And the women Shane had seduced with his Adonis-like good looks were usually more vulnerable than this smart young lawyer who knew how to handle herself in the courtroom and equally well in the bedroom.

'Do you like the feel of my sopping wet panties on your cock?'

'Yeah. It feels kinda weird.'

'Weird?'

'Yeah – I've never had lace on my cock before.'

'You should try it sometime when you play with yourself. I'll loan you some of my old panties if you want to.'

'Wow, you're weird.'

Marlene just laughed and kept squeezing the swollen head of Shane's cock. It was clear to her that when gifts had been handed out, Shane was at the front of the cock line and somehow never made it over to the brain section. But then again, Marlene kept telling herself that she wasn't here in bed with this young stud to have him quote Shelley, Byron or Keats to her. She looked at his athletic form reclining on the bed, arms crossed behind his head, smug, empty-headed smile on his face, apparently admiring his mammoth stand twitching under her fingers' touch, and Marlene quickly resolved to enjoy the exceptional collection of male equipment presented before her for what it was – a dick with a body attached to it as an afterthought.

'Do you like to have your balls played with?'

'Yeah – yeah, that feels good.'

At least he didn't describe it as 'weird', thought Marlene as she kneaded one of the two ripe orange-sized testicles with one of her hands whilst casually stroking Shane's cockhead with the other. Marlene spread her fingers wide and pinched the shaft between her thumb and forefinger, placing the maximum pressure she could on the lace that just managed to cover the massive blue vein that sprouted from deep within the root of Shane's cock and climbed defiantly upwards. In strict coordination with her jerking of Shane's cock, Marlene increased the pressure on his balls, squeezing and pulling the scrotum roughly.

'Ouch. Hey, be careful . . .'

'Oh, come on, big boy, not afraid of a little pain, are you?'

'No, but you're really weird.'

There was that 'weird' again. The realisation that Shane liked his sex straight and uncomplicated was taking a little of the fun out of Marlene's late afternoon romp. She backed off from the squeezing of Shane's balls, and went back to wanking his erectness with both of her hands. With her tongue she licked Shane's cockhead through the lace of her come-soaked panties, planting heavy-duty sucking kisses on the gigantic slit at the top of the purple coloured fist-sized cock. Her own juices mingled with Shane's sweat and salty pre-come to present her with quite an unusual concoction of taste sensations. There was something about eating her own panties on Shane's hardness that ignited flames deep inside Marlene's cunt. It seemed so primal, so animal – so very crude to see this fine specimen of male pride encased in come-soaked lace. And then to rake her teeth on the bulging cockhead of this tanned young man kick-started her cunt into sexual overdrive. She increased her pace and pressure on Shane's dick noticing for the first time that the vacant smile had been wiped away by her increasingly frenetic advances. Shane had closed his eyes and was grimacing under her lust-craved on-slaught.

He may have a huge cock, but he has no more resilience than any normal man, surmised Marlene as she saw her body's experienced fucking technique gain the upper hand. Shane was now rolling and twitching under Marlene's calculated fondlings. It was time to nibble his balls, she decided, and in doing so she did not miss one beat of her masturbating motions. Whereas for most men she would be able to suck on both testicles at once, it was physically impossible to do so with Shane's gonads. Instead she focused solely on one, nibbling the fleshy sack and sucking tightly on the ball itself. As Shane writhed under her oral ministrations she reduced the force of her kisses and gradually slowed down to long lashing licks that traveled all the way up from his balls, to the stem, up the foot-long shaft to rest once more, vampirelike, on the vulnerable head.

Shane was now whimpering with anguish. He'd clearly never encountered such sensations with as much intensity as Marlene's capable mouth and hands delivered. She could have kept the poor boy in suspense indefinitely, but felt the need to bring matters to a head. She arched her back, releasing her grip on Shane's cock. At this point he could hardly tell the difference as his body underwent pre-orgasm spasms evidenced by the curling of his toes, by the repeated licking of his lips and of the supreme arching of his magnificent dong. Marlene wrapped the lace of her panties once more around the girth of Shane's cock and stood above his sexually charged body.

What a sight it must have been for the voyeuristic occupants

34

of other downtown high-rises lucky enough to own high-powered binoculars with which to see Marlene's statuesque body, legs astride this behemoth of a man, her breasts gently swaying as she gradually lowered herself onto his towering penis. She had no need to guide the member inside of her, preferring to sit gently on its concretelike straining form. Marlene had never taken in her cunt a cock of this size. At first her cunt muscles refused to take in the lace-covered dick until after a few moments of bearing her full weight, the head of Shane's dick forced open Marlene's labia, the cock gently sliding backwards and up her cunt. It was Marlene's turn to whimper.

'Oh, oh my god. It's so fucking big.'

'Yeah – you're gonna like this.'

Shane's lack of eloquence somehow understated the sensations that pervaded Marlene's sex. The lace of her soaked panties slid tightly against the walls of her cunt adding an odd sensation to the equally odd sensation of having such a huge cock inside her. Marlene imagined that the tingling sensations she was feeling must be something like giving birth, so stretched inordinantly wide her cunt felt. And in the length department she had difficulty as she could not take the dick's full twelve straining inches inside of her, but was forced to squat on her bent legs, just a few inches from the base of Shane's cock, supporting herself on Shane's chest with her stately arms. The whole scene looked like some kind of perverted exercise video.

Shane would like that, she thought – and one, and two, and three, and legs bend and squat on that cock – all done to some trashy disco music. Marlene smiled at the view her mind's eye gave her of a room full of people doing 'fuckerobics' with some obnoxiously happy teachers engaged in a calorie-reducing carnal embrace.

Marlene's wandering mind jumped back into the reality of the situation as she felt the huge cock within her beginning to pulse rapidly. The throbbing of Shane's giant cock made her whole body pulse as if her insides were actually expanding and contracting under the pressure of the insistent cock. She gripped her thighs closer together to force her cunt muscles to grab that much tighter a hold of Shane's tool. In doing so, the lace of her panties slipped and pulled at the flesh of Shane's cock, thereby never giving the poor boy the slightest release from that delicious fucking sensation caused by an extremely tight cunt being modulated by lovely taut thigh muscles. Even as Marlene relaxed, the constriction of the panties pulling on Shane's sensitised flesh continued its relentless sensory assault. The texture of the lace slipping and sliding within her was hard to describe. It felt as if there were additional hands or small creatures inside her vagina, toying with her cunt and Shane's cock with playful abandon. At times the feeling was not totally pleasurable, but Marlene was not about to stop the merry-go-round and get off. It was worth the soreness she'd feel tomorrow for the sensations that wracked her body today.

With each of her long strokes of Shane's cock she was able to take the gargantuan throbber deeper inside her as her pussy expanded to accommodate the cock's fullness. Fucking such a monster was an art, Marlene concluded, that required patience, cunning and a more than capable cunt. But apart from the sheer size of Shane's cock and the intensely pleasurable pain it caused on its pistonlike ramming of her pussy, Marlene had to give herself additional stimulation to bring her orgasm closer to the brink. Shane appeared oblivious to Marlene's desire to reach fulfilment, somehow accepting that the sheer size of his unit should be enough for any woman. Under Marlene's fucking, Shane felt like he was doing his job just to keep his proud dong as fully erect as he could and to shoot his load into her desirous receptacle, which moment, because Shane was not known for his restraint, was imminent.

Marlene experienced Shane's release as one of the longest male orgasms she'd ever had the pleasure of sitting upon. She felt it first in her bottom as she sat down fully on Shane's apparatus. His balls seemed to push back on her as if buckets of sperm were being loaded into his cannon of a cock to be launched outward at her. Marlene pushed back against the pressure with her buttocks and thighs, reaching behind with both of her hands to grasp each of Shane's testicles in her hands and roll them between her fingers. With her back arched, reclining backwards on his dick, Marlene's breasts swung to her sides and jiggled under Shane's thrusts. Marlene stopped sliding her cunt over his length, content to use her strong muscles to bring off Shane's orgasm.

The response was increased writhing from Shane who didn't want the long languorous motions to stop. Marlene was bucked up and down like a cowboy being bounced around by an unruly steed. Throughout her ride she held on to Shane's testicles, fiercely pulling the hairy objects and squeezing those large orbs with little care for Shane's body.

It didn't help Shane's comfort that Marlene's lace panties were now thoroughly wrapped tightly around the root of his shaft, constricting his erection into new heights of hardness. And Marlene's calculating thigh muscles added just that extra pressure to his cock, driving the usually calm and in control Shane into fits of come-desiring motions. He wanted to get off and end the pleasure that started at the tip of his mammoth penis and spread throughout every nerve of his huge body.

His wish was granted as his balls released their maximum load into Marlene's already full-to-capacity cunt. She felt the hot liquid spurt forth from Shane's cockslit and spread like melting butter throughout her warm insides. The orgasm seemed endless in its ability to fill every nook and cranny of her tasty quim. Soon she felt the liquid dripping out of her hole, down over Shane's balls and on to her satin sheets. As she began to move again on his cock, more come squeezed out of her stretched opening like a squashed fruit giving up its sweet juices.

Marlene entered the realm of desperation fucking at this moment. She felt curiously unsatisfied with the huge dick inside her. It was so long that she was unable to grind her clitoris down on Shane's pubic mound adding that desired titillation of her hot little button. A more aware gentleman might have assisted her with his hands, but Shane was too into his own body to contemplate the subtleties of fucking. Now that he'd shot his massive load he appeared uninterested in the whole proceedings. Marlene was having none of it.

'Oh no you don't. You keep that dick of yours hard while I ride it, or I swear you'll be limping out of here.'

'Hey, no problem . . .'

It was during this part of the early-evening fuck that Marlene noticed the shadow cast by Shane's tree trunk of a cock, and her imagination had wandered to thoughts of ancient druids as her fingers played with her throbbing bud. Shane's cock had withered slightly, making it that much easier to ram its remaining fullness inside her. It was as she realised how boring this fuck was becoming that she had an idea that would at least make it more enjoyable for her. Marlene was fed up of looking at Shane's stupidly smug expression as she rode up and down on his cock. There was something about the view that was none too erotic. She could have closed her eyes, but she felt that such an action would be cheating. To her back was a magnificent vista of the Los Angeles coastline and the setting sun. She decided to face the ocean.

As she reached the top of Shane's cock she quickly pivoted around completely. The view was much better. Marlene rested on her knees and was able to slide up and down on Shane's dick with just a small bend of her delicious limbs. She focused on the setting sun and the rippling shadows it cast over Los Angeles, conscious that her ass was staring at Shane. She wished he'd have the brains to play with her bottom – stick one of his thick fingers up there as she slid up and down on his dick – but Shane seemed oblivious to the possibilities.

Looking down from the horizon, Marlene noticed the swell of Shane's balls between his legs. With one of her hands she hefted the sack towards her and began to rub it hard on her clitoris. The massive ball contorted around her flesh massaging her button in every possible direction. Combined with the full sliding movements of her body up and down Shane's cock, Marlene at last began to feel the rise of her orgasm building. As the warmth within her spread she pressed the testicle harder and harder against her until she was practically digging her nails into the flesh.

'Hey Marlene, take it easy.'

'Just ʾuck me, just fuck me and shut up. Stick your finger up my asshole.'

'Wow – no way.'

Marlene paid no attention to the big lug's apparent reluctance to touch her bottom. She didn't let up one iota on his testicle, pounding the fleshy sack into her cunt with ever increasing ferocity. Underneath her she could feel Shane wriggle and twitch as if he were trying to escape her onslaught. His motions only made her more determined to bring herself off in this manner.

It began with no small subtlety. Marlene was used to orgasms that slowly rolled through her pussy like the distant Pacific Ocean crashing on the beaches of Los Angeles. For some mysterious reason this orgasm was more like a tidal wave erupting from the deep without the courtesy of a storm warning. The intensity of her release hit Marlene like a hurricane, literally devastating her body. With an ear-piercing scream she folded forward, continually racking her cunt with Shane's balls. To prevent his dick from being done a mischief, Shane was forced to sit up, amazed at the ferocity with which this apparently demure lawyer fucked.

Wave after wave of electric come-draining intensity shot from Marlene's pussy, jolting her body. She slid further towards the end of the bed, extricating her body from Shane's dick, releasing his balls, and ending her orgasm at the foot of her bed staring at the descending orange ball of the sun. As it sank lower and lower towards the horizon, Marlene was sure that the distant orb winked at her.

Shane gingerly removed the tattered remnants of Marlene's panties from his rapidly softening cock, and poured himself another glass of wine. Marlene seemed to be out cold, so he decided he'd treat himself to a nice hot shower before he popped the question to her. Marlene dimly noticed Shane's movements but was content to let the young stud wander around her apartment.

When Shane returned from the shower wearing a small towel wrapped quite modestly around his waist, Marlene was sitting in a light blue silk robe at her dresser.

'Have a nice shower?'

'Yeah, I feel great.'

'That's good.'

The conversation was a little stilted. Finally, Marlene decided to bring matters to closure.

'Look, Shane – I've got to get ready for a party I have to go to this evening, so could you see yourself out and walk the couple of blocks to your car?'

'Well, I could, but hey – why don't I go to the party with you? I have a change of clothes in my car. We could then have more fun afterwards.'

'No, Shane. I really can't take you to this party.'

'Ah come on, Ms Neumann. I want to be a big movie star just like Arnold Schwarzenegger. I work out at the same gym he started at, and I just need to be discovered. I even speak better English than him.'

Marlene was about to say that that statement could easily be debated when it dawned on her that she hadn't told Shane the details about the party. Marlene's prosecutorial mind kicked into gear.

'What makes you think that this party has anything to do with the movie business?'

'Well – I kinda used my brain, Ms Neumann. Since I sort the mail I know who a lot of your clients are, and I kind of put two and two together. When you said you had a party to go to I figured it had to be connected to the movie business.'

Shane seemed proud of his reasoning abilities. Marlene was ready to tear them apart.

'But what made you think the party was business related? It could have been a bunch of my old law-school buddies just as much as a movie-business party.'

Shane suddenly developed a guilty look.

'Well, I have to admit I did something sneaky. When you were in those offices in Burbank today you left your appointment book in the car. I looked through it and saw that you were going to Neil Waslinger's party tonight, so I thought . . .'

Marlene interrupted his confessional.

'So you thought you'd fuck me and get an invitation to the party.'

'No, no – that just happened.'

'Sure it did.'

Marlene was fuming at the thought of being used so transparently. She knew she'd made a mistake in fucking Shane. It was now time for damage control.

'Look, Shane – I cannot and will not take you to this party tonight. And don't think there will ever be another of this evening's little flings. There won't be. And if you have any brains you'll realise that it would be to your advantage to keep things quiet. If I hear just so much as one word out of your mailroom buddies then I'll personally see to it that you couldn't get a job cleaning the toilet of any one of the movie studios. Ever.'

'Hey, take it easy – I won't say anything.'

'You'd better not. It was just a one-night – an early-evening – stand. Leave it at that. And if you ever mention the slightest peep to anyone I'll deny it completely. And I can make things very difficult for you. So just let it drop, OK?'

'Yeah, sure.'

Shane grabbed his effects and slipped into the bathroom to change, his tail literally between his legs. As he returned and motioned to leave, Marlene decided to finish her threats with an incentive to Shane to keep his end of the bargain.

'Look, Shane – I'll see what I can do to find out if there are any openings at any of the studios in their mailrooms. If you work on the lots it will be easier for you to get discovered. Just remember our deal.'

'Sure, Ms Neumann – thanks, Ms Neumann. Thanks.'

Marlene watched the big oaf saunter out of her bedroom and out of the front door of her life. Within a week he'd be working at some little studio in Burbank, no longer a potential threat to her position at the law firm. Marlene sighed a reprimanding look at herself in the dresser's mirror. Looking at herself with those piercingly ice-blue eyes, she spoke slowly and surely.

'Never fuck a man whose dick is bigger than his brain, especially if his ego is by far the biggest part of him.'

Duly chastised she poured herself a glass of wine, toasted the setting sun and stepped into the shower to cleanse herself of the remnants of her one-night stand's indulgence.

8 p.m.

AN ALLEYWAY BEHIND THE ROX-BOMB
NIGHTCLUB ON SUNSET BOULEVARD

If Cassandra closed her heavily made-up eyes tightly and tried
to think of those seemingly endless summers long ago where
she'd spent many a happy moment growing up on the sands of
well-to-do Laguna Beach, a small coastal town just a short hour
and a long lifetime south of Los Angeles, she could easily forget
where she was and what she was doing. Behind those closely
shuttered, brightly coloured windows to the jumble of her mind,
the drone of the incessant Saturday evening traffic on Sunset
Boulevard did sound remarkably like the rolling of the Pacific
Ocean crashing on the slippery rocks of yesterday, dulled ever
so pleasantly by the numbing fog of oh-so-long ago.

Cassandra was the only child of a well-to-do family with
everything that money could buy, including the peculiar problems of the wealthy. Precocious to the point of being dangerous,
she'd lost her virginity at the ripe old age of thirteen to a business
associate of her father's, whom she'd found most remarkably
dishy and very willing to pork his partner's daughter in the
swimming pool one hot August night. Her first sexual experience
other than at her own hands occurred after one of those boring
business dinner parties that her father was always throwing where
everyone got drunk and acted like kids, and in Cassandra's case,
the kid acted like an adult.

Sex rapidly became an obsession for Cassandra. She was
pretty, but not beautiful, mature for her age and when she fucked
somebody – anybody – they at least paid attention to her, unlike
her parents who seemed occupied only with waging a war against
each other.

Cassandra had been just fifteen when her mother had over-
dosed on sleeping pills, Valium and red wine because her father

had demanded a divorce so that he could marry his secretary, whom he'd been fucking for pretty much all of Cassandra's childhood. Cassandra didn't even wait for the funeral. She left the seemingly idyllic community of Laguna Beach in the beat-up Volkswagen bus of a surf-punk band who were down at the seaside for a weekend of surfing, sex, beer and drugs. Cassandra had hitched a ride with the five-member band and fucked each one during the ride back to Los Angeles. During a particularly thick patch of traffic on the 405 Interstate she'd even fucked the driver by sitting sideways on his lap. It was her first introduction to rock-and-roll sex. Landing feet first on the streets of Hollywood, Cassandra had never looked back, quickly gaining a reputation as one of Hollywood's most fuckable groupies.

In the eight years that passed so traumatically on the somewhat less glamorous side of Hollywood, Cassandra never saw or talked to her father ever again. She'd never been back to Laguna Beach and avoided even the closer Los Angeles beaches because of the memories that crashing waves and wide-open expanses of sand tended to rekindle. She'd become a creature of the night, vampirelike, pale and hauntingly enticing. She'd fucked some of the greatest names in the rock-and-roll business, as well as some of the lowest ones. She'd never gotten close to anybody – she was sure there was no place in her life for sentimentality – but every so often memories of Laguna Beach and what might have been assaulted her mind's eye with images of her misspent youth and lost childhood.

Tonight was one of those times. It was flashback time. The grunting and snorting of the sweaty individual thrusting his slimy rubber-covered hardness into Cassandra's well-worn cunt bore an uncanny resemblance to the bellicose utterances of the big black harbour seals, those comical inhabitants of California's coastal waters, as they challenged each other for tasty morsels of fish.

Opening her eyes to dispel the thoughts of a long ago, born of a nostalgia Cassandra would never openly admit to, she couldn't help but think that the hulk who held her pressed tightly against the alley wall of the Rox-Bomb nightclub did look in no small way like one of those seals. His long greasy hair was slicked back and gathered into a ponytail that draped down his sweaty back and glistened just like the marine mammal's shiny skin as it basked languorously in the sun. The effect was emphasised by numerous tattoos of vaguely satanic origins adorning the roadie's limbs, thereby creating a sheen that in the evening twilight could easily be mistaken for the lustre of a seal's water-repellent coat. The human's three or four day growth of sweat-soaked beard stuck out from his face like a seal's whiskers dripping salt water. The heavy-metal roadie's hands, dirty from the moving of crate after crate of electronic equipment and gargantuan amplifiers, pawed over Cassandra's white skin like a seal's flippers tearing through the surf.

It was time to lay off the heavy-duty hallucinogenics, Cassandra told herself. Such disturbing visions so early in the evening didn't bode well for what little of her sanity remained. To shake her senses back to the here and now she swigged carelessly out of the Jack Daniel's whiskey bottle that dangled half-heartedly from her hand, spilling as much as she consumed. The whiskey bit at her throat, causing her to cough. To the English roadie with his cock inside Cassandra's pussy, the sounds she made sounded quite like she was moaning in ecstasy.

'Nice bit of dick, uh?'

Cassandra smiled back through shiny red lips that contrasted starkly with the paleness of her face. The glistening red of the lipstick complemented her heavily made-up but very bloodshot eyes that peered out from underneath a spiky mop of long, jet-black hair. She neither agreed nor disagreed with the roadie's boast. It was just another dick. One little link in the chain that would lead her to her ultimate goal for the evening: an all-areas unlimited access pass for tonight's sold-out show of England's latest rock sensation – Momma's Nails.

The transaction had been negotiated easily enough. Roadies were, after all, an extremely predictable bunch. And the location of the Rox-Bomb on Sunset Strip made gaining their attention childishly convenient. The band's equipment-laden trucks were forced to park right in front of the club on that most famous of Los Angeles roads, and the sweating roadies had to wheel the equipment up the back alley and into the club. Cassandra casually strolled by at precisely the right moment. She was dressed ever-so-appealing in her thigh-high black leather boots that made her thin five-and-a-half-foot figure seem a towering six foot tall. The paleness of her thighs shone through her red fishnet split-crotch tights, the contrasting whiteness of her exposed flesh heightened by a black plastic miniskirt and black leather halter bra. Cassandra was not voluptuous – she was skinny – but still highly desirable. To sex-starved roadies she was like a magnet to iron filings.

Words were exchanged, drugs were promised, alcohol was mentioned and a deal was struck. Once the band was loaded in and soundcheck completed Cassandra would fuck the roadies in exchange for a pass.

A fair exchange, thought Cassandra. There were three of them and they wouldn't last long. They had been on the road for several weeks, and from what Cassandra could tell from their conversations, they hadn't had much pussy. This observation was confirmed by the impatient comments voiced not too discreetly by the next-in-line roadie.

'Get a bloody move on, 'Arry – I don't have all night, me old son. The bleedin' bus is leavin' in a few mo.'

'Sod off, Nobby. We can fuckin' walk back to the friggin' 'otel, so shut ya gob. I'm savourin' the moment, ain't I?'

There were various mumblings and grumblings and stamping of feet as Harry gave Cassandra his full attention once more.

'So sorry, my dear, to have been interrupted by those louts. Now where was I?'

'Somewhere about here, I think?'

'Oh yes, my dear – oh yes – oh yes indeed.'

Cassandra had reached between their heaving bodies and was grasping Harry's balls tightly with her long black fingernails. The heavy sacks were ripe with sperm that boiled so quickly underneath her skilful touch. Realising that his share of the bargain was almost over Harry decided he should get as much as he could.

'Wor – let's have a look at yer titties.'

Cassandra didn't object but she didn't help. If Harry wanted to look he would just have to help himself. And that he did, pulling roughly aside her black leather chrome-studded bra to reveal Cassandra's small breasts. The sight of such delicate miniatures excited some deep perversion in the roadie, whose libido was now working overtime. He slobbered over Cassandra's tiny nipples, rubbing his rough growth of beard harshly on her white skin. Amidst his droolings he couldn't resist revealing his lecherous thoughts.

'Wor – how old are ye then, love?'

Cassandra was, as ever, brutally honest.

'Twenty-three.'

'Wor – such little titties. They look like a little girl's knockers. I've always wanted to fuck a . . .'

Harry didn't have time to finish describing his Lolita fantasy to the bored Cassandra. Her fingers had done the job. She lacked the motivation to clench tight her cunt muscles the way she knew she still could. She had every confidence in the ability of her nails to have the desired effect. With two other roadies to go she didn't want to tire herself out.

'Thanks, luv.'

Harry stepped aside and carefully zipped up his Levis. Cassandra found it curious that he'd not bothered to take off the condom. Perhaps he was overcome with emotion? Perhaps he was just absent-minded? Or perhaps he believed in recycling? The thought made her smile.

Harry took Cassandra's show of humour as a sign of friendship and of satisfaction.

'Nice, uh?'

'Yeah, Harry, it was nice. Now give me the pass.'

' 'Ow about the others?'

'They'll get theirs, OK – just give me the pass now or I start screaming and nobody gets any more pussy.'

'All right, all right.' Harry handed over the prize.

'Now you didn't get that from me, all right?'

'All right. My lips are sealed. Now send in the next one. You can watch if you like.'

'I don't think Nobby would like that.'

'Suit yourself.'

Cassandra didn't bother to pull down her black plastic skirt or rearrange her small breasts into her bra. She didn't even bother to close her long skinny legs. There was no point. It would be just so much wasted effort. Cassandra just stood there propping up the bricks in the dingy alleyway wall. She took another swig of Jack Daniel's whiskey and awaited her next visitor.

She wasn't kept waiting long. No sooner had Harry had turned the corner than did Nobby emerge. He was aptly named, thought Cassandra.

'Cor, what a sight for sore eyes. Ya looks lovely. And oh so wet for me. 'As old 'Arry been good to ya then? Getcha all ready for the star of the show, did he?'

As he spoke he ran his gnarled hands over Cassandra's cunt, roughly probing her pussy lips, toying with her wetness. Once more Cassandra started to hallucinate. The scene reminded her of a perverted X-rated version of *Snow White and the Seven Dwarfs*. She would be Snow White and one of the dwarfs – the naughty one – would have been called Nobby or something like that, and he would have looked exactly like the aged roadie. Thankfully, the necessities of modern sex brought Cassandra back from the land of sexual fairy tales.

'Here – put this on.'

Cassandra handed Nobby a condom.

'Right you are then. Foreplay over and done wiv.'

Cassandra couldn't help but smile at Nobby's feeble attempt to be a man of the nineties. That he even knew what foreplay was shocked her just a little. He didn't look the kind of guy to indulge in such niceties. Nobby was – what was the best word to use to describe him? – nobby. He was short – at least a foot shorter than Cassandra was in her high-heel boots. His beady little eyes peered through a wrinkled prunelike face at just the right height to stare into Cassandra's cleavage – if she'd had any. Nobby was almost completely bald except for a few straggly brown survivors that crawled down from his rather round ears to his neck. His mouth closed more than it should due to his almost complete lack of teeth. Nobby's nose was huge, round, bulbous and extremely red from its sudden exposure to the bright California sun.

For just the faintest of moments Cassandra was curious as to how old the impish creature might be, but it quickly dawned on her that it really didn't matter. Nobby looked like he was seventy but was probably more like forty. He'd probably looked the same when he was born, all the way through school and adolescence.

He probably hadn't changed his tour T-shirt since the whole odyssey had begun just a few weeks before. Nobby had the unmistakable air of being a perpetual Nobby. A perpetual roadie too. Just one look at his caricature of a body convinced her that Nobby had been a roadie all of his life.

Cassandra gulped another mouthful of Jack Daniel's carelessly, letting the overflow trickle down her chin to provide a steady stream of whiskey between her small breasts. Nobby smelled the nectar immediately and wasted no time in taking his fair share.

'Always was a whiskey-and-tit man meself.'

Cassandra shuddered as the coolness of the whiskey trickled down the skin of her neck to be slurped by Nobby's hot tongue. His steamy breath evaporated her sweat and the bristles of his beard burned roughly against her tender white tits. With whiskey on his already rank breath he sucked rabidly on Cassandra's tiny nipples. The rough stimulation excited the small buds into bulletlike points, causing her to spill more whiskey down her neck in a stream that Nobby happily consumed as he turned his attention quickly from one breast to another.

'You're my kind of woman you are. I much prefers whiskey to milk any day of the week.'

Nobby giggled hideously at his rude observation. Cassandra thought more than just a moment about smashing the almost empty bottle over his head but eventually decided against such a drastic course of action. Nobby would have probably enjoyed it. He looked like the sort of pervert that always smashed empty bottles on his head just for the fun of it. She consoled herself with the knowledge that this would all soon be over and she could enjoy the fruit of her labours.

Nobby in the meantime was fumbling with his trousers, attempting to extricate his member from its dark confines. He didn't want to miss a drop of whiskey so he wasn't about to stop any of his oral mauling of Cassandra's bosom, but it was difficult for him to remove his trousers which were overly sticky from the sweat of humping packing crates. Cassandra was not about to help him lest Nobby mistook her desire to hasten the end of their 'lovemaking' as a sign of her attraction for him. Finally Nobby lost his patience and backed away from Cassandra's whiskey fountain.

' 'Ang on a mo.'

Nobby quickly pushed his trousers down around his ankles. He wore no underwear. And his dick, Cassandra noted with passing curiosity, lived up to the rest of Nobby's aptly named form. His dick was – well, there was no other word for it but knobby. The shaft was thin and ridged with veins of all colours culminating in a huge red knob of a head that seemed to swell and wink at Cassandra's gaze. Whomever coined the phrase 'one-eyed trouser snake' as slang for a penis had obviously had a close encounter with Nobby's member. With the condom pulled tightly over his cock, the view it presented reminded Cassandra of a robber with a stocking pulled tightly over his face distorting his features so as not to be recognised in the dastardly act. Visions of rogue robber penises holding up banks at dickpoint and raping the virginal tellers danced bizarrely through Cassandra's imagination. With a shake of her head and a wave of her hand she let the almost empty Jack Daniel's bottle fall to the ground. All these visions of things looking like other things were beginning to get to her. She'd already vowed to stay off the hallucinogenics – now she'd have to go a little slower on the booze. The whole world was starting to look like some surrealistic painting. Pretty soon she'd be seeing dead fish and melting clocks everywhere. This early on a Satuday evening to be in such a mood was not a good sign at all. Cassandra tried to shake herself back into the here and the now.

'Fuck me, Nobby – fuck me. I haven't got all night and I want that dick now.'

Getting back to the basics always helped.

'Only too glad to oblige a lady.'

Nobby stepped forward and, by virtue of his small stature, had to stand on his tiptoes to insert his throbbing member inside Cassandra's sopping cunt. It amazed her how wet she got even when she wasn't really interested in fucking. Long ago Cassandra had decided it was just a redirection of her tears. Crying never really did any good, so at least those precious juices were now put to some use, she reasoned. But no matter how wet she got, Cassandra rarely came. Orgasming during sex with a man was a pleasure that she only distantly remembered enjoying.

To fuck Cassandra's cunt Nobby was forced to pull his body

up inside the taller woman by grasping her shoulders and heaving himself off the ground. Even given the passion of the moment, the precarious position was somewhat uncomfortable for the small man, but he seemed not to mind as he pulled himself in and out of Cassandra's cunt with his muscular arms.

'Phew – it's like doin' bleedin' exercises in the bleedin' army, ain't it?'

Cassandra smiled a vacant stare and closed her eyes. She wasn't in the mood for idle chatter, but she decided to aid in Nobby's plight. The manner in which he was fucking her was quite stimulating to her cunt – surprisingly so, in fact. The sexual shockwaves battering Cassandra's psyche must have had something to do with the way Nobby's rather large, bulbous cockhead was penetrating the opening of her cunt. As he pulled himself eagerly upwards and then slipped reluctantly out past her clitoris, thereby complying with the laws of gravity and returning his feet to earth, he stimulated her cunt more than she was used to. Cassandra felt strange feelings build within her, and she decided to add to this unusual sensation. With a randy determination born of a rapidly escalating lust, she wrapped her arms around his waist, grasped his saggy little bottom, dug her jet black nails into the mottled flesh and tugged Nobby to her in motions that more than matched his erstwhile pull-ups. Something primal and debased ignited within her, sending intense lurid shafts of hot and dirty pulses up from her usually dull clitoris, through her rapidly flooding pussy, temporarily ricocheting around her stomach, playing pinball with her nipples and finally blasting like a nuclear bomb in her chemically suppressed brain. Cassandra bucked against the brick wall of the alley, threatening to do bodily harm to her skinny frame, and in doing so bring to rubble the legendary Rox-Bomb nightclub that had for so long withstood the onslaught of many decibel-proud rock-and-rollers. Suddenly cognisant of the magnitude of the erotic forces at work around him, Nobby was surprised by the intense violence of Cassandra's reaction. He wasn't used to having this effect upon women.

' 'Ere, steady on love – you'll tear me bum off.'

Cassandra paid no attention to Nobby's protests but continued to pull his flesh towards her, leaving huge red welts on the white-as-snow terrain of Nobby's ass. To Cassandra it felt as if she was sitting on one huge dildo, and by pulling it into her she was able to wrap her legs tightly around the thrusting form. The sensations were intense. Nobby didn't exist for her any more. She was fucking herself with an abandon she rarely felt in these hardened days of denied emotions. Her breathing began to exaggerate as she gasped for oxygen to feed her rampaging brain. She was experiencing a rush that bordered on a perpetual orgasm. Cassandra's skinny frame broke out in a cold, clammy sweat as Nobby was literally tossed around like a rag doll on the crashing waves emanating from the jaded young woman's quivering thighs.

'Oh me bum – oh me . . .'

'Oh, shut up and fuck – don't stop.'

Cassandra was unusually insistent. She was experiencing the first orgasm she hadn't faked in quite some time. Most roadies and rock stars were so taken with themselves that they gave little consideration to their 'partners' for the evening. In most cases of band sex it was just a way to relieve the excessive build-up of sperm gathered during those long lonely drives from city to city across the vastness of the United States. The sex act was reduced to just so much masturbation. Even so, the egos of stars demanded that they feel that they'd satisfied the woman, and ever careful to please such vanities, Cassandra had become skilful at faking her release. It had become almost a regular way of having sex for Cassandra. Slightly before the thrusting male form on top of, to the side of, up against of, or underneath her willing body began to squirt forth his load, Cassandra would begin to squirm her hips and moan in a high-pitched agonisingly helpless staccato whine. Her head rocked to and fro, shaking her long spiky black hair in sensual ripples as she bit tightly on her fingers. The combined effect of these motions was invariably an insatiable desire on the part of the man to fuck her harder. In a desperate bid to fulfil her wishes, he would invariably comply with Cassandra's apparent orgasmic cry, thereby leading to the inevitable release of several c.c.'s of seminal fluid. There would be several more gratuitous thrusts, a few more moans and then an uncoupling, a few cigarettes and one more notch would be added on to Cassandra's collection of rock-and-roll penises.

It was somewhat like stamp collecting. No one who is seriously philatelic would ever conceive of actually licking their prizes, slapping them on an envelope and using them for their prime purpose of paying for mail delivery. Oh no. The act of collecting – of accumulating specimens – is worth much more than the act of postage itself. So too with Cassandra and rock-and-roll stars, their assorted entourages and bonking. She never fucked rockers for the pleasure of it any more – in many ways there really wasn't that much pleasure to be found in such one-night stands. Cassandra fucked the rock-and-roll industry purely for the notoriety it afforded her. Except here in the alley a chink in the armour had materialised quite unexpectedly. Here she was, like some inexperienced little schoolgirl, enjoying herself backstage after her first concert. And to make matters even more strange Cassandra was giving her all to the most unlikely of prospects.

Nobby for his part was very relieved to feel his cock arch inside Cassandra's shuddering quim, indicating the imminent explosion of his hard-won orgasm. His body was black and blue from Cassandra's pummeling and small drops of blood dotted the landscape of his bum. In his final thrust up deep inside Cassandra's come-ravaged opening he penetrated the furthest her pliable furrow would allow. Nobby stiffened every muscle of his body as he came inside the rubber sheath, in the process releasing his grip on Cassandra's shoulders. She had long since released Nobby's ass as she spread her arms wide against the Rox-Bomb wall to prop up her own sex-racked body. The scene was surrealistically sacrilegious – a perverted crucifixion that lasted but a moment before Nobby, completely lacking of any support, fell with a loud slap back on to the concrete of the alley. A grimace of pain spread across his face as his already-punished bottom received the worst of the impact. Twitching like some dying animal, his cock continued to spurt forth come into the distended condom.

Cassandra knew nothing of Nobby's plight. She didn't even hear him struggle to his feet and make his way out of the alley to the safety of the band's equipment van. She remained propped against the wall at a slight angle. Her long skinny legs were spread-eagled resplendently in her thigh-high boots and red fishnet split-crotch tights revealing the dark wisps of her cunt hair, wet from her recent fuckings. Her tiny breasts heaved slightly as she caught her breath. Her jet black hair lost some of its hairspray-induced stand and fell enticingly further in front of her eyes. She felt lost to the whims and vagaries of this world, and was therefore completely unprepared for the third roadie who made his presence known with a slight cough and a shuffle of his sneaker-covered feet.

'Er – hi. Are you all right?'

Cassandra didn't start at the sound of the voice but slowly turned her head to where the sound came from and hesitatingly opened her eyes. The sight that greeted Cassandra confused her well-worn senses. She wasn't sure what to say, so she chose the easy way out.

'Hi.'

The third roadie looked at his worn-through sneakers and shuffled uncomfortably, apparently trying to cover the holes through which his toes poked. Cassandra eyed him carefully, trying to appraise herself of his mood. When she'd struck her deal with Nobby and Harry, this roadie had been busy in the Rox-Bomb packing up the last of the crates. She'd assumed he would be just like them. She was wrong. Dead wrong. She tossed around the possibilities in her confused mind, but before long her musings were disturbed by the unmistakable tones of Harry and Nobby egging the other seemingly reluctant roadie on.

'Get a move on, Jimmie. We don't have all bleedin' night. Dip ya wick and let's bugger off.'

Cassandra could see Harry and Nobby's eyes glistening in the dim light of the alley. She suddenly felt a tremendous sympathy for Jimmie. He could have been just eighteen, but was more like seventeen or even a well-developed fifteen-year-old. He was actually sixteen. He wore the standard heavy-metal uniform of the day. He was probably a runaway from some small middle-American town who'd talked his way into roadie-ing for Momma's Nails when their tour passed through his usually quiet home environment. A modern-day rock-and-roll version of running away to the circus. Only in the rock circus the lions really did bite. Cassandra knew all about that. She'd been bitten many times. Her heart had the scars to prove it. Through all that past agony she felt a strange fondness for this youth. It must have had something to do with the rush of emotion she'd just experienced. She decided to be friendly.

'Jimmie? Is that your name?'

'Yeah.'

'Where you from?'

'Indianapolis. Just outside of . . .'

'You like Momma's Nails?'

'Yeah. I got all their CDs.'

'Cool.'

'Yeah.'

'Axle Greeser's pretty neat, uh?'

'Yeah. He signed my shirt – see.'

Jimmie stepped closer, apparently overcoming his fear in the camaraderie of showing a fellow fan his proud adornment.

'Neat.'

'Yeah.'

And there they stood, the twenty-three-year-old groupie and the sixteen-year-old fan, inches apart but closer than they could ever imagine. Cassandra saw so much of herself in Jimmie. The thought of where he might end up frightened her slightly. Would he live in alleys giving hand jobs for favours? Or would he be one of the ones that make it to stardom and the bigtime? And would she still be in the alley waiting for him? Doing god knows what to get a backstage pass to his show? Would he even remember her?

'You want to be a rock star?'

'Yeah. Spickle – the guitar player – he's been teaching me some riffs. I get to fool around with their axes when we're setting up the stacks. It's cool. You're really pretty.'

'Thanks. You've never done this before, have you?'

Jimmie started, his male ego rising to his defence.

'Yeah – tons of times.'

It was a hollow answer. Jimmie sounded like he was trying to convince himself. Cassandra stared at his pimply face and the fuzz on his upper lip. His scraggly blond hair was unkempt, framing a face that really should have been back home just outside of Indianapolis at the dinner table enjoying some of Mom's apple pie and lectures about getting his hair cut.

'Yeah – me too.'

They both laughed as Cassandra put her arms around his neck and pulled him to her, her hands cradling his face as her lips moved closer to Jimmie's. There was a momentary pause, and then experience overcame naiveté and Cassandra pressed her lips against Jimmie's inert form. She could hear the muffled titters of Harry and Nobby from around the corner. They too had probably figured Jimmie for a virgin and were trying to have a laugh at his first time expense. Cassandra thought she'd give them a show to make the two well-worn road dogs jealous instead. She kissed Jimmie long and tenderly. Her tongue coaxed Jimmie's out of its shyness in an intricate mating dance of slippery probing. It was clear he had little experience with women – or with girls for that matter – but he did know enough to let Cassandra do all of the work. She held him close in her embrace and could feel his youthful hardness beat against her. Typical of the inexperienced male embarrassed by the betrayal of his excited state, he tried to shift his weight so as not to rub his erect dick on Cassandra. It was a touching gesture to the woman who thought she'd seen it all. From Jimmie's lips she slid her tongue over the pale skin of his face and kissed his ear lobe. At the same time she whispered words of encouragement to the reluctant Romeo.

'Don't pay any attention to those guys and don't worry about this. Just trust me.'

The 'this' that Cassandra referred to was Jimmie's throbbing boner which was visibly emitting all manner of effluent through the worn material of his ripped-up Levi jeans. As she spoke Cassandra gripped the bulging form firmly. Jimmie could barely speak under her expert touch. Swallowing quickly the lumps in his throat, he gasped, 'OK.'

From the corner of her eye she could see that the smiles of Harry and Nobby had disappeared to be replaced by looks of wonder and envy. She was pleased with her calculated manoeuvres, but there was little time to reflect on elements of strategy. It was clear from the expression on Jimmie's face that his imminent eruption was just moments away. Cassandra acted fast. It would not do for the boy's first fuck to end before it had had time to begin.

She expertly unbuttoned his jeans and eased them down his hips. He wore Bart Simpson boxer shorts whose discovery seemed to cause Jimmie even further embarrassment. Cassandra choked back her smile and pretended not to notice, although it was quite difficult not to burst a blood vessel or two at the sight of Jimmie's penis sticking out of Bart's nose.

With jeans and boxer shorts safely around his ankles, Cassandra took Jimmie's twitching cock in her hand and squeezed it tightly around the shaft as she rolled a Durex over the virgin cockhead. It was a technique she'd learned many years back to keep some of the sex-starved road guys she'd bonked from coming too soon. The constriction intensified the hard-on, but prevented a weakening release of sperm, thereby allowing Cassandra to enjoy the delicious feeling of cock-riding she used to look forward to so much. Jimmie's cock was small but firm, and the way it twitched in her hand she could hardly wait to get it inside of her.

Somewhere at sometime in his pubescent curiosity Jimmie must have read an erotic work of fiction, the letters section of a men's magazine or perhaps have been given some advice by a more experienced friend, for in response to Cassandra's handling of his penis he felt obliged to reciprocate in some fashion. He didn't feel bold enough to touch her cunt, but instead he seized her small tits, touching them at first through her studded leather halter, gradually sneaking his way to touch flesh. He didn't squeeze the nipples the way Cassandra liked them to be treated, but rubbed the little mounds with the palms of his hands in a cupping motion.

'That feels good, Jimmie, but here, do this.'

Cassandra took his hand and squeezed his fingers on to her hardened nipples. She rolled the points around his hands, feeling the sweat of his palms glide over her cool white flesh. Satisfied that he now knew what to do to please her, Cassandra reached behind Jimmie and pulled his bottom towards her. With her other hand she took his penis and slowly inserted it into her moist cunt. Her slippery opening easily parted for the small cock and warmly welcomed it to its temporary home. She relaxed her leg muscles and let her high-heel boots slide away from the wall, causing her body to settle on to Jimmie's smaller frame. Jimmie needed no words of encouragement to instruct him on what to do next. Some things, Cassandra reflected, do come naturally.

Jimmie thrust his cock inside Cassandra with all the fervour that a first fuck can unleash. Each thrust seemed like a lifetime of sex. Each sensation spoke volumes of erotica to his raging libido. With each push and slide he felt his experience grow. A voice deep within kept saying 'You're fucking a girl, you're actually fucking a girl – and a real pretty one too.' He was moving in and out of Cassandra with a speed that blurred his actions. No amount of fantasising, no amount of wanking, could have prepared Jimmie for this moment of moments. Cassandra felt like she should really slow him down, but decided against it. One cannot halt the progress of sixteen years of sexual evolution easily, and Cassandra was enjoying the way Jimmie's pubic mound was banging so rapidly against her clit. The experience was decidedly pleasurable, made even more so by the thought that she was this young boy's first fuck. He may not have admitted as much to her, but there was no hiding the facts that his young and inexperienced body readily revealed.

As quickly as it started it was over in a flash. Jimmie released his load into the condom whilst desperately trying not to cry out as the hot fluid was pressed out of the small slit at the top of his cock and forced around his swollen cockhead. The sensation was heightened by Cassandra's cunt grabbing tightly a hold of his orgasming dick and milking as much of the virgin sperm as she could with electric quivers of her warm box.

After a few more pulses she could see that the sadness so typical of the male animal exhibited after fervent love-making was taking control of Jimmie's body, and perhaps the embarrassment of his actions too was causing him to wish he was now elsewhere. Around the corner she could hear Nobby and Harry applauding. She wished somehow she could shut them up, but she knew better. Life on the road was inherently cruel, and Jimmie she was sure would learn to handle himself. She had given him the best start he could ever have asked for.

Cassandra slid the full condom off Jimmie's still-hard dick and kissed him slightly on the cheek.

'So don't forget me when you're a big star, OK?'

'Oh, I won't. You bet I won't.'

'I'm sure you won't. Here, I'll give you something to remember me by – at least for a short while.'

Cassandra grabbed the retreating boy's hand and forced it between her sopping thighs. She ground her cunt into his fingers coating Jimmie's hand with her juices so that the haunting miasma of their lust would stay with him for the near future. Throughout the night, at odd moments when he thought no one was looking at him, Jimmie would sniff at the odour coating his hand and carry it proudly, like a badge of courage triumphantly announcing the fact that he was no longer a virgin. It would be quite a while before water washed that intoxicating smell away from his hand.

And with that same beguiling smile, now not so innocent, he pulled up his Bart Simpson boxer shorts and his torn jeans and actually ran out of the alley to join his compadres. Cassandra could hear the jocularity between them as they made their way back down Sunset Boulevard to the band's hotel. Jimmie was now one of the boys – life would be a little easier.

Cassandra straightened her clothing and checked her make-up in the small multipurpose mirror she kept in her purse. She clipped the all-access pass to one of the straps of her halter bra and strode out of the alley to the hustle and bustle of just another Saturday night in Los Angeles. She checked her watch and concluded she had enough time to have a small meal, a few drugs, a long shower, choose the most stunning outfit she owned and still be back before the band returned to the Rox-Bomb. It would be important to be there when they arrived so that Cassandra could make her presence known to the lead singer, Axle Greeser. He was her target for the evening, the scalp she desired, the prize for which she'd fucked three very different roadies just a few moments ago. And as she walked down Sunset to her apartment on Highland Avenue, paying no paricular attention to all the whistles and comments from men with raging hormones cruising around for a good time in their expensive cars, she couldn't help thinking about Jimmie.

Would he remember her when he was a big star, or would she be just another one-night stand?

Maybe so, but the twinkling lights of Hollywood gave Cassandra the small comfort that they knew – oh yes, they knew – that she was his first one-night stand.

9 p.m.

THE 405 FREEWAY: FROM THE VALLEY TO
BEVERLY HILLS

'Bye, Mom.'

'Bye, honey – have a good time at Sherry's. Say hi to Mrs Williams for me.'

Tawny Peters never heard her mother's farewell. The front door had firmly closed on her departing utterance, and Tawny was already halfway down the suburban garden path that led to her own bright-red convertible Japanese car parked haphazardly in the Peters's driveway. Mrs Peters shrugged her shoulders and turned to her husband.

'Kids these days – always in such a hurry.'

'Huh.'

Mr Peters was engrossed in the latest issue of *Sports Illustrated* and wasn't paying attention to his wife or his daughter. He may have if he'd have known that his precious seventeen-year-old Tawny wasn't going to spend the night at her best girlfriend's house but rather in the clutches of a perverted Hollywood movie producer whose penchant for kinky sex would have raised even the most decadent of eyebrows. But Bob Peters had no idea what his daughter was up to so he stayed glued to an article about baseball while his loving wife went about the important tasks of being a Valley housewife.

It took but a few minutes for Tawny to drive to Sherry Williams's house. After the cursory smalltalk with Sherry's parents, the two teenagers retired to Sherry's room, ostensibly for the age-old custom known to teenagers the world over as 'dressing up'. To Tawny it was just another step in the elaborate deception that she was forced to perpetuate every time she wanted to visit Otto Verge. It involved deceiving her parents, it involved fooling Sherry's mom and dad and it even required that Sherry be misled.

'So when am I going to get to meet this drop-dead dreamboat hunk of a guy of yours? Uh?'

'Soon – soon. He's very shy.'

Tawny's excuses were running thin.

'Well, you owe me, Tawny. I've been covering for you for the last few months.'

'I know, Sherry – and I'd do the same for you.'

'Well, doesn't this Brad guy have any friends? Couldn't we go out on a double date?'

'It's not like that, Sherry. He's very quiet. He really doesn't go out. He's very private – reclusive. You know what rich people are like.'

'So you just stay at his fancy house all night and fool around.'

'Sherry!'

'Well, I'm curious. And you can't blame me. You sneak out of here once my parents have gone out, and you get back just before dawn, and all you ever tell me is that it was wonderful. You always have this real dreamy look on your face when you get back so what am I supposed to think?'

'OK, OK. I'll talk to Brad, and maybe we could arrange something. I'm sure he'd like to meet you.'

'All right. I'm dying to meet him.'

Tawny was indeed sure that Otto would love to have another young girl to chain to the wall, but how would Sherry react to find that the dreamy Brad didn't exist, but a seventy-year-old famous producer named Otto did? Tawny wasn't sure that Sherry could handle the shock. Tawny and Sherry were best friends, but like most best friends they were night and day different. Tawny was at seventeen the essence of California beauty, whereas Sherry reflected the homeliness of a Valley wallflower – not unattractive, but definitely not as stunning as Tawny. And certainly nowhere near as unruly. Tawny was adventuresome, with an untamed wild streak that ran through her lithe body, craving perversion, whereas Sherry still put pictures of rock stars on her wall and dreamed of them falling in love with her. Sherry was the perfect foil for Tawny, but one day there would be no stalling her easily fooled friend any longer.

Tawny kept telling herself that she would cross that bridge when she came to it.

Now that Sherry was pacified the girls went back to the business of trying on clothes and putting on make-up. All panties and bras, they modelled for each other until they heard Mr and Mrs Williams leave for their weekly visit to the movies.

'Don't wait up for us, kids. We'll be back late. We're going to see a double feature.'

'OK, Mom, Dad. Have a good time.'

Poor Sherry. She had no idea how everyone around her deceived her. Her parents never went to the movies. They traveled into nearby Burbank to the home of one of Mr Williams's friends where they engaged in an evening of good old-fashioned spouse-swapping.

Sherry and Tawny were glad to see the parents finally leave – it allowed the two girls to complete in relative secrecy the dressing-up of Tawny for her date with mythical Brad.

'So how do I look?'

'Terrific. Brad sure is a lucky guy, Tawny.'

'Thanks. You're a great friend.'

Tawny hugged Sherry and said goodnight, making sure that the window was open and that the small ivy trellis was still attached to the house so that when she returned just before dawn she would be able to climb up into Sherry's bedroom. Once safely inside Tawny would quietly climb to the upper bunk bed and remove from under the covers the bundle of clothes designed to pass as a surrogate sleeping Tawny. Replacing the bundle with her well-fucked body, she would drift off into a rather deep sleep, thereby creating the impression that she'd been a very good girl all that Saturday evening.

She would be good, but not quite in that way.

The transformation from the cutely dressed Tawny Peters to the sex-kitten Mistress Tawny took place in the bathroom of the Shell Petrol station on Victory Boulevard, just below the Interstate 405 on-ramp. Tawny always stopped at one of several petrol stations in the general vicinity of the freeway to fill up her bright red convertible for the drive into Beverly Hills and to change into the garb Otto required of her.

Tawny felt she was being quite the cautious operator not to stop at the same station at roughly the same time over a period of weeks, but she underestimated the observational prowess of bored petrol pumpers. Word had quickly spread amongst the stations close to the 405 to watch out for the cute blonde in the red car. Strategic holes had been drilled in the women's bathroom's walls and two-way mirrors installed of the kind the station used to protect its cash registers. The greased-up voyeurs could watch Tawny's unsuspecting show in relative comfort. And it took but a quick call on the local CB radio from whichever station Tawny chose for her quick change to alert the other stations. By the time Tawny had finished pumping petrol and pulled her car next to the bathroom door, an audience of perhaps ten to fifteen randy beer-drinking perverts had gathered to enjoy the show. Some brought Polaroid cameras, some brought video cameras, but all slurped huge gobs of grease on their turgid members as they wanked off to Tawny's unsuspecting striptease.

It was quite the thing to do on an otherwise boring Saturday night in the Valley.

Tawny was meticulous in her preparations for Otto. He was a perfectionist in his sex life as he was in his screen epics. Otto scripted everything – what she would say and what she would wear throughout the evening of debauchery, and he even provided her with a custom-made costume appropriate to her role. She kept the costume in a compartment underneath her car's spare tyre so as to hide the strange garments from her parents. After extracting the bag of goodies from the boot and quickly making her way to the women's lavatory, she always began her disrobing by locking the bathroom door to prevent an unwanted disturbance. Little did she know of her secret audience.

Her first step was to remove the cute little dress that she and Sherry had agreed was just the thing to wear for the fictional Brad. It was a flowered summer dress that flared at the waist into a multitude of bright pleats that swished enticingly with Tawny's provocative walk. She removed it by undoing a yellow-brick road of small buttons from just below the neck down to her waist. For no apparent reason Tawny performed this tantalising act directly facing the mirror. Perhaps it was that she enjoyed watching herself undress, to see her perfectly proportioned five-feet-eight-inch, one-hundred-and-ten-pound, seventeen-years-young body emerge from its little-girl covering, to cast off its cloak of innocence and emerge, bared, stripped down, lewd and ready for lust. It always excited her to undergo this transformation, made all the more filthy by the fact she was completing it in a smelly petrol station bathroom underneath the roaring Interstate freeway.

Button by button she undid with deft precision until no clasp remained fastened. Slowly Tawny's hands traced the path of the flowered material down from her neck to just below her navel, and ever so slowly again her sleek fingers worked their way up the dress gradually baring her body underneath, pausing briefly at that delicious space between her breasts, where the flesh was so soft and comforting to touch. Tawny never took her eyes off of the mirror as she disrobed. And neither did her audience, two of whom had prematurely shot their loads at the seductive emergence of Tawny's virginal white lingerie.

Tawny was tanned a seductive golden brown, emphasised all the more by the whiteness of her matching bra and panties. Her golden blonde hair matched her skin in the way that only unadulterated beauty's could. Her pubic hair was also a rich golden colour, creating an overall effect reminiscent of someone's idea of what a goddess must have looked like to mere mortals.

Turning completely around, Tawny carefully folded the dress and placed it into her bag. Next it was time to remove her underwear. Leaning over the bag she unhooked her bra by its front clasp and let the dainty garment fall down her arms to join the dress in her bag. This action kept her back to the mirror which drove several of the surreptitious audience to near hysterics. It was lucky for them that the noise of the freeway obscured their moans, groans and encouragements from Tawny's unsuspecting ears.

Still facing the garment bag, Tawny bent ever so slightly and hooked her hands into the taut elastic of her lacy white panties. Slithery, the dainty white knickers were removed from her bottom by her long-nailed fingers, revealing a pouting set of pussy lips for the petrol station perverts to ogle. Four more of the pumpers came at this point in the striptease show, their climax made all the more exciting by the way Tawny accidentally caught the hem of her knickers on the point of her black high heels. The thin white fabric stretched almost to the point of tearing, but then the stress was relieved by Tawny's delicate fingers. The panties were carefully placed in the bag.

Three more petrol pumpers orgasmed in torrents as Tawny turned to face the mirror quickly to doctor the goody-two-shoes make-up job she'd allowed Sherry to assist with. Tawny's full thirty-six inch bosom swayed gently as she pivoted on her black high heels, her golden bush glistening under the stark white light of the bathroom. She pouted her lips and adorned them with an intensely red lipstick that matched her nails. Her eyes received a deep blackening of liner to emphasise their natural deep blue. Powdering her face to bring out her tan, she couldn't resist the dusting of her breasts and her pubic mound. Reaching behind her she patted her bottom, as she did this girlish act her breasts jiggled lewdly. The remainder of the audience came at this point, and she hadn't even begun to put on her intriguing outfit that Otto had had specially made for Mistress Tawny.

Turning and reaching into the bag Tawny retrieved the garment and began the intricate process of slipping into it. The basis of the sex-kitten uniform was a pair of roughly one-inch-wide criss crossed black leather straps that intersected somewhere just above Tawny's navel, went up past her cleavage, over her shoulders, crossed again at the small of her back, wrapped around her thighs to meet back a few inches above her flat stomach. One could hardly call this outfit an item of clothing but perhaps a pair of elaborate belts. At strategic locations on the straps there were a variety of rings and poppets and studs for attaching the rest of the outfit.

The first attachment to be added was a tight leather choker that fastened tightly around Tawny's neck and connected to the diagonal straps by elasticated bright red ribbons. At the centre of the choker was a huge three inch diameter brass ring that dangled invitingly above Tawny's pertly full tits. Additional red ribbons were wrapped around the straps around Tawny's thighs and these were used for the exceedingly important task of holding up the sheer black nylons that Otto had found for her. The stockings had a firmly reinforced top band of a much heavier material than the sheer black nylon. This heavier material was punctuated with brass ring reinforced holes through which the red ribbon garters could be woven. Otto had gone to extreme lengths to find the stockings – after weeks of searching through the nylons sections of every department store in every shopping mall of Los Angeles he'd finally given up and had them special ordered from the legendary Playmates lingerie store on Hollywood Boulevard, saying that he needed them for one of his movies. Almost true.

Tawny balanced precariously on one high-heeled foot while she slid the black nylon sheath over her extended naked leg. In a motion that drove the covert audience to new heights of masturbatory pleasure she pivoted daintily, like a naughty ballerina, her back to the two-way mirror, and twisted her upper body so that she could observe whether the all important black back seam was straight. It was a picture of intense eroticism that was partially wasted on the majority of the uncouth audience unused to the nuances of such fetishes. The fact that she repeated the whole exercise for her other lovely leg, achieving a kind of sexual symmetry both in clothing and in a perfect young body willing to experience the heights and depths of lustful depravity meant little to the perverted pumpers. To them this was just like watching an X-rated movie at the local porn house, only better because it was live like the twenty-five cent peep shows. The majority of the audience expected Tawny to sit spread-eagled in front of the mirror and start playing with herself. They had no idea that this transformation had a purpose beyond the obvious titillation of seeing an extremely beautiful young woman undress.

Next came the footwear. They were red leather Victorian style high lace-up boots that snuggled tightly against Tawny's calf muscles. The laces were black velvet that provided a sensual link between the sheer black nylons and the red leather of the boots. To put on the antique footwear, Tawny had to prop herself against the bathroom wall, bend her leg at the knee and insert her pointed foot into the boot, extend her leg to its maximum length while pulling firmly on the top of the boot to settle her leg fully inside the snug red leather sheath. The hidden voyeurs were treated to an exquisite view of Tawny's long legs covered in the sheerest of black nylon being extended, flexed and bent for the audience's secret pleasure. The few true connoisseurs of women's nylon-covered gams that were amongst the petrol-pumpers paid keen attention to the way the dark-reinforced heel portion of the nylons disappeared in a tantilising fashion into the boot, as it did so rippling and creasing in such a perfect demonstration of seductive imperfection. So too, as Tawny bent her legs to insert her foot into the boot, delicate black nylon wrinkles emanated from just behind her knee and crept over her goddesslike thighs and calves. The vision was a voyeur's dream come true, although most of the secreted petrol station workers were too worked-up to notice such sexual nuances. They had, somewhat understandably, fallen into a predictable rut.

'She wants it bad . . .'

'Yeah, we should go and fuck her . . .'

'Yeah, man – after you . . .'

'Hey, Ernie, pass the Vaseline – I'm gonna have another wank.'

'Save some for me, Bert. I feel like another quick one.'

'Who's got the beer? Where's the brews, man?'

And so it continued, almost as if the greased-up petrol pumpers were watching a football or baseball game on national television. And there really wasn't any danger of the audience molesting Tawny. Oh, they might talk all right, but it was generally agreed that a girl that weird should be left alone. Secretly they were all afraid that she carried in her big black bag a really big carving knife specially sharpened to wop off offending penises. Much discussion had surrounded the reasons for Tawny's elaborate garb and the unconventional way in which she changed into it. All of the petrol station employees agreed that most probably Tawny was some sort of feminist avenging angel out to wreak vigilante justice on rapists and perverts that the courts seemed to want to ignore. Like a black widow spider she'd entice them with the outfit she wore and then *wham* – off it would come with one swift motion of her sexy hands. That's what the guys called Tawny – the Black Widow – and despite their macho bravado none were about to test the hypothesis.

Tawny, who was of course quite oblivious to her reputation, was completing her costume by the addition of appropriate breast and pussy coverings. The costume, as it now stood, basically crisscrossed between her full tits, leaving them completely exposed. Likewise framed, but not covered, was her blonde pussy with the black leather straps wrapped around her thighs. Otto had thought this openness perhaps a mite too obvious, so he'd prepared a bra and panty set of sorts. The bra was the first to be donned. It was made of red leather and fashioned to hook conveniently to the leather straps as they descended down Tawny's sculptured back. It was more of a wraparound kind of bra like those shoulderless types worn with bikinis at the beach, except it did have one noticeable difference. Matching in brass to the large ring attached to the choker were two smaller rings that framed two small holes in the red leather through which Tawny's nipples were to be exposed. It took Tawny quite a bit of fiddling with her breasts to get her nipples through the holes, but once so exposed the coolness of the metal insured that the firm buds of flesh remained pointing through.

It was the observing of this exercise – the moulding of Tawny's tits under her own hands, the squeezing of her nipples through the tiny brass rings by her red fingernails – that caused several of the valiant pumpers to orgasm yet once more. Exhausted they sat watching the final dressing act. All but one or two of them remained masturbating, determined to save their second release until the final moment.

It was not long off as Tawny stepped into the red satin panties that were tied with red elasticated cords to the black leather thigh straps. Bent over to one side she delicately tied a dainty red bow around the black leather and repeated the act on the other thigh. The crotch of the panties was split but covered by a flap of satin such that a prying finger or cock could easily gain entrance. The outfit was now ostensibly complete.

Standing before the mirror, admiring her lustful form, Tawny added her final preening touches. Otto had gone to great lengths to emphasise the need for Tawny to have a few blonde pubic curls exposed through the red satin flap of the panties. Opening her legs slightly, Tawny reached underneath her crotch with her long fingers and pulled some of her golden tresses out of the flap. She had to repeat the act several times before a sufficient quantity was poking through the gap in the material. Wetting the hairs with her fingers helped considerably in this endeavour – an action that reduced the die-hards in the audience to quivering spouts of sperm.

With a final tease of her hair and the throwing over her shoulders of a light long raincoat that she buttoned loosely around her, Tawny was dressed for the part she was now to play. She turned and headed for the bathroom door but paused before she left and did something quite innocent that caught the audience unawares. Looking at herself in the mirror she blew herself a kiss and said, 'You look gorgeous.' It was a simple compliment that anyone taking a considerable amount of effort to get dressed for an occasion would do before venturing out – understandable enough. Yes, indeed. But to the wanked-out petrol pumpers the obvious became a subject of much debate. It seems they mistook this innocent action and assumed that Tawny was completely aware of their sly observations and was deliberately putting on a show for them. By the time a consensus of opinion had been reached amidst the circle-jerkers, Tawny was proceeding south on Interstate 405. It was just nine o'clock, and if the traffic stayed as light as it was she should be on Otto's Beverly Hills doorstep within thirty minutes.

Tawny drove her red convertible with extreme care. It would not do to be pulled over for some minor traffic offence by one of the ever vigilant California Highway Patrol officers who might then wonder what the seventeen-year-old Tawny Peters was doing dressed up like something out of the Marquis de Sade's worst nightmare. Being pulled over by a cop might involve tremendous explanations that would result in phone calls to parents and then the whole balloon would go up. Not worth it reasoned Tawny. And so she drove at the speed limit of fifty-five miles per hour as all manner of cars zoomed passed her doing at least seventy. It really didn't bother her. She was in no hurry. The drive gave her time to compose her thoughts, to prepare her lines, make sure every so often that a small amount of blonde pubic hair was still sticking invitingly out of her red satin knickers.

Before she knew how much time had actually passed by she was turning into the large driveway of Otto Verge's monstrous mansion. The iron gateway was open, awaiting her arrival. By virtue of a closed-circuit video camera that had announced her approach, the gate creaked shut the moment her small car had passed through.

According to the script she was to park at the end of the driveway and walk to the door of the mansion. Tawny did as instructed, feeling the tingling of apprehension as she walked in pitch blackness along the heavily wooded driveway. It was, as ever, vaguely terrifying, just like the time she had first met Otto Verge. She had been drawn to him like a moth to a flame. He had been obliged to make a small speech to her high-school English class as part of the high school consenting to let his movie company use the school for a location shot for one of his movies. He had been witty and charming, full of anecdotes about movie stars and writing movies and literature. His teutonic accent and aged vitality commanded the respect of the class in a most unusual manner. The students were captivated, and one in particular, Tawny, was enthralled and consumed. Otto, of course, had more than altruistic notions for giving the lecture. He had hoped that there would be some bright young thing that he could possess – and indeed there was. He had spotted Tawny and she had fallen under his spell. After class she had stayed and had asked if she could visit the movie studios. Otto was gracious and gave her his card. She called the next day to arrange a time. That was two months ago. It had taken but a week for Tawny to assume the sex-kitten role. It was, she knew deep inside her young and willing body, what she had been craving from the moment her luscious body and mind had discovered sex.

After a final few crunchy steps on the gravel driveway, Tawny reached the imposing front door·of the mansion. The huge building appeared deserted, foreboding, in much the way that the house in *Psycho* had seemed to the attractive Janet Leigh. Making sure that her raincoat was tightly closed about her she rang the doorbell. Once. Twice. Three times. As she rang it a fourth time the door creaked open and Otto appeared dressed in a silk robe, monocle in one eye, cigarette in a long-stemmed black holder in his free hand.

'Yes?'

'I wonder if I may use your telephone. My car has broken down, and I need to call for help.'

'It will be difficult to obtain service at this time of night, but you may try. Enter if you will. Follow me, young woman.'

'Thank you. You are so kind.'

Tawny meekly followed Otto as the script he had given her required. They descended a staircase and entered an elaborately paneled room opulently decorated with turn-of-the-century erotica. Otto motioned for Tawny to sit in a chair next to the phone.

'Here is the phone – the number of the garage is in the book. Would you care for some wine while you wait?'

'Yes, yes – that would be nice. I need to calm my nerves. You are so kind.'

'Yes, I am.'

Otto handed Tawny a goblet of wine from which she sipped as she dialed the fictitious number. As detailed in the script she dropped the receiver and her goblet.

'I – I feel strange. I think I'm passing out.'

'Yes, yes, you are. A small potion in the wine that will render you helpless for a short while. When you wake up you will be totally and unconditionally at my mercy.'

'Oh . . .'

And with that understated exclamation Tawny passed out. Although she really didn't because the wine hadn't really been drugged, as Otto had scripted it she was more than happy to oblige. She felt his strong arms encircle her, and carry her off to the dungeon and the fates that awaited her there.

A short while later she 'came to,' acting, as she was supposed to, thoroughly confused and disoriented and, according to the script she had so diligently memorised, struggled in vain against the chains that held her bound and spreadeagled to a dark brick wall. Huge flaming torches burned above her head, giving the undeniable impression of being imprisoned in a medieval dungeon. She tried to cry out but the leather gag in her mouth prevented all but the merest of whimpers from escaping. Her eyes focused on Otto. He still wore his huge silk robe and that detestable monocle. His bald head glistened and shone under the flaming torchlight. In his hand he held what looked like a cat o' nine tails. Tawny's eyes bulged at the sight of the intimidating object. Seeing her shock, Otto began his monologue.

'Do not struggle. It is futile. I could give you all the boring technical details about the tensile strength of heat-treated steel sunk by eight-inch rods into the finest of stone, but suffice it to say, your most delectable form has nowhere near the strength to break those bonds. No one ever has. No one ever will.'

Tawny struggled once more and then succumbed to Otto's words.

'You will also be much more comfortable if I take that gag out of your mouth. I do detest loud screaming, and there would be no point. This chamber is soundproof. I have tested it with the most severe of sounds, and my servants have slept through the most unspeakable of acts. So if I take the gag out of your mouth please do not anger me by screaming. Yes?'

Tawny nodded, her blonde curls falling seductively in front of her charming face. Otto removed the gag. As Tawny began to spout a thousand questions – demands – Otto held up his hand to stop the verbal onslaught.

'One moment, one moment and I will explain. I can understand your anger at your predicament, but let me explain. May I?'

'Go on.' Tawny sounded suspect.

'You are my prisoner. There is no hope of escape, but fear not. I will do nothing that you yourself do not want to happen to you, and you can leave whenever you wish. Just say the word and I will let you go. I will even have my chauffeur drive you to wherever you need to go, and you can rescue your car in the daylight. But if you desire sexual experiences of the kind you have only ever pretended not to dream about, stay and play my wicked game. No harm will come to you, only an excess of emotion and sexual release that your young body has no idea it contains.'

'And I can leave at any time?'

'At any point in the proceedings you may ask me for your release, and I will give it to you. You have my word on the matter.'

'Well, your offer is quite intriguing, and as you can tell from my garb, I was looking for sex of the most bizarre kind. I am tired of boring boys and their bungled attempts at arousing my sex. I want a man who knows how to handle my cunt with the authority it demands.'

Tawny had now made the transition to the sex kitten Mistress Tawny.

'Indeed, I am that man. The gods of lust brought you to me tonight. Your nipples swell with anticipation of my lash. I should reward their straining with a few well-placed strokes.'

'Oh please, please – beat them, but be careful with my tender buds. They have never been touched so. Be gentle at first.'

'Tonight will be the first of many such raptures for you – mark my words and mark my lash.'

And with that oratory Otto Verge brought the velvet cat o' nine tails down across Tawny's breasts, making sure to drag the lashes thoroughly around the young woman's nipples as the swollen buds poked through the brass rings of the red leather bra. Otto didn't hit Tawny hard enough to cause real pain, but the electricity of having the soft velvet pulled roughly across her tender nipples made her cry out, not with agony but with the discomfort of too much sensation.

'Ah – I can tell you will be a true devotee of the velvet lash. Perhaps you would like to feel its caress somewhere perhaps a little more sensitive – a little more wet?'

Tawny had let her head fall forward, her long blonde locks obscuring her face. Jerking her head upwards she peered through the mass of tangled strands with a feral stare. This was indeed a much better form of sex than sucking off members of the football team.

'Yes, master, yes – whip my cunt with your lash. Let me feel its nine fingers on my sex. Frig my box with your naughty tool so that I may juice for you.'

'As you wish, you nasty wench. Spread your legs wide. Strain against your chains.'

Tawny did as ordered until she was almost unable to stand, the steel chains holding her body in its vulnerable stance. Her inner thighs pulsed under the tension, her cunt gaped wide. She could feel small drops of her moisture begin the journey down the twisty path of golden pubic hair that protruded, as required by Otto, from between Tawny's open red satin panties.

'Let me first arrange your quim to be more accommodating of my lash.'

Otto Verge took his seventy-year-old hands and matter-of-

72

factly began to pull aside the red satin panties, fingering in the process Tawny's tender young mons. Otto, skilled in navigating the terrain of a woman's cunt, quickly uncovered the throbbing bud of Tawny's clitoris. He squeezed the pink delicacy between his thumb and finger. Tawny winced and gasped at the shock such rough handling caused.

'Ah, I can tell you are ripe. A few well-placed strokes of my lash and you will bear fruit.'

Tawny could only whimper.

'Lean forward from the wall so that your pert young ass is not touching the bricks. Good, good – you are an obedient sex kitten. And you will see that in the position you are now in, the lash strokes will be all the more enjoyable. The full length of the velvet cat will wrap themselves up between your legs, up between your bottom, and as I pull the lashes fully down they will slide between your ass cheeks, over your cunt hole and across your pleasure knob. Delightful.'

'Please – please do it. Whip me – whip my sex.'

'As you wish.'

Otto did just as he described. Holding the whip loosely in his hand he lowered it to the ground and brought it forcefully upwards between Tawny's exposed thighs. The velvet lashes immediately found their tempting home and became covered with a delicious ooze of sweat and musky cunt juice. Otto then pulled the whip up towards Tawny's mouth, dragging the lashes over her engorged clitoris in a slow and telling process. By the time the whip handle had reached her mouth and she was allowed to suck the leather in gratitude for its job well done, the last of the lashes were slipping off of her titillated bud. It was as if she were sucking her own clitoris in some perverted kind of dream in which all manner of depravity was made possible through a most pliable body and an exceedingly long tongue.

Over and over again Otto repeated the action, each time lingering tauntingly a little longer on Tawny's clitoris as she sucked gratefully on the whip's bound-leather handle and her master's curled fingers. Otto felt genuinely lucky to have found this girl at the Valley high school of all places. She was a most remarkable find, willing to do anything as long as it involved kinky sex. The boys back at Encino High School just didn't know what they were missing.

After several applications of the velvet lash, the nine strands were becoming soaked through with Tawny's juices. As Otto directed the whip up between her ass and passed her cunt, Tawny increasingly shook with the release of further moisture. She licked her bright red lips as she could hear the slippery sounds of the lash as it journeyed from between the tightness of her ass, pausing briefly at her dripping cunt to gain momentum for the exquisite dance it was to do with her clitoris. She welcomed the whip into her mouth as a small token of her gratitude for the naughtiness it allowed her. This was sex at its very best for Tawny, better by far than the bumbling boys who, try as hard as they could, could not please the desire buried deep within her young, quivering thighs. It was sex that was better than the moments when she brought herself off with her long nails, toying with the bud that was being tantilised so by the lashes. Up until these moments with Otto it had been her own playing with her cunt on those warm Valley nights that had been the peak of sexual frenzy for Tawny. Now she had discovered that the deep and dirty thoughts that she used to bring her to climax under her own hand were indeed not only the province of her imagination. They had a life of their own in the form of Otto's lurid fetishes.

Otto sensed Tawny's impending release with all the keenness of a vulture sniffing out dead meat. He noticed how her soaked thigh muscles began to tremble, and how her head snaked back against the cold brick wall as her lovely throat began to emit deep guttural moans. Otto had nestled the whip between Tawny's ass cheeks, this time pulling the hard handle down past her reddening cunt, spreading her flushed pink lips to dance nastily across her bursting clitoris before plunging the warm handle deep inside the young girl's stretched wide opening. Tawny sank on to the shaft with a fond oblivion that relished her sex-slave role. To be chained against the wall, to be dressed in the perverted clothes that she'd furtively changed into, to have Otto – a seventy-year-old man – live out his fantasies on her young body was a freedom that excited passions within her that normal people only ever read about.

* * *

'Tonight is to be a special night for our lust, my dear Mistress Tawny. I have several new adventures planned for us, that judging by your most recent performance under the lash, I am sure you are most ready for.'

'As you wish, Otto. I trust in your judgement.' The script so diligently prepared by Otto was not completed. It was time to improvise.

'Then let me release you and introduce you to the horse. I think you will enjoy riding this stallion.'

Otto unchained the come-drained Tawny and offered her his hand in a most gentlemanly fashion – even though he stood quite naked before her. He had disrobed while she recovered from her sapping release, and the sight of his proud erection had greeted Tawny as her eyelids fluttered open. Otto's was a majestic cock of strong proportions. His balls were swollen with lust and his slit was sticky with telltale fluid. Tawny marvelled at the fineness of his gray pubic hairs and the tautness of his ageing body. Otto worked hard to stay in shape, swimming several miles a day in his Roman fresco swimming pool. The results of his aquatic exertions showed in the tanned firmness of his muscles, and the exercise his stiff penis received showed in the eagerness with which it beckoned Tawny to feast upon its rapture. It was all she could do not to drop to her knees and swallow it whole, but Otto had said that he had something special for her – something about riding a horse. Bizarre and frightening thoughts danced in the pit of Tawny's stomach, heightening the lust dripping from her cunt.

'Behold – the horse.'

The object had been hidden behind a black satin curtain that Otto had ceremoniously pulled aside. The horse resembled a vaulting horse used in gymnasiums the world over, but it had been modified in quite a special way. The seat was made of black leather and there were no handles – just a statuesque ebony erect phallus sticking provoking upwards from the rear in much the way that a show horse's tail will stand erect. The way the huge dildo strained upwards at a slight angle reminded her of the beautiful curve in Otto's bulging member, and then it dawned on Tawny that he had probably modelled the artificial dick on his own more than capable tool. Otto was definitely quite egotistical and most vain.

'And what do you think of my latest toy, Mistress Tawny? I had it specially built for you.'

'It is – it is exquisite. I cannot wait to ride it.'

'You will, my dear, and quite soon. But please examine the beast closer. Become intimate with your stallion.'

Tawny stroked the horse as if it were a living animal. She inspected every inch of its body closely, as if communing secret thoughts to its inanimate form. Underneath the black phallus, the front and back faces of the horse seemed to be finished in a jet-black marble as were all the four legs. The horse stood in a shallow trough which appeared to have in it a small drain of some sort, for some soon-to-be-discovered unspeakable purpose, no doubt, surmised Tawny. The prospects caused her cunt to quiver in anticipation. She licked her lips.

'Ah, I neglect your comfort so. Please indulge your body in some wine. Drink – drink your fill. It is required.'

'I drink to your health, Otto.'

'Indeed. Drink your fill, little one, for I am to have mine.'

Tawny gulped down the red wine, letting small amounts trickle out of the goblet and down her neck and on to the large brass ring between her breasts. The sight caused Otto's penis to twitch noticeably.

'It is time. Mount the horse, Mistress Tawny.'

'As you wish, Master.'

Tawny climbed on to the leather seat and inched her way back and over the hard ebony penis, bending the hard rubber of the dick forward as she took her stance. She settled slowly on the huge shaft making sure her clitoris rubbed properly upon the seat as she allowed her full weight to be taken by the horse.

'Now lie forward. Put your arms down the front legs of the horse. Let your legs rest on its back legs. That is good. You look most inviting. How do you feel?'

'I feel ready to serve your desires by offering you my body.'

'Do you feel vulnerable?'

'With you I am always vulnerable. And now more so that you have given me such a fine present.'

'There remains but one last touch. I must bind your limbs.'

'I had hoped you would.'

Otto took bright red cords and slowly tied Tawny's stockinged legs and then her tanned arms to the horse's marble legs. Upon completing the process, he kissed her on the back of the neck, her face being pressed against the black leather seat. He whispered in her ear his wishes.

'I take it you know what you must do.'

'I do – and I will.'

'I have longed for this moment. You are a treasure to make my dreams – my fantasies, my perversions – such a charming reality.'

'Please don't delay any longer,' she gasped. 'I need your sex in me.'

'Your wish is mine, my dear Mistress Tawny.'

Otto walked over to a nearby table and picked up a small clear container. He walked over to the horse and momentarily drank deep the sight that greeted his eager penis. Tawny's tanned red-satin-covered bottom was thrust forward invitingly. Her long black-nylon-covered legs strapped to the black marble of the horse, the immaculately straight seams of her stockings disappearing into the red leather Victorian boots, was a sight that would have made a lesser man ejaculate forthwith. But Otto was made of sterner stuff.

'I must remove your panties to insure correct positioning – it will take but a moment.'

'Take whatever you want, Otto, and however long you want. I am yours to do with as you please.'

Otto undid the ties that held the panties to the leather straps and slid the soaked garments from underneath Tawny. He slipped his hand underneath her sex and slid her body slightly backwards on the black dildo so that she would have slid off the horse if it were not for the surrogate dick and the restraining straps on her limbs. In this position her bottom was thrust outward – a perfect target.

Otto took aim at the bull's-eye of her anus.

'A little lubrication is helpful.'

He poured the contents of the container he had retrieved from the table over Tawny's ass, making sure that plenty of the warm oil coated her anus. With his largest finger he smeared the oil deep inside the tight opening, causing Tawny to shake from the force of the sudden penetration. The excess oil could be heard dripping from the black leather on to the marble of the trough, dominating the chamber in the way the ticking of a clock dominates a silent room.

Otto coated the end of his cock with the warm oil and positioned himself just above the trough. It was a perfect height – his cockhead exactly matched the level of the small buttonlike opening of Tawny's arse. Slowly or quickly? He debated. It took but an instant to decide the speed and violence of his intended entry. Without any warning he forced his member completely inside the virgin sphincter, causing a scream of intensely desirable pain to be emitted by the bound young woman.

'Oh God, oh God – oh, Jesus – oh, Christ . . .'

'I'm afraid they are unable to help you at this moment, my dear Mistress Tawny. Trust me – the pleasure will overcome the pain quite shortly.'

'Oh, oh, it has – it has – oh Christ – no matter how much I ask you to, don't stop. Please don't stop.'

'I shall not, my dear. Do you like the way my cock feels up your ass? Do you like the way it can be felt against its twin inside your pussy? Is it not delightful to have my shafts inside you? One stonelike and perfectly smooth, the other alive and pulsing so that you can feel every minor ridge and bulge twitch within you.'

Tawny wanted to say what a truly unusual feeling it was to have two such large cocks inside of her, and how she could feel them grinding together between the membrane of her cunt, but she could only scream as she felt her insides seemingly being torn apart. The pain was almost unbearable, almost causing her to beg the perverted movie director to stop. But she couldn't – she wouldn't. She knew what was required of her.

With each thrust of his muscular form Otto ass-fucked Tawny's body which was fucked in turn by the inanimate resistance of the horse – her already ravaged clitoris rubbed by her weight and the force of Otto's thrusts into the leather of the seat. She bit tightly into the rich blackness of the horse to stifle another loud scream as Otto's penis tore through her, the taste of the leather acidic and intoxicating to her, pacifying the intense feelings of agony and ecstasy.

Otto enjoyed watching the slap of his pelvis into the young woman's ass – the way the taut tanned skin of her buttocks strained under the straps of her garment, the way her golden thighs rippled in the black nylons. It was perhaps his greatest sexual moment to have taken her virgin asshole in this way. He had procured many young women in his time, but there was something about the eyes of this one that spoke to his inner being – he dared to think that perhaps these encounters would lead to something more than his usual one-night stand of perverted sex and uncomfortable morning-after breakfasts. Certainly Tawny seemed to enjoy his aberrations as much as he, and that was a good sign. As much as she screamed in pain as his large penis bored into her, he knew that she would not have it any other way.

Such thoughts played havoc with Otto's psyche as the tightness of Tawny's asshole gripped his shaft with growing vigour. She was crying with a lustful abandon, tossing her blonde locks to and fro as if to dissipate the intensity within her. The sight of Tawny in the throes of orgasm and the sensations her frenzied motions produced were too much for Otto to bear. His moment was nearing. His swollen balls banged against the face of the horse, slapping indecently against the marble. Otto had refused to play with himself all week long and had forsaken all other forms of sexual release in preparation for tonight. He was primed for the tight constriction of Tawny's ass and its unrelenting sucking pressure on his shaft could not be denied any longer. He was going to come. It was time for the *pièce de résistance* of his fetishes.

Tawny was in sexual heaven, or perhaps hell – she wasn't too sure of anything other than the way her body seemed to be melting from the tip of her clitoris to the depths of her brain. From her toes to her nipples she was one quaking mass of sexual fervour. It had been wise of Otto to fasten Tawny's body to the horse. She could have never voluntarily subjected herself to this debauchery, but with no choice in the freedom of her movements she readily enjoyed every thrust and every slap of her thighs as she dissolved into a pool of constant orgasming desire.

Her reverie was disturbed by Otto's insistent cries.

'Now, Tawny – now, my dear, release your precious cargo – please!'

Otto was screaming at full volume as he released his pent-up load of steamy come inside Tawny's shuddering bottom at the very moment that Tawny complied with his perverted wishes. Thanks to the specially designed seat of the horse, it was surprisingly easy for Tawny to unleash the flow – it just seemed like such an extension of her seemingly continuous orgasming. To Tawny it felt as if her thighs were melting into a pool of steaming flesh.

Otto was at first disappointed because in the throes of his own orgasm he did not notice the warm sensation enveloping his genitals, but quicker than this uncertainty could take over his mushing brain, he felt Tawny's hot urine surround his cock and his balls in a warmth that simultaneously dissolved the bones in his legs.

Otto felt a deep sense of satisfaction in knowing that his perverted design actually worked. The fluid mechanics of the horse's specially crafted seat performed flawlessly, directing and deflecting Tawny's yellow stream against his balls as Otto fucked her from the rear. The passion of the moment consumed his being as the full force of Tawny's emission engulfed his heaving testicles. Otto gasped, feeling that at last he could understand what a woman's orgasm must feel like.

'We are one – you and I ... I am your body, I am your come.' Otto rambled almost deliriously under the spell of his revelation about feminine release. He truly felt as if he were out of his seventy-year-old body, as if this Nirvanalike feeling was what it was like to die. Appearing drunk or drugged, Otto slumped forward on top of Tawny but lost his footing in the ooze that such messy lovemaking created, thereby collapsing backwards to the floor, an exhausted old man writhing in the effluent of his perversions. happier than he could ever have imagined possible.

Tawny had no idea of Otto's lack of control, for she too was lost to the normal niceties of civilised life. As she kept pissing in happy relief – the wine desperate to complete its transformation – she felt as if she was experiencing one continuous orgasm the like of which she would probably die from, such was its violence. She wished she could reach under her wracked body and frig her clitoris in the warm yellow ocean in which it swam, but since her hands were restrained she was forced to content herself with the ample writhings of her athletic hips. Under her motions, the warmth cascaded over the marble and around the black dildo and down to the trough, waterfalling over the ecstatic form of Otto Verge. In between a fading vision of reality, Tawny finally understood the need for the small drain in the trough.

Otto moaned his desperate feelings of complete sexual satisfaction to a passed-out Tawny. Stumbling through the mess of his depraved lust he made his way to the front of the horse and cradled Tawny's head in his hands. Otto wept as he mumbled incoherent compliments to the shattered seventeen-year-old about how she had fulfilled long-standing desires of his.

'You have made me a happy man, Mistress Tawny, but tonight isn't over by far, my dear young thing. Tonight I shall repay your performance here by taking you out. That's right. Tonight we shall venture out in public – you and I together in full view of the world. It shall be your coming-out party.'

Tawny slept peacefully on the horse, oblivious to Otto's weeping testimonials and promises, completely unaware of Otto sitting in the trough, his tears dripping on to the cold marble, intermingling with her bodily effluent, combining briefly to flow in a poetic unison down the small drain and into the Beverly Hills sewer system.

10 p.m.

Near Los Angeles Airport and the Freeways Thereabouts

'Here's a fifty-dollar bill – just get me out of this fucking airport to some place dark and comfortable where I can kill this fucked night.'

'Sure, you're the boss. Anything you say.'

As the yellow cab pulled away from the International Terminal of LAX, otherwise known as the Los Angeles Airport, Australian lawyer Sydney Nats breathed a deep sigh of frustration. If all had gone well he'd have been roughly halfway to England by now. But it hadn't. And he wasn't.

The prim and proper British Airways counter assistant with extremely pert breasts, who under more of an ideal setting would have entranced Sydney no end with her firm, up-turned nipples, had been as polite as humanly possible. With an unflappable optimism that was born deep within her pointy bosom she had shown an uncanny aplomb in informing the increasingly angry passengers that the 5 p.m. flight to London Heathrow had been delayed due to a problem with the incoming aeroplane. The new scheduled departure time had been set for 7 p.m., and then 8 p.m., and then 9 p.m. – and then the prim and proper and now somewhat embarrassed assistant whose breasts no longer seemed in the slightest bit pert to an enraged Sydney, had with great apologies announced that the weary potential passengers would have to wait for a replacement 747 to arrive, and consequently the earliest they would leave for England would be 8 a.m. the next morning. Sorry and all that – bit of a bother but we do appreciate your patience. We'll be sure to get you to old England just as soon and safely as possible, and oh, by the way, have a complimentary stay at an airport hotel and a smashing free British Airways biro on us as a token of our regrets at having prolonged your stay in jolly old America.

Sydney was, to put it mildly, royally pissed off. He hadn't wanted to come to America so soon after his last encounter with the country and the entrancements of one of its cocktail waitresses, but business knows no room for personal malaise. So here he was in Los Angeles – at least it wasn't Silicon Valley – but he still couldn't help jumping just a little at the appearance (and in Los Angeles it happened quite frequently) of a long-legged blonde with a feisty attitude.

In between these bouts of over-the-shoulder neck-breaking gyrations Sydney timed his weeklong infuriating meetings with the arsehole American agent of his highly wealthy English show-biz client to be completed no later than Saturday morning. At least that part had gone according to plan, but in order to catch the flight he did have to bow out of a fancy Malibu Beach party that was being held by the arsehole agent. Normal business etiquette would have demanded his attendance after completing the lengthy negotiations, but Sydney had desperately wanted to catch the now-mythical BA flight 286 to London Heathrow in time to be back in England and at The Fosters' Oval for the Sunday play in the fifth test of this year's Ashes. England and Australia were tied at two games all in the series, and it had taken the pulling of some heavy-duty strings to get Sydney a ticket. Now he'd miss the Sunday play, and he had to be in court on Monday and Tuesday. Anger rose deep within as he came to the inevitable conclusion that there would be no chance personally to partake in the ritual rivalry between his native country and his adopted country. To add insult to injury, he was now sure that under the fucked-up circumstances of his life in general the Poms would win the Ashes back from the Aussies. No wonder he was upset and in need of a relaxing drink or two – or ten.

As the cab negotiated its way through the airport congestion and out on to Century Boulevard with all of its hotels and car-rental offices, the cab driver tried to engage Sydney in conversation, as cab drivers that speak English are wont to do with their usually frazzled passengers.

'Bad night, uh?'

'Uh huh.'

'Feel like a woman to make it better? I knows a real good . . .' Sydney interrupted the erstwhile pimp-cum-taxi driver.

'Look, I just want a drink – or maybe a couple. I don't need a hooker, OK?'

Sydney's tone implied a not so subtle 'just leave me alone', but the cab driver knew too little of subtlety.

'You maybe wants a boy?'

'No.' Sydney was emphatic.

The cab driver was insistent. 'OK you maybe like to watch women? You know, dance. I knows a great –'

Once again Sydney felt compelled to shut the amateur psychologist up, but carefully weighed his strategy in achieving this goal. As an experienced lawyer Sydney was a practised reader of the peculiar mannerisms of people. He immediately deduced that it would be better to agree to something – but not just anything – just to shut the chatty cabby up.

'If the place serves good drinks, fine. Just get me there as soon as possible, OK?'

'Yeah, sure, OK. Dis place is real classy.'

As surmised by Sydney, the taxi driver closed his mouth in the satisfaction of having been helpful and concentrated on getting to his chosen destination as quickly as possible.

It took but a few minutes to arrive at the Jet Strip A Go-Go. Garish neon signs announcing a plentiful supply of nudes and liquor greeted Sydney as he extricated himself from the taxi and its full-of-advice driver. A burly doorman opened the door to the strip club for Sydney without comment. Inside it was dark and the beat of highly amplified disco music assailed his ears. A grim passageway adorned with extremely faded pictures of once beautiful women in various stages of undress led him to the box office where a gum-chewing female asked Sydney for his money without even looking at him, careful not to be distracted from the demanding task of filing her nails.

'Ten dollars, two drink minimum. The girls do accept tips.'

As he pushed his money through the grimy slot in the counter Sydney reflected on the cab driver's description of the Jet Strip A Go-Go as a 'real classy place'. Sydney was secretly glad that he hadn't taken the driver up on his offer of a 'real good' hooker.

Through a foggy haze of cigarette smoke and flashing lights Sydney made his way to the bar where he staked out a seat roughly in the centre of the room. Mirrors were strategically placed so the dedicated drinker could sup intently without missing any of the action on the stage. Sydney ordered a gin and tonic from a barmaid who didn't look old enough to be serving alcohol. The drink was expensive – eight bucks – but the view of the young barmaid in skin-tight jeans and a black lace bustier bending over to mix his drink was worth the expense. Sydney was starting to feel just a little bit better.

On the stage a rather emaciated black woman was wrapping herself around a brass pole and sliding up and down the object in a most lewd fashion, all to the noise of some highly synthesised version of the seventies hit, 'Shaft', by Isaac Hayes. The sight didn't really captivate Sydney, who was more interested in the athletic prowess of the young barmaid and the peculiar manner in which she opened beer bottles. Sydney's amazed gaze was disturbed by a lull in the music and a loud announcement by a hyped-up DJ.

'A big hand for Sirena. Wouldn't we all like to give her a big hand, huh? Just kidding, guys. But seriously, folks – would you put those big hands together to welcome our Texas rose, the star of the Lone Star State. Watch out for her six guns, you guys down front – let's here it for Miss Kimberly Duke.'

Convinced that Kimberly Duke would be as interesting as Sirena's fumbled pole vaulting, Sydney decided it was time for another gin and tonic. The disco music was replaced by some rock-and-roll version of an old-time cowboy song emerging from the sounds of welcoming cheers and applause. This occurrence generally reinforced Sydney's conviction that a real beefy farm girl was about to take the stage, so he turned his back and concentrated on the barmaid. The room started to erupt, but Sydney was oblivious to all the excitement as he tried to figure out how best to make a move on the young barmaid. The careful planning of his seduction strategy was interrupted by the fleeting glimpse of a reflection in the behind-the-bar mirror that did more than catch Sydney's well-trained eye. The young buxom barmaid with skin-tight jeans never stood a chance after that. Sydney didn't even order another drink. He forgot his thirst and turned to stare at the vision that had taken centre stage.

It was Miss Kimberly Duke direct from Austin, Texas, but as far as Sydney was concerned she might as well have been an angel from heaven. Amidst a wall of synthetic fog and strobe lights Miss Duke was cracking a bullwhip to the beat of the music – side-on profile shot, Kimberly was stunning in the freeze-frame effect of the strobe lights. It was like looking at a movie frame by frame, and what exquisite frames they were.

Kimberly was tall, at least six foot. Her hair was a golden blonde that shimmered like honey under the starkness of the lights. Her legs were bare and stockingless – for good reason; her long limbs were as golden as her hair and Sydney could swear he could see the soft downy hairs of her thighs radiating that same golden hue. For a man that had promised himself he would never fall for a long-legged blonde ever again, Sydney was on dangerous ground as he moved closer to the stage. He was mesmerised by the perfect vision of natural beauty before him; the few ice cubes left over from his gin and tonic were melting in the glass held loosely in his sweating hand. Just as he reached the periphery of the crowd at the front of the stage the strobe lights halted their somewhat annoying dance and a spotlight of high-intensity white illuminated a full-frontal view of the Texas rose.

The crowd gasped. Compared to the other women working the seedy club, Miss Duke was in a league all of her own, and by the look of her tanned face, she knew it. She held every man in the room in the palm of her long-fingered hand as she stood motionless, her breasts heaving as she caught her breath, legs astride, facing the audience. A white cowboy hat was cocked playfully on the back of her head, exposing her plentiful cascading blonde curls which dangled delightfully over her shoulders. Her lips were the brightest red, perfectly emphasised by the deep blue of her eyes. Her smile was full and kissable – she had the kind of mouth that men would gladly trade their hands for. The rest of the outfit she wore would on anyone else have been perhaps even a trifle clichéd and gaudy, but on Kimberly Duke it positively shone with originality. The crowd focused on her large rippling bosom which was meagrely covered by the slightest of white leather, rhinestone-studded waistcoats that strained underneath the pressure of her confined cleavage.

As the beat of the music picked up, Kimberly strutted around the stage, cracking the whip once more. The vision was illuminated now by the spotlight rather than the strobe, and it was now much easier for the increasingly rabid audience to see how the whipping motion caused Kimberly's large breasts occasionally to expose themselves from underneath the tiny leather waistcoat. Long white satin gloves with black frills covered her hands up to her elbows, contrasting seductively with the golden brown of her tanned limbs. She wore the merest of white leather frilled miniskirts, held together by an easily released zipper. The frills began their tantalising descent at just below Kimberly's pubic mound and continued to the golden terrain of the middle of her perfectly proportioned, tanned thighs. Underneath the frilled skirt she wore a white satin G-string from which small blonde hairs poked naughtily through, delighting the lucky members of the first few rows of the audience. The string of her panties disappeared between the firmness of her tanned buttocks in a most come-hither manner. Around her waist Kimberly was adorned with a theatrical six-gun with a white pearl handle encapsulated in a rhinestone-studded gun holster, replete with rhinestone-studded bullets that sparkled under the starkness of the stage lights.

No such outfit would have been complete without the obligatory pair of cowboys boots – in this case white leather with jewels decorating the heels and bright silver spurs spinning as she walked. Miss Kimberly Duke looked like the very essence of down-home Americana erotica. Her skin was tanned so perfectly golden it looked almost as if it had been painted on her luscious frame – the gaudy outfit highlighting the captivating tones – and she was simply the most stunning woman Sydney had ever clapped eyes upon.

He stood there in awe, empty glass in hand, gaping at the bullwhip-cracking woman, not really sure what he was going to do to win her attention. Sydney stared right at her taut body, willing her to notice him. All thoughts of England winning the Ashes were long gone at this moment. And any fleeting vignette of a possible Aussie victory was banished by Kimberly drawing her gun, pointing it right at Sydney and pulling the trigger, thereby releasing an almighty bang, a brilliant flash and a cloud of smoke. She fired again and again and repeated the action until she had discharged her load of fake bullets into the surprised body of Sydney Nats.

Through the haze of the Jet Strip A Go-Go he saw Kimberly Duke lift the smoking barrel to her lips and blow the last wisps of gunsmoke away from the barrel towards him. She kissed the gunsight, staring all the while at Sydney. He turned quickly to look behind him to see if there were anyone else she could be aiming her attentions at, but there appeared no obvious candidates and when he turned back he could have sworn that Kimberly nodded towards him as if to say that yes, it was him she was looking at.

Kimberly then slipped the gun down past her chin, tracing a line down her throat to rest in the nest of her cleavage. Slowly she masturbated the silver barrel between her tits, bending her legs in unison to the motions of the gun. Each time she came up from a crouch she stared directly at Sydney, who stood transfixed, wondering what strange fate had ordained that this all-American beauty should be putting on a show apparently just for him, even though they were in the midst a crowd of raucous males craving the merest of her attentions. It was just too good to be true, Sydney kept telling himself, hoping all along that it was his lucky day after all.

After the audience had been whipped, quite literally, into a feeding frenzy by Kimberly's gun-barrel masturbating, she decided it was time to bring her act to a climax, so to speak. She didn't want the gorgeous chap with the dazed expression, expensive suit and an empty glass to get away. He stood out amongst the crowd like a corned-beef sandwich backstage at a Morrissey concert, and perhaps – perhaps – this likely-looking guy could be Kimberly's ticket out of this dump and on to the big time. If not, not to worry. He at least gave the impression that a good time could be had by all.

Thinking of how best to approach him, Kimberly used the barrel of the gun to unhook the clasps of her white leather waistcoat while she writhed on her back on the stage floor. She quickly zeroed in on a plan and decided to get her act over with a little sooner than usual. It was an easy matter to shed the garment as she rose from the stage floor, standing before Sydney – and, incidentally, the rest of the crowd – bare-breasted, swaying provocatively to the country and western music, her tits driving home between Sydney's eyes more effectively than if she'd fired real bullets at him just a few moments ago. Kimberly spun around a few times to give a nearer audience a lovely shot up her miniskirt at her white-satin-covered cunt, while those farther away got their eyeful of her rather full tits swinging around her body as she spun, the tanned golden globes lifting and pointing outward under the delightful effect of centrifugal force. With a bow that betrayed her classical dance background, Kimberly backed off stage, leaving the obnoxious DJ to improvise and the crowd to wonder what the hell was going on.

Kimberly's spell was broken by a rather hefty brunette introduced by the obnoxious DJ as Olga, the 'legendary' Russian mud-wrestler. Olga writhed in an oversized inflatable child's backyard pool filled with mud, challenging any of the audience to the best of two falls or a submission. Sydney thought it was time to get that drink he'd been distracted from by the Texas rose, so he made his way through the swelling crowd that was leaving the stage area and Olga's challenges. It took Sydney almost fifteen minutes to work his way to the bar and attempt to order his drink. He was about to shout 'gin and tonic' to the young barmaid who now, after Kimberly's performance, held not the slightest appeal for the befuddled Australian lawyer, when he felt a frim tap on his shoulder.

Sydney almost died.

It was Kimberly Duke.

'Buy a girl a drink, mister?'

Sydney cranked his mouth slowly off of the floor and thought fast. He needed all of his *je ne sais quoi* to come up with just the right response. It was a good one.

'No.'

He paused slowly.

'I'd hardly call you a girl. A lady – yes – girl never. But I'll buy you one.'

'Why, thank you, mister . . .'

'Nats. Sydney Nats.'

'Hi, I'm Kimberly.'

'I know.'

'I guess you do have quite the advantage on me. Perhaps over a drink I can catch up?'

'Certainly. What will it be?'

'Margarita – blended.'

'Certainly.'

Sydney ordered the drinks, feeling ten feet tall, and would someone be sure not to wake him from this super dream, thank you very much.

'Would you like to sit down? I have a booth over here, in the corner?'

'Lead the way.'

Sydney was amazed beyond his naughtiest dreams, but quickly the lawyer in him began to gain control of his palpitating heart. As they sat down in the darkness of the booth Sydney's mind raced with the obvious questions. Why me? What does she want? Am I being set up? He kept his concerns to himself so as not to appear nerdish, but still he fought hard to keep his guard up. It wasn't easy staring into those deep blue eyes with their disarmingly flickering lashes. Sydney, like any lawyer worth his salt, began interrogating Kimberly as if she were a witness undergoing a cross-examination.

'If you're from Texas – Austin, I think the guy said – where's your accent?'

'Why, I'm surprised at you, Mr Nats. Not everyone from Texas sounds like something out of a cowboy movie. Oh, I can talk like a country hick if you'd like, but I thought if I wanted to get ahead in this town I ought to speak proper American. But if y'all want tah hear a Texas drawl, ah can oblige yew. And then of course thar are times when ah just can't help mahself, and my little ol' accent comes rollin' right on out.'

'And when might that be?'

'Now, Mr Nats – is that any question to ask a sweet Texas lady?' Kimberly fluttered her eyes as if hiding behind a wavering fan.

Sydney laughed. It was time for Kimberly to ask the questions.

'So, Mr Nats, what brings you to this fine establishment tonight?'

Sydney recounted his travel ordeal to the sympathetic Kimberly Duke.

'And why were you in Los Angeles in the first place? Business, I'll bet?'

'How did you guess?' The question was facetious. Sydney continued telling her about his profession and the reasons for his being in the city of one-night stands. Kimberly Duke interrupted him when Sydney mentioned who his client was, who he'd been seeing in Los Angeles.

'I knew it! I knew it! I knew you were the one. Tonight is my lucky night. He is my favourite actor, ever since I was a little girl.'

'I was the one what?'

'Oh Sydney, I'll be honest. I want to get out of this dump. I've been in Los Angeles just one month – it's the same old story you've heard a million times. I'm a dancer, I've been classically trained, so I thought I'd come to LA to find my fortune, and the only way I can pay the bills is to strip for these morons. The only fortune that came my way before tonight and you was when some overweight Japanese businessman offered me $1000 to sit on his face.'

'I'm not going to offer you a $1000 to sit on my face.'

Sydney was starting to get suspicious. There was a nasty feeling growing in his stomach.

'No, no. Nothing like that. I'm not on the game. I just saw you through the crowd looking so well dressed compared to this lot, and I said to myself, Kimberly, that is the kind of man you should get to know. So I thought I'd get your attention. Worked, didn't it?'

'That it did – but I don't know how I can help you.'

'Oh, we'll see. In the meantime you've got a Saturday night to kill and I've got time on my hands. So what'll we do?'

'You don't have to dance?'

'No. I quit – well, I'm going to quit. And you're responsible for that.'

'Me?'

'Yeah, you. I cut my act short to get off stage and find you in case I'd scared you off. Mr Crayola is hopping mad, and unless I'm very much mistaken, that the little shit over there is

91

looking for me. It would probably be for the best if we ducked out the back. Joey Crayola is four feet nine inches tall, a short Italian with a very nasty temper. It would be best if we left – now.'

'Lead the way.'

Once out of the back door of the Jet Strip A Go-Go they faced a typical Los Angeles stumbling block – transportation.

'Where did you park?'

'I didn't – I took a taxi. Don't you have a car?'

'No, I ride to work with one of the girls at the club.'

'I guess we could call a cab? But what are we going to do?'

'I don't know. Just drive? It's such a nice night.'

'Well, why don't I rent a car, and then we can go wherever we like? Just drive?'

'Yeah, let's get a convertible. I want to feel the wind in my hair.'

The Australian lawyer and the Texas rose walked down to Imperial Boulevard where they were able to rent a red Chrysler Le Baron convertible for the amazing price of $39.95 per day with unlimited mileage from Low Budget Limos Rent-A-Car. With their complimentary map of the Los Angeles area in hand they negotiated the airport streets to the Interstate 405 freeway. Sydney turned on to the North on-ramp heading towards the city. Overhead jets streamed in and out of the busy airport, masking the roar of the constant rush of cars. Sydney looked up at the planes and said a small prayer of thanks to the god of air travel for stranding him this one more night in Los Angeles. It was then that Sydney had a fateful idea that was going to change Kimberly Duke's life.

'Say, I was invited to a party tonight at the agent Neil Waslinger's house in Malibu. Do you want to go? There will be lots of movie and entertainment types there – you might even get discovered. I mean it's the least I could do after causing you to leave your last position.'

'For sure! Are you kidding? I'd love to go, but speaking of my last position – there is a new position I'd like to get into.'

Sydney knew better than to ask something dumb like what position that would be. Kimberly's fluttering eyelashes told a complete story.

'I've always wanted to do this. Just drive, Sydney – just drive.'

Sydney smiled. He thought she was going to curl up on his lap, all cuddly and warm, but she went further and began unzipping his trousers. Deftly her hands unbuttoned his fly and reached in and encircled his growing cock in her palms. Sydney fought to maintain his composure and his driving skills. Part of him denied that it was happening. He was hardly able to believe the strange turn of events that had overtaken his life since the fateful cancellation of flight BA 286.

'Kimberly, what – what . . . I'm driving!'

'I know you are. Just drive, Sydney – and enjoy the ride.'

'But, but –'

Sydney's objections faded into the hot wind of the Los Angeles summer night as Kimberly's warm breath stirred his penis to rigid attention. Her hands parted his trousers so that the turgid member could be caressed by her bright red lips. Gently she kissed his penis hesitantly, carefully, as if it were some delicate priceless sculpture.

Sydney dared not look down at the sight of Kimberly's golden locks cascading over his crotch. He dared not look to the passenger side where her full pleated skirt had ridden high on her thighs, exposing her tender golden skin. Just like in the strip club Sydney could discern the soft golden hairs on her legs – they made her limbs shine in the night with a freshness that not even moonlight could convey. On her feet she wore the same white cowboy boots, this time minus the spurs, the jewels glistening under the oncoming flash of the freeway lights overhead.

The scene had a surrealistic quality about it that heightened Sydney's passion. His cock strained and arched and he was forced to shift position slightly. He let out a small moan of pleasure. Sensing the effect she was having on him, Kimberly changed her sucking tactics. She wanted this to last.

'I can see the lights reflecting off of your cock each time I lick it and get it wet.'

Cradling Sydney's penis in her palms, Kimberly licked the throbbing shaft from its nest to its tip with long deliberate motions of her tongue. Using just the very point she glided her tongue over the ridges of the pulsing dick, careful to trace a path of saliva over the shaft. At the ridge of the shaft she would tickle underneath the flesh with her tongue, causing the penis to buck wildly as if being shocked by an electric current. Once at the tip she would insert her tongue into the slit of Sydney's dick and flick the head backwards and forwards. The sensations were phenomenal. Sydney had to fight his body's wishes to floor his foot and charge like a demon into the night. Using all his self-control he slowed down instead and tried to keep in the rightmost lane, hoping he wouldn't have to overtake someone going slower than he. To say it was difficult to concentrate on the road would be an understatement.

It became even more difficult to drive when Kimberly shifted her position and kneeled on the passenger seat to gain a more effective purchase on Sydney's dick. In this basic praying position she was able to move her head fully up and down the large length of Sydney's tool, taking the whole object slowly down her throat where her natural gagging action added further intensity to Sydney's glorious discomfort. Kimberly felt as if his dick was sliding down her throat and entering her cunt through her body. Her juices began to flow with each deep suck of her mouth as she imagined being impaled on the fullness of the shaft. She saw herself swallowing the huge purple head and moments later it would poke out from between her legs, titillating her clitoris as it retreated back through her womb and out of her mouth. The vision was shockingly disturbing and perfectly erotic, driving Kimberly's sucking to new heights of passionate frenzy.

Under such an oral onslaught Sydney was forced into shaking his head and blinking his eyes the way a really tired driver would to keep awake on long-distance all-night journeys. Only Sydney wasn't in danger of falling asleep. Oh, no – far from it. Sleep was not the problem. It would have been all too easy to pull over to the side of the road and have a wild passionate fuck, running the risk of being interrupted by one of the ever-present California Highway Patrol cars, but that would have been cheating. There was something very exhilarating about being sucked off while driving on a crowded freeway on a Saturday night. 'Just drive,' she'd said, and Sydney intended to comply with this forceful young woman's wishes.

In doing so Sydney had to improvise rapidly. The freeway

exit for Malibu came and went, because Sydney didn't want to start driving in the stop-and-go traffic of Sunset Boulevard. Not wanting to be interrupted by the stare of a red light it was better to stay on the freeway and enjoy Kimberly's long lashings of tongue, so over the hills Sydney went and into the San Fernando Valley.

At this point Kimberly started kneading Sydney's balls with her fingers, all ten digits probing and squeezing testicles firmly and forcefully. She pressured the swollen sacs as if she meant to burst them like overripe grapes, but backed off before the sensation turned into intense pain. Each time she did this Sydney's balls would roll around in her palms as if trying to escape her grip. It was as he turned the car on to the Hollywood Freeway from Interstate 405 that she matched the fingers' probings with her mouth's nibbling of Sydney's cockhead. It was too much to take for Sydney, who had been the very model of self-restraint, up until now releasing only the barest of soft moans.

Kimberly looked up from staring into Sydney's cock.

'Do you want me to stop?'

'No, no – I'm enjoying this too much. Keep sucking, suck my dick right off of my balls. Squeeze my sacs dry!'

Sydney was almost screaming the words in a state of complete frenzy. He had become like an automaton in one respect – a part of his brain solely dedicated to the mechanical task of driving precisely and as carefully as possible under the circumstances, and the rest of his cranium had been given over to enjoying the bloodlust of Kimberly's expert sucking. It was as if his concentrating on driving was freeing a part of the brain that never really got to enjoy sex, thereby heightening the pleasure and sensations in much the way a blind person's hearing becomes more acute when the brain doesn't have to worry about the job of seeing.

This was sucking at its best – pure unbridled oral sex with no care for the niceties of modern love. It was primitive fucking the way two savage pre-historic creatures would have used each other's sex, enraged by the sights and sounds of each other's bloodlust to daring feats of erotic excess.

Under the light of the freeway signs and the occasional rush of a passing car's headlights, Sydney could see the bulge his cock made in Kimberly's cheek as she swallowed his dick deeper and deeper until the outline of his swelling slipped passed her cheeks and down her throat. Deliberately she guided his shaft with her tongue against the roughness of the inside of her mouth to titillate and tease the sensitive nerves of Sydney's penis, sending knifelike ripplings throughout his brain and down to his toes and into the mechanical orgasms of the car as it found its way down the Hollywood Freeway and into Los Angeles.

As the Le Baron convertible passed Universal City and dipped into the lights of Hollywood the prevailing wind changed direction, whipping Kimberly's shirt up into a flurry of pleated pink material. Her exquisite tanned behind was adorned with the same type of white satin G-string in which she'd danced. The shimmery material shone in the dark in an eerie fashion every time Kimberly's ass bobbed upwards and her skirt got caught in the breeze. Sydney tried to steer the car with one hand and finger Kimberly's bottom, but it was too far to reach and Kimberly showed no interest in anything other than being a totally committed sucking machine. Her motions were frenetic – practically bouncing up and down on the car seat, at times anchored to the speeding automobile solely by her sucking of Sydney's dick.

They were fast approaching downtown LA, which caused Sydney a moment's hesitation – which way to go? He wasn't too sure of his directions, but any hope of making an intelligent decision was removed by Kimberly's sudden shift of her hands from the kneading of his balls to the wanking of his long and sucked shaft. Sydney, a well-practised masturbator – knew too well that delicious feeling, accomplished by just the right pressure of a finely tuned hand – but imagine accompanying that with the equally resonant pressure of a carefully placed pair of lips, and the feelings imagined couldn't have come close to what Sydney experienced as he let the car turn south on the Interstate 110 Harbor Freeway. If it was generally in the right direction, fine – if not, if they ended up driving off the edge of the world and into a timeless abyss, so what? At this point nothing mattered to Sydney but achieving a cock-splitting orgasm to end all possible orgasms.

Kimberly enjoyed the sensation of the wind sweeping up her dress and cooling her sweaty cunt. She was lubricating fiercely and her exertions were combining with her natural moisture to soak her inner thighs. The warm night air was cooling, but not cold, keeping that sense of impending sex pulsing between her cuntlips and making her suck Sydney's dick all the more violently. She hoped that there were people in other cars, in trucks, on overpasses who could catch a glimpse of her fine body in action. She knew that they would like what they saw and probably go quickly to some private place where they could wank off and squirt come all over their hands and chest, thinking of that ass they saw bobbing up and down and how good it would be to have that ass to themselves.

The car found its way on to the Santa Monica Interstate 10 freeway heading west as Kimberly had visions of hundreds of dicks squirting hot steamy come into the night. She thrust her ass skyward, imagining that she could feel the hot wet juice splattering across her ass and staining her satin-covered crotch as if she were the star of a cheap porno movie. Tightening her two-fisted grip on Sydney's dick she raked her teeth underneath the bulging head and pulled the skin agonisingly upward with each sucking cycle. Sydney screamed the wail of a mandrake torn from its earth as his orgasm was rent from his shaft. Deep within his balls, it bubbled and boiled until under Kimberly's rough attentions it felt as if it had completely melted away his cock.

How he managed to maintain control of the car he never knew. Almost ten miles of black tarmac were a complete loss and he finally regained composure as the car approached the intersection of the 10 and 405 freeways. He'd come in a complete circle that had taken almost an hour of driving and sucking. Shaking with the relief of just being alive, Sydney resumed the journey north on the 405 towards Malibu Beach and Neil Waslinger's party. His dick still remained hard inside Kimberly's mouth. In the moonlight he could see small rivulets of his semen and her saliva trickling down her chin and into her hair. He tried to wipe up the mixture of juices but she brushed him aside. Unable to speak clearly with his dick inside her mouth she mumbled something that sounded like, 'I'm OK. Just drive . . .'

She'd curled up into a fetal position, her ass staring at Sydney invitingly. He reached over in an attempt to repay her affections, but she restrained him and mumbled something that sounded like, 'Later, later — we have all night.' Sydney pulled his hand away and stroked her golden hair instead. She was right. They might have only one night together, but they did have all that night.

'Drive,' she'd said. And he did.

11 p.m.

A SMALL HOUSE IN SANTA MONICA

The digital clock next to the computer had just added one precise red glowing minute to the hour of eleven o'clock before the phone rang. Sighing, Nancy Thorne saved the word-processing document upon which she was avidly working on to the hard drive of her desktop computer and picked up the phone, knowing already who was on the other end. She had hoped for a quiet Saturday night so that she could try to finish the latest version of her screenplay. Apparently there would be no such luck. She was scheduled to be on call at eleven, and she told herself she shouldn't complain too much. She did need the money – at least until she got that elusive call from a studio.

Nancy worked as a technical writer for Consolidated Big Machines during the day, authoring user manuals for the purchasers of CBM's high-powered computers. By night she was a phone fantasy artiste, creating sexual escapades for the caller, and in between she worked hard at writing a screenplay that perhaps one of the giant movie studios would say yes to, and Nancy Thorne would become a household word – and rich too. At least that was the dream that kept her typing away through the small hours of the morning in between calls from sex-hungry men who found themselves womanless and randy for the evening.

Flattering herself with the small comfort that it had taken just two minutes for her telephone talents to be requested, she resigned herself, if her phone kept ringing with such frequency, to a non-productive evening as far as writing was concerned. Well, not to worry, reasoned Nancy as she answered the call, at least there might be a few ideas for characters from the varied people who called Fancy Phone Fantasies tonight.

'Hello?'

'Nancy? It's Amber. I have a call for you. He asked for somebody with imagination, so I chose you.'

'Great. Give me the particulars.'

Nancy tried to sound enthusiastic as she scribbled the details on to a pad of paper as Amber matter-of-factly conveyed the strange sexual desires of the customer.

'His name is Andrew Benjamin. He's English. The phone number is a beach number – he sounds educated but shy. He's paid for an hour on a platinum Amex card, and he specifically asked for somebody with imagination, who likes dressing up in lingerie, who doesn't just make sucking noises into the phone. Sounds like you, ha ha. Have fun . . .'

'Thanks, Amber.'

Nancy Thorne trundled to the kitchen and fed her yowling cat, Biggles. The feisty feline always seemed to sense when Nancy had to make a call and seemed to discover his vocal chords at just the wrong moment. It was hard to talk sexy to a man who was masturbating at the other end of the phone when a marauding moggy was wailing in her face. A can of tuna usually did the trick, and Nancy rationalised that this was a small price to pay out of her $50 commission from the average fifteen-minute call.

With Biggles quietly stuffing his face Nancy poured herself a glass of very ordinary white Zinfandel wine and curled up on her couch. From the notepad she read the number and dialled – the call was local so she didn't have to bother using the operator to reverse the charges. One ring, two rings – the phone was answered on the third.

'Hello?'

'Hello, Andrew?'

'Yes.'

'Hi – it's Nancy from Fancy. I understand you'd like to have a phone liaison with me this evening.'

'Yes, yes – that's right.'

Nancy quickly detected the shyness that Amber had alluded to. After a year of dishing out phone sex, Nancy was well versed in the multitude of ways of breaking down the antiseptic barrier of the phone.

'Well, how are you on this hot Saturday night?'

I'm fine, doing very well, thank you. And you?'

'Good. Good. Perhaps I should describe myself to you so that you can picture me in your mind's eye. Can you do that? It's kind of like painting a picture from my words.'

'Yes, yes, I can. Please do.'

Nancy had succeeded in breaking the initial ice – now it was time to start melting away the remaining chunks. Amber had said that Andrew appeared intelligent and wanted to talk with someone with an imagination, so consequently Nancy decided to turn on her esoteric qualities. Rather than go for the typical vital statistics replay followed by a brief description of sexy clothes and how wet her genitals were at the thought of sucking the caller's cock, Nancy decided to engage in a little phone foreplay.

'Well, Andrew, where should I start? How about my eyes? Yes, that would be the best place to start. Imagine that they are floating in front of you right now, staring at you, watching your every move. They have long black lashes and are an emerald green in colour. If you stare at them long enough they will hypnotise you, and I'll be able to make you do quite unspeakable things – but I'm much too much of a lady to do anything like that.' She gave a little wicked laugh. 'I wear a light pink pastel eye shadow that blends subtly with my skin. I can undress a man with my eyes, Andrew, and I'm doing that with you. Right now. Item by item I'm stripping you naked with those eyes.'

Nancy Thorne did not have emerald-green eyes. They were a muddy brown and she never wore make-up. Her skin was ruddy in complexion, so much so that no amount of make-up, even if she'd have worn any, could have made her colouring any more appealing.

'After noticing my eyes most men immediately avert their gaze to my breasts. I'm quite tall – five feet nine inches – and almost too slender, only one hundred and ten pounds, but I think most of my upper body weight is concentrated in my bosom. It is a very full 38D. I'm very athletic so my breasts are incredibly firm for their size – I work out at the gym three or four times a week and it really shows. I'm even able to go without a bra in some of the skimpiest dresses you've ever seen, and my titties support themselves. I'm very proud of them and judging by the way you seem to be staring at them I think you like them too.'

Nancy Thorne did have 38D breasts – that part of the description was at least true to life – but the rest of the story was not too accurate. She was five feet two inches tall, 160 pounds, she didn't exercise – if she didn't wear a tent of a bra her mammoth mammaries would sag down to her knees – and she never wore skimpy dresses. By definition, any dress she could fit into was not skimpy.

'I can tell you like the way the full curve of my breasts strain against the material of my dress. Just thinking of you looking at the way my titties swell makes the nipples harden under the white lace bodice I'm wearing. The lace is extremely thin as it curls over the curve of my breasts. It is exciting to feel the long auburn curls of my hair brush against the lace covering of my pointy buds in their extremely sensitised state. You'd like my hair, Andrew. You could run your fingers through my long silky locks. Sometimes I wear it piled high on my head with dainty slender tails of hair falling down around my face in a very Victorian manner. You could take out the satin bow that holds my curls in place and let them fall down into your fingers. If you were extremely good I might let you wrap your cock up in my hair. It is so silky – almost as soft as my pussy. I'm sure I could make you come just by letting my hair fall into your lap and swishing it around, ensnaring your cock in my locks – whipping it with thousands of silky lashes until you shot that lovely cream into my auburn curls.'

Nancy Thorne had very short black hair that was styled in no particular fashion other than one of minimum maintenance. She had often thought of growing it longer – especially since it would have made her face look thinner – but practicality always won the day with Nancy, so she kept it militarily short.

Nancy continued weaving her fantasy web.

'The dress I'm wearing was made especially for me. It is like one of those huge ballgowns worn by the aristocracy before the French Revolution. The top is a white lace bodice and the skirt billows out from my tiny waist like a huge bell, covering all of my long legs. The skirt is made of a lustrous pale blue silk embroidered with a delicate off-white lace trimming that matches the bodice. It looks like it is made of Wedgewood porcelain – and I am a china doll encased within. It teases you so to see me dressed this way, because I know that you can only guess at what lovely things I have on underneath. I curtesy to you so that you can ogle my huge cleavage, and I can tell by the way that your penis arches towards me that you are pleased with the sight. You are wearing nothing – naked – except for an elaborate feather mask that hides your eyes and therefore your identity. I am fully clothed in my formal gown. We meet in the centre of a grand ballroom. An orchestra, all immaculately dressed in the finest of tuxedos, is playing a waltz. We are the only guests at this decadent ball. You naked, except for your mask, me dressed in the essence of a lady – my exquisite body partially, tantalisingly revealed by my gown. You ask me to dance. I consent.'

Nancy closed her eyes and easily visualised the scene she was describing – it was like a dream sequence unfolding in those precious early-morning moments between being full asleep and partially awake, when the most vivid of dreams usually occur.

'You take my hand and we strike a formal pose before beginning our mating ritual. You hold me tight, your erect throbbing member poking into the stiff material of the dress. I cannot feel it touching my skin because the dress flares out so, but I can sense its presence as we float around the dancefloor arm in arm. One hand holds mine and the other cradles my waist as we pirouette around the dancefloor. Your hand around my waist slyly drops to my bottom and continues down to my thigh, feeling through the silk of the dress for the telltale signature of my suspender belt. Your hand finds the confirmation it desires as it negotiates the slight ridges the lace suspenders create on my buttocks. All the while you are fondling my ass your eyes never leave mine as I struggle to guess your identity and you attempt to uncover my degree of virtue. Through the mask I see your eyes and cheek muscles wrinkle in a smile as you feel the suspender – happy in the knowledge that I'm wearing the stockings that you so fantasise about. I avert my stare from yours and cast an admiring glance at your proud tool. Your cock seems so familiar – large and encouraging. I'm sure I've had the pleasure before, but I just can't put my finger on when – and where?'

Nancy's practiced ear could distinguish the unmistakable sounds of a hand-cream-covered cock being stroked at the other end of the phone. She found the sound comforting, an indication that her words and her fantasy-weaving were having the desired result. Nancy was pleased with her story telling capability, especially her attention to details so small as the English 'suspender belt' instead of the American 'garter belt'. She hoped Andrew appreciated such a thoughtful touch and was pleased with the wide erotic vocabulary that incessant reading had given her. She sipped the wine and was about to continue when Andrew's voice interrupted her. Nancy was a little startled – the more usual clients never spoke, just wanked, moaned, came and hung up. She began to get the idea that Andrew was no ordinary client.

'You don't recognise me because I am your dream cock. I am the dick that you slide between your legs in the dark of night when your lover is sound asleep beside you. I am the portal into your cunt that opens you wide and exposes your pink flesh to everyone's sinful cravings. I am every dick you have ever wanted. I am your fingers – each one a lovely fat dildo dick with which you fuck yourself into oblivion, dreaming of me, wishing your lover could be this good. You have never seen my face and perhaps you never will – knowing my identity may break the spell. So here I dance with you, my maleness fully exposed to you but my face, my face – only your pussy lips will ever see it.'

Nancy could still hear the delicious slippery sound Andrew's hand made as it slid up and down his cock who knows how many miles away. She felt the beginnings of excitement build as she listened to Andrew's almost whispered utterances. His English accent was soft and lilting, making the filthy words sound all the more decadent. The word 'cock' just seem to roll off of his lips with an understated elegance. Nancy could imagine moulding her lips around his cock and rolling the firm member around. Such randy thoughts caused Nancy to shift her buttocks on the couch and take a long sip of calming wine. She placed the glass down and let her free hand casually fall between her legs. She wore sweat pants that fit her abundant frame loosely. It was an easy matter to slide her hand underneath the waistband and probe her way between her fleshy thighs to find that knob which made all the lonely nights that much more bearable. She was about to continue her story when Andrew interrupted once more.

'I do hope you are enjoying yourself at this moment. It is important to me that you gain as much pleasure as I. I hope you have your hand between your legs, as I would if I were there with you.'

Nancy was a little taken aback but quickly drew on her creative writing skills to regain composure. Treat it as a story – imagine you're typing these words on your computer, she kept telling herself as she struggled for a response. Nancy was on unfamiliar ground – it was usually her that was doing the story telling. She found herself in a new situation where her client had become as much a part of the fantasy as she. Nancy knew she was in danger of losing control and it bothered her not in the least. She was starting to enjoy this game.

'My hand is there to guide your hand as it moves between my legs.'

It was a line that she probably would have edited out of a story upon further review, but the spoken word affords no such luxuries. Andrew was not about to be deflected by ambiguous statements.

'Are you stroking yourself? Please – I must know. Be honest with me.'

Andrew's voice was insistent, firm, and very demanding. Nancy considered briefly before answering, but decided to be truthful.

'Yes, yes, I am. I don't usually play with myself when I make a call but I must admit I feel quite excited by your words.'

'Good – good. Now I believe we were in the ballroom.'

'Ah, yes, yes. The ballroom.'

Nancy closed her eyes and let the fat part of the side of her hand slide up and down the folds of her thighs, rubbing every so often against the hidden knob of her sex, her fingers toying with the sensitive flesh around her cunt-opening. Like ice cream melting under the intense heat of the summer sun, her juices began to flow under the firm pressure of her hand's motion. It was a decadent feeling, made all the more so by her role as a phone-sex artiste. She had never masturbated herself while talking to a client before, even though she had had hundreds of such fantasy calls. None of her clients had ever shown the slightest interest in actually participating in the development of fantasy – especially one that pleased her as much as it did the caller. Most

wanted to hear a few four-letter words, a lot of sound effects, a
ego-boosting description of their capabilities and the telling
conclusion – 'Have you come yet?' Nancy hated those kind of
calls, but they were by far the majority and the most lucrative,
taking just a few minutes and no mental effort. And now, out of
the darkness of what had promised to be a very ordinary night,
came Andrew's surprising interruption. His words, their content,
the images they carried played on her own vivid imagination.
The result of her musings made Nancy feel more a part of the
fantasy than if she was merely reciting one of her stories – as if
she were living the fantastic sex she was describing. She began
to imagine the possibilities . . .

'As we swirl around the room keeping a precise time to the
sweeping orchestral music you begin to swing my body around
you in ever-increasing arcs. Your hard penis slaps against your
thighs as you spin with me. It makes the most lewd sound – a
sound of filthy wet lust – almost like the sound you are making
now as you pour more cream on your dick and jerk it faster to
my words. It excites me to hear the naughtiness of your dick –
and I get wet in anticipation of your advances. I think you can
sense my moisture. It beckons you to act, and act you do. You
surprise me with your speed, spinning me first one way, folding
up your arms to encase me in your embrace, and then spinning
me forcefully out of your grip, around and around to the classical
waltz of the imperturbable orchestra. I think you are spinning
me so fast so that you might be able to cause my full skirt to
blossom upward, and then you would be treated to a glimpse
of my sexy lingerie that has so far remained intriguingly hidden
from your lustful gaze. My dress defeats your purpose – the silk
maintains its full shape, revealing nothing more than my trim
ankles, perfectly formed and delicately supported in white high
heels with blue ankle straps.

'Unable to see up my dress with your masked eyes, your penis
strains harder as your frustration rises. You repeat the spinning
motion but this time as you spin me away from you, your hand
slyly slips to the waist of my dress and grabs tightly at the
fasteners. As I am thrown away from your grip you snatch at
my dress, tearing off the buttons, pulling the full skirt of my dress
away from my body as you spin me across the dance floor, my

stocking-covered thighs exposed to you, to the orchestra. Finally you can ogle my lovely lace-encased figure – you can see the suspender straps that you could only feel just a few moments ago. You can peer closely and see the dark outline of my bush, partially hidden by white lace panties already moist from the anticipation of that straining member between your legs and the pleasures it proffers.

'I continue to spin in large pirouettes, my hands above my head, thrusting my breasts forward out of the lace bodice as I arch my back like a seductive ballerina. I try to appear unperturbed by your tearing-off of my skirt – as though the violence of the action was completely expected of you. You stand across the ballroom floor, amazed at my movements – at the realisation of your deepest fetishes – only a few steps away from your eager cock. My dress is still in your hand. You drop it to the floor and run towards me, your cock hard and angry seeking me like a arrow to a bull's-eye. The orchestra plays on, providing a soundtrack to our erotic ballet.

'You stop my spinning and pull me by my shoulders to your embrace. My arms, still above my head, fall earthwards around your shoulders, and I pull you tightly to me. We lock in a long kiss, my silk-stocking-covered thighs sliding up and down the naked flesh of your legs, first one and then the other. As our lips kiss, I kiss your body with my legs. The silk feels exquisite on your flesh. With our lips locked, our tongues entwined, you angle your body so the purple head of your swollen dick is brushed by my thigh as I raise my leg along yours. I press my leg tightly against your thigh, catching your angry dick between our limbs. Through the diaphanous lace membrane I can feel every bulge, every ridge, every pulse of your aching shaft pressed warmly against my soft thigh. I roll the member up and down, the silk of my stocking tantilising you wickedly.'

'What – what colour are the stockings?'

'Ah, Andrew – you are ever the perfectionist. They are ivory, embroidered with off-white lace at the top. The suspender belt is a matching Jasper blue to my dress that you most recently disposed of. The paleness of the stockings makes the deep colours of your swollen manhood stand out more vividly. It is an impressive contrast.'

'I've wrapped my dick in a stocking just like the ones you are wearing. It feels lovely – the nylon soaked with the cream feels unbelievable as I stroke myself.'

'Wrap the stocking around your balls and pull it tightly with your hand as you masturbate yourself, and when you come, pull as hard as you can – it will be like you are pulling your release from deep within you rather than squeezing it out.'

Nancy had no idea if that was true – she was improvising, her own hand's travels unleashing thoughts she rarely voiced in fantasies. Andrew and Nancy had developed a strange rapport between them that spontaneously unleashed passions that neither of them ever got the chance to experience on a intimate level, one to one, with another person, in the flesh. This was no longer a business call to Nancy. She was making love to Andrew – and by his responses it appeared as he was doing the same. They played a kind of erotically charged verbal tennis. Backwards and forwards they volleyed, lobbed, forehanded, backhanded and served their filthy thoughts, feeding off each other's wanton ideas.

There was a brief moment's silence as Andrew adjusted himself. He did have a stocking wrapped around his cock, although it was not the same colour as the one Nancy was supposedly wearing. It was black and quite well used.

'Ah, you are right – that feels so much better. You naughty wench – someday you will have to tell me how you came by such amorous knowledge.'

'Perhaps someday I will. There are many things I'm sure you would like to know of a lady such as I.'

'Indeed. I can tell you are no ordinary woman by the way you kiss so passionately, dressed so sexually, in front of all those men in their tuxedos, pretending not to look at your sex-goddess body, but all the while ogling you at every opportunity. It excites me to think of these men – strangers – watching you rub your sex on me, watching me slide my cock up and down your ivory-stocking-covered legs. Ah, such limbs – such towering pillars of sexual enslavement. It is too much for me to take. I want to throw you to the ballroom floor and mount you forcefully, tearing off the dainty white lace panties that barely cover that dark bush of yours. The music quickens as the orchestra senses my impending intention, and in preparation for

108

my entry I reach between your legs and underneath the elastic of your white lace panties. Once inside the domain I slide apart your musky cuntlips. They are sticky with female moisture. I savour the aroma and all that it betrays. I survey the scene. Your eyes are closed awaiting the insertion of my penis, your tongue licks your lips in anticipation of that sumptuous feeling of my hardness filling your cunt to its capacity. Your arms are stretched wide in an appearance of submission. It would please me to enter you now, but suddenly I have the most wicked of thoughts. With no warning I place my arms around your waist and hoist you skywards with all my might. You are momentarily disoriented at being lifted off the ground. You fear for your safety – perhaps I will drop you? – but you realise that my firm hands and muscular arms can easily support your trim figure.'

Nancy couldn't help but smile – in fact, she had to stifle a little laugh at the thought of this chap hoisting her off the floor and trying to support her. In her mind's eye she could see them teetering around the ballroom until Andrew's legs gave way under the strain of her bodyweight and they collapsed on to the floor, a heap of tangled flesh. Luckily, Andrew knew none of the true details of Nancy's size, so he was not distracted from the fantasy he was weaving by the mundane details of her overweight reality.

And the thought never crossed Nancy's mind that Andrew was likewise not the epitome of a muscular male god with a taut, tanned body and well hung to boot. He was not. Andrew had never rid himself of his pudgy baby fat and the excess of too many business lunches had taken their inevitable toll. Andrew looked like an overweight schoolboy with a beard whose penis, even in its fully erect state, had a hard time poking out from underneath several layers of belly fat. He was not an attractive sight, but it was his words, not his physique, that enchanted Nancy. If she'd thought about the situation long enough she'd probably have come to the conclusion that Andrew was very much like her, preferring the solitude of the phone to the ridiculing glances of those 'beautiful' people who seemed so plentiful in LA. One of the reasons Nancy had taken to writing and then to phone sex was that it helped fill the void in her life caused by her own shyness, by her own self-consciousness of her

109

less than sleek figure. Rather than going out and facing the real world she preferred her own imagination's comforting freedom. None of the callers that she talked to knew what she really looked like, and through the use of her imagination she could cast any spell she desired.

And in much the same way Andrew found himself on the other end of the phone. Shy, finding it difficult to be taken seriously by the gorgeous beauties of LA, he had concluded that fantasy was much better than reality. Andrew lived in a fantasy world fuelled by novels and movies, and phone sex gave him the perfect way to exercise his fertile imagination on a member of the opposite sex.

'Lifting you as high as my arms will take you I am able to press my mouth against your sex. I bite through the flimsy lace of the panties so that I may press my face against your unprotected cuntflesh. The feathers of my mask tickle your soft thighs making you wriggle even further upon me. You latch your legs around my neck, and like a pornographic ballet we dance around the floor, each jarring step sending my tongue deep inside your tight furrow. The music carries us around the room as my tongue dances inside your cunt. I press against your bottom with a swaying motion as I dance, making your sex vibrate against my face in undulating waves of high-energy contact. With every one of my teetering steps your own weight forces your cunt on to my tongue so that as I lick your precious little button you writhe delightfully on my wet lips. Your cuntlips, my mouth, pressed tight together – as tight as any new lover's kiss – I drink you deep.

'Intoxicated by your lust I stagger around the room until I feel unable to keep my balance a second longer. With the last of my strength I slide you down my body, your dripping cunt smearing itself along my naked flesh. You leave a musky trail from my lips, pressing tightly against my throat, matting my chest hairs with your juices, pausing ever so slightly at my belly button to rub your own little cunt button there, and then, and then, I hold your body paused above my penis. Erect and arched it awaits your wet opening. Your legs slide down from my shoulders and grip around my waist. I stare into your eyes and then you toss your head back awaiting my entry. You look exquisite in your dainty lingerie – your ivory stocking-covered legs wrapped around my body, the pale blue suspenders framing the object of my desire, your full tits peering out of the white lace bodice, your statuesque shoulders, your kissable neck, your long arms draping earthward to the cold wood of the floor. You cast a seductive portrait that a mere mortal like me has not the powers to resist. I want you, I need you – with the every sap of energy I have left in me I gradually enter your heavenly opening with my sacrificial tool.'

Nancy was imagining the scene described by Andrew. It struck a pleasing chord with her because she absolutely adored ballet. She often fantasised about being a neat trim ballerina being hoisted aloft by one of those muscular dancers. How their hands would hold her body firm, feeling discreetly in all of those special places – it was perceptive of Andrew to have recognised this fantasy of hers. With increasing wonder she lost herself in his words, rubbing her cunt with growing urgency.

'Slowly at first, I place my sticky slit at your door and gain entry delicious millimetre by millimetre. As my dick progresses inwards you become more and more agitated. Those submissive arms begin to flail in a frenzy of lust. You bite your fingers savagely willing me to fuck you harder, faster, harder, faster. But I won't. I continue to slide you up and down my cock as slowly as I can. As we sink gradually to the floor in a slow motion fall like the last leaf of autumn, again you scream, your cries overshadowing the orchestra. You beg me to have my way quickly with you. But I resist – I am determined to fuck you slowly. Hard, but slowly. No matter how loud you scream for me to fuck you harder, faster, deeper, quickly – I won't.'

'Oh, you will, you will! You must – it is what you really want.'

Nancy almost screamed those words into the phone as she bucked ferociously on the couch. She had quite sometime ago forced her sweatpants down around her ankles and was frigging her sex violently – much more so than she ever did when lust demanded its regular release. She heaved her body up and down on her hand, imagining it was Andrew's cock and not her plump fingers that were doing this most intimate dance around her quim. She splayed her fleshy cuntlips as wide as her flabby thighs would allow and pulled the mons far apart so that her fingers could play with the delicate flesh surrounding her opening. It drove her to a frenzy that bordered on the verge of unconsciousness. She was close to orgasm when from the deep blackness surrounding her reeling brain, Nancy heard Andrew's proper tones.

'You know me well, Nancy. It is what I want and I know it is what you want – to be fucked savagely hard, not just to be fucked but to be impaled on this ballroom floor by my stiffness. I cannot hide my desires from you, no matter how I try. I had thought to tease you, to fuck you slowly, to repay you for dressing so invitingly in that saucy lingerie – but I am just a man. I cannot control my drinking at your Aphrodite's fountain. I want to plunge in and out of you like the furious pistons of a steam engine. I must have you now. Now!'

In her own crazed fingering, Nancy sensed that Andrew was climaxing at the other end of the phone. A year of phone sex had taught her what to do in such situations. She quickly picked up from where Andrew's orgasming had forced the cessation of his narration.

'We spin around on the ballroom floor as I squirm on your magnificent dick. I ride you like a bucking stallion inciting you to dare to throw me off. We wrestle each other, rolling around, fighting each other for the upper hand. We are impervious to the hardness of the floor and its discomfort. I have something much harder inside me. I feel it pulse between my thighs as my cunt sucks you dry. Like a vampire I drink your come with my thirsty quim as if it were my life's blood. We fuck hard and fast with no care for anything but our own sexual pleasure. The orchestra plays wildly on, occasionally missing a note here or there as one of the players is distracted by our fucking. They respond to our urgings, matching the crescendo of their playing exactly with the pulse of our loins. Our lust has created a symphony of excess. In perfect harmony with the ethereal sounds filling the room I moan loudly and wetly as you come, forcing my own – my own – oh my, my . . .'

As rule Nancy didn't try to make fake orgasm sounds just for the benefit of the caller, and tonight was no exception. She brought herself off under her hand's ministrations and under the captivating spell of Andrew's words. By the sound of heavy breathing at the other end of the phone line, it was clear that Andrew had also achieved his desired release.

For the next few minutes nothing but the teeming static rush of electrons and the occasional gasp for breath could be heard from either receiver. Finally, Nancy broke the spell.

'Andrew, Andrew . . .'

'Yes, Nancy . . .'

'I don't know what to say.'

'Neither do I.'

And again they lapsed into a stunned silence, content to listen to the serenade of each other's exhausted breathing. After what could have been minutes, maybe much longer, Andrew spoke softly into the receiver.

'Nancy – may I call you again?'

'Please – please do, but don't go through the service. Please call me here at home – any time. If you have something to write on I'll give you the number.'

'Just a minute.'

And Andrew Benjamin, forty years old, a shy, overweight, divorced aerospace executive originally from England but now living in the sleepy seaside town of Hermosa Beach, stumbled naked around the dark of his bedroom, dripping globules of sperm and hand cream around the room as he hunted for a pen and paper. Nancy Thorne, twenty-five years old, an overweight technical author who dreamed of becoming a great screenwriter while she earned extra money and more than a few ideas dishing out phone sex, lay exhaused on her small couch in her small rented house in Santa Monica, soaking the cushions with her juices. She gave Andrew her phone number and encouraged him to call her any time of night. She stopped short of asking him for his – she wasn't sure why, but it seemed the right approach. If it was more than a one-night stand he would call again, and then she could ask him for the precious seven numbers. As she hung up the phone she noticed the red glow of the digital alarm clock. It was just past midnight. She watched the glowing red figures change almost magically before her eyes. Already she was counting the minutes until the phone rang again, hoping it would be the shy Englishman with an untamed imagination and a dreamy voice.

113

Biggles yowled in the kitchen. He was hungry again. Nancy dozed on the couch, trying to ignore the cat's insistent cries. At almost the same time the phone rang and Nancy sat bolt upright and grabbed the phone. Biggles walked in from the kitchen and watched his person with an admonishing cat stare.

'Yes?' Nancy was full of anticipation.

'Are you through? This is Amber – I hadn't heard from you after your last call, and the lines are all lit up tonight. It's been almost two hours.'

'Oh, oh – I'm sorry. I must have dozed off and forgot to call you.'

'Must have been an exciting call then . . .'

Nancy could tell Amber was fishing. Nancy didn't take the bait. 'So who's next?'

Amber gave Nancy the details. His name was Frank and he was a travelling salesman staying at a motel near the airport. He sounded like a five-minute moaner, or at least Nancy hoped he was. She wasn't really in the mood to deliver phone sex to a travelling salesman after her aural intercourse with Andrew.

Biggles yowled again as the phone was set down in its cradle.

'OK, OK, I'll feed you. One more bowl of tuna coming right up.'

Biggles smugly led the way into the kitchen. Nancy had barely finished dishing up the cat's meal when the phone rang again. Nancy took her time to get to the receiver and picked it up in a bad frame of mind. She had decided it must be Amber with another client for her to call after she'd got Frank off with a few well pitched moans and slurps.

'What?' Her tone was impatient.

'Nancy?' His tone was soft and flavoured distinctly English.

'Yes, Andrew? I'm sorry – I thought it was the agency.'

'I hope I'm not disturbing you. If you're busy I could call back . . .'

'No, no – I'm glad you called.'

There followed an uncomfortable silence generally referred to by novelists, screenwriters and other pretentious LA residents as a 'pregnant pause'.

All at once they both started speaking, recognised their respective faux-pas, simultaneously laughed and in perfect synchronisation said, 'you first', followed by more uncomfortable laughter. Finally, Andrew got the verbal drop on Nancy.

'I was wondering if you'd like to get together. You know – meet.'

Nancy was quick to respond. This was better than she had hoped for. Caution flew right out of the window.

'Sure. I'm free pretty much all of next week up until about eleven or twelve – then I'm on call – and I also have Tuesday and Wednesday completely off.'

'I was thinking – well, how about tonight?'

'Now?' Nancy was shocked at the shy Englishman's bravado.

'If you don't mind. I mean I don't really do this a lot and I hope I'm not being presumptuous – but we did hit it off rather well . . .'

'Yes, we did, but – but I'm working.'

'Can't you call in sick?'

'Andrew – you are so persistent.'

'I am when I know what I want, and I want you. Not the fantasy – I want the real Nancy.'

'You may not like what you see.'

'And you neither. So what have we to lose except each other and a night in which we both could be wonderful . . .'

'Well, since you put it like that . . .'

'I do. I do.'

'Look – let me get rid of the next call in line and then let's meet somewhere. I'm in Santa Monica – where are you?'

'Hermosa Beach. Why don't we meet in Manhattan Beach at the pier? Whenever you can make it. I don't mind waiting all night. We could even have breakfast together . . .'

'At the pier then, but give me lots of time just in case I have to do any more calls. Shall we say three a.m.?'

'Three it is – at the pier. Right at the very end – over the ocean.'

'And Andrew, how shall I recognise you?'

'I'll wear a white carnation in my lapel. There shouldn't be too many overweight English people on the Manhattan Beach pier dressed like that at three in the morning.'

Andrew's honesty about his appearance brought forth a similar admission from Nancy.

115

'Andrew – I don't look like how I described myself earlier.'

'I know. That was fantasy. This is reality. It will be much better.'

'But I'm not beautiful. I don't want to disappoint you.'

'The only way you could possibly disappoint me is if you didn't show up. Please say you'll be there.'

'Oh, I will – I will. Till three then.'

'Till three. Bye.'

'Bye.'

Biggles was disturbed in his late-night snack by the shrill shrieks of Nancy's yells of joy, and the rather loud commotion of her dancing around the room applauding herself. The cat looked at Nancy with a puzzled look and considered running for cover, but hunger won out when Biggles satisfied himself that it was all just another one of those strange human mating habits and went back to devouring his bowl of tuna. Nancy, enthralled with the prospect of her tryst at the beach, made a few more circuits of her living room and danced off to take a shower and decide what to wear.

And Frank the travelling salesman fell asleep in his hotel room with his floppy dick in his hand, naughty magazines spread strategically around the bed, waiting for a phone call that never came.

Midnight

Malibu Beach

'I say, please don't come in the hot tub – only it does make such a frightfully gooey mess for the rest of us.'

The amorous couple to the right of the aged British actor paid not the slightest attention to his polite remonstrations. He thought about tapping the fornicating duo on the back, decided against it, then felt that it was his right as one of Her Majesty's subjects to complain as strongly as possible when the bounds of civilised conduct were breached and he wasn't included in the fun, even if this was America and all that rot. He tapped one of the couple on the shoulder as they surfaced. He wasn't sure whether it was the male or female protagonist because they kept rolling around and disappearing under the bubbling water, and to make identification worse they both had long blonde hair à la LA style.

'I say, would you mind . . .'

He didn't get a chance to finish his complaint as the fucking couple were too far gone on several doses of mind-altering substances to register any kind of bad karma.

'Cool, man – not in the least. There's plenty to go around. Hey, I can go both ways, babe – join in . . .'

The aged British actor had no time to explain the confusion and was rapidly drawn by a number of limbs into the whirlpool of flesh and superheated bubbling water. Over his cries of 'Oh I say', and 'Madam – please', the amorous couple became a writhing *menage à trois* as the aged actor became an integral part of the submarine orgy.

'Archie certainly seems to be enjoying himself.'

'Pardon me? Oh, hello, Mr Waslinger. I'm not so sure he is a willing participant.'

'Trust me, Marlene, I've known and represented Archie Steele

117

for decades. Despite what he may say and appear to want, he's thoroughly enjoying himself and getting a bit on the side in the process.'

'Well, you're the boss, Mr Waslinger.'

'Neil – please.'

'Neil. You do have quite a history with our star there.'

'Yes, I do – and thanks to you and your stern negotiating talents it appears that Archie and I will continue our long and profitable relationship.'

'Why, thank you. I must admit that Archie's lawyer did prove a trifle difficult.'

'The Limey was a pain in the ass . . .'

'He's Australian, Neil. But you're right. He was a pain in the ass.'

'I can't say I blame him. I must add being a pain in that nice ass of yours would be quite appealing.'

Neil Waslinger patted Marlene Neumann on her taut bottom, lingering perhaps too long for comfort. There followed an uncomfortable silence during which Marlene debated her best course of action. She had been warned about 'Naughty Neil' by her colleagues, but it was not wise to anger a man so powerful that a word from him could ruin her chances of law firm partnership. She decided, quite figuratively, to turn the other cheek.

'Neil! What would your wife say?' Marlene turned her body so that her bottom slipped out of Neil's hand.

'Oh, she'd probably want to watch . . .'

Marlene laughed a strained titter. 'I'm going to get some more champagne.'

'Fantastic idea. And why don't I give you a tour of my humble abode here in the quaint seaside village of Malibu Beach.'

'That would be lovely. Lead the way.'

Neil Waslinger placed his firm tanned hand on the small of Marlene's back and steered her from the poolside area. Marlene hoped that she would see someone she knew, someone whose presence she could enlist as a buffer between her and her extremely wealthy, powerful and frisky client. As they worked their way past frolicking couples in and around the swimming pool Marlene began to think of evasive manoeuvres. A headache wouldn't work – Neil's reputation gave every indication that he wasn't the kind of man who worried about how the woman felt. 'That time of the month' was reputed only to excite him further, like a great white shark enraged into a feeding frenzy. No, none of the old standbys would work. She cursed herself for getting trapped in Neil's presence, especially after she'd been warned by the other women attorneys that had at one time or another had responsibility for the Waslinger Entertainment Agency account.

Neil Waslinger was Hollywood. He owned the town, and owned its key players. It was a standing joke around the entertainment business that they may have very easily have replaced the big white 'HOLLYWOOD' letters on the hill with 'WASLINGER'. It would only have formalised what everyone already knew – this was Neil's dominion and he ruled his empire with a steel dildo in a velvet condom. He was handsome and charming. Tall, tanned with silver-gray hair, athletic beyond his fifty-five years of age, he was desirable. There were worse people that Marlene could sleep with – or rather, have sex with. This afternoon's romp with Shane for example, but at least with that encounter it was over and done with. She'd heard that somebody like Neil Waslinger didn't let go easily until he was tired and bored, and by that time he'd have done his demanding damage. One of her closest friends had told her that Neil Waslinger was an attractive young woman's vampire – desiring, chasing, ensnaring, enslaving, using and destroying the very beauty he craved.

And to make matters worse he owned, albeit very discreetly, the high-profile law firm for which Marlene worked. Now just one year away from achieving the status of partner, she could not afford to anger this man whose vengeance supposedly knew no bounds.

Neil and Marlene – his hand still sliding all over her back and bottom – made their way around the palatial twenty-room mansion through numerous ornamental gardens until they reached a small area close to the roaring ocean. The walkway towards the beach was lined with anatomically correct white marble statues. Neil was obviously enjoying showing off the trappings of his wealth to Marlene. She tried hard not to be swayed by his Malibu Beach ostentation.

'These statues are from Greece – they represent male virility. Impressive, aren't they?'

'Beautiful. They are so perfect.'

'Go ahead. You can touch them – feel the cool stone against your skin. It is reputed to make women swoon.'

'Really? And does it?'

'Touch it and see.'

Marlene cherished the opportunity to escape from Neil's confining hand. She walked up to the nearest statue and placed her hand on its chest, right between the breast bone. She held her palm pressed tight against the cold stone. It was smooth and comforting. She swore she could feel the distant murmur of a beating heart – as if the statue was somehow alive.

'Are you swooning?'

'No, I'm afraid not. You'll have to send them back – they must be fakes.'

Marlene laughed. Neil appeared undeterred.

'I believe you are supposed to stroke the phallus. Legend has it that that is where the statue's source of internal energy is concentrated.'

Marlene didn't like the direction in which this conversation was going. One minute the statue, the next Neil – she could see his mind working overtime – but there appeared to be now no way out of the predicament. And then there was the possibility that perhaps he would get off just watching her fondle the statue . . .

Marlene let her hands fall to the statue's genitals. She cupped the stone balls in one of her sweating palms and wrapped her long fingers around the shaft and squeezed the coolness tightly. The cock had been sculpted exquisitely. Every ridge and nuance had been faithfully reproduced – she could almost feel it grow under her languorous touch.

Marlene practically fell over backwards as the statue's cock grew erect. The stone expanded under her touch to a steely hardness of mammoth proportions. She jumped back with a girlish squeal, her demure black pleated skirt swirling upwards in the process, revealing to Neil her shapely long legs and the promised land not far beyond. Marlene's hand leapt to her mouth in a stifling expression of shock. She stared again at the statue and blinked to make sure it was not an optical illusion. No indeed it wasn't. There before her eyes was a raging twelve inch hard-on where before a small stone penis had been. In her state of shock she failed to hear Neil Waslinger's raucous laughter. Finally, the peals of hilarity broke through her dazed confusion and she turned to face the source.

'What the hell?'

'Oh, I apologise, Marlene, but I couldn't resist. They are all fake. A friend of mine at SFX special effects studio built them for me. Cost a small fortune – but the look on your face was worth every penny.'

'Neil, you – you –'

'Oh, come on now, Marlene – don't you feel just a little bit more comfortable now? You were so sure I was going to take you behind the bushes and have my wicked way with you.'

Marlene started laughing at her own embarrassment.

'Well, there are stories . . .'

'Yes, there are plenty of stories in Hollywood and most aren't true. So perhaps now we can be friends as well as business acquaintances?'

'Certainly. I mean – I always thought we were.' Marlene knew she was being apologetic without any real reason for her feeling so, but Neil Waslinger had made a career out of inducing such emotions in people. To stop herself from talking she turned her attention back to the statue, which was now shrinking back to normal size.

'It is activated by your body heat. Temperature sensors pick up your warmth and heated hydraulic fluid is pumped into the cock. The stonelike material has special thermal properties that cause it to become pliable and expand, and presto – a big hard-on there for your pleasure as long as you keep supplying your lovely warmth. You should see these things on hot days – all ten of them standing out at attention. Amazing, isn't it? Quite like the real thing.'

'Yes, really – amazingly so.'

Marlene thought of Shane and how she'd ridden his engorged flesh with a lustful abandon just a few hours earlier. At the thought of her recent escapade her excited brain coaxed a small wetness to spread from her quivering thighs. She could still feel the swelling of Shane's dick within her. Neil's voice interrupted her musings.

'Forgiven?'

Marlene was quick to respond. 'Oh, Neil, I'm sorry to have believed those stories. Please don't hold it against me.'

'Consider the matter forgotten, Marlene. Let's start afresh. And now that you hopefully trust me not to maul you, perhaps you would like to go up behind those bushes. I think you'll find the view totally spectacular.'

'Really?'

'Would I lie? I'll lead the way.'

'Please do.'

Marlene wasn't quite sure why she agreed to accompany this egotistical man whom just a few moments earlier she was in mortal dread of, but she felt she could not refuse as a matter of face. If she was to make partner in the law firm and command this man's respect she would have to appear in command, self-assured – not flustered by a man's advances. Heaven knows, she'd seen enough of that in her climb up the legal ladder – now was not the time to shy away from the challenge. Why she had been so afraid before puzzled her. Neil Waslinger was just another man, albeit a powerful one, and Marlene knew very well how to handle, manipulate and command the men around her. Acting like a scared schoolgirl virgin just wouldn't do. And so she agreed, her confidence buoyed and her defences temporarily relaxed by the levity of the statue's rise and her own amusing reactions.

Arm in arm, Neil and Marlene made their way up a small grassy knoll to a bluff that overlooked the Malibu coastline. A stiff ocean breeze whistled up from the shore, blowing Marlene's dress skywards. Struggling to keep her modesty, she secretly enjoyed the cool wind on her sex. The statue experience had titillated more than just her imagination. Her body had now begun to acknowledge the delight she inwardly felt at the thought of her bringing an inanimate statue to full erection with the warmth of her caress. The cool ocean wind soothed those lustful feelings that she felt best belonged under control. One mistake today was enough.

Neil stood behind her his hand once more cradling the small of her back. He pointed out the magical sights.

122

'The beach below is all mine. The yacht to the right of the small boat anchored to the pier is mine – she sleeps ten comfortably. You'll have to join me on one of my fishing trips to Mexico. It is the most relaxing way to forget all of the insane demands of this town. Far to the south you can see the lights of Santa Monica, and beyond that the occasional aeroplane taking off from LAX. I often come and sit up here throughout the night. It is so refreshing – so cathartic. I feel cleansed by my time here high above the ocean, death just a footstep away. I walk away from this place like some medieval knight ready to battle once more with the infidel hordes of the Sodom and Gomorrah of Hollywood and Burbank.'

Marlene turned to face Neil Waslinger. He stared out at the ocean oblivious to her gaze, perhaps enjoying a rare private moment. Marlene didn't interrupt, but faced the immense blackness herself. The ocean wind whipping more fervently at her clothing with increased determination. Neil's deep voice mingled with the roar.

'Marlene, I think you'll find that you'll have much the same effect on me as you did on the statue – but perhaps quicker, more responsive.'

Marlene whirled around to see Neil Waslinger's cock protruding from his trousers. Her eyes flashed from the immense head to Neil's face and back to his cock. He sensed her confusion.

'Yes, you're right. The dick on the statue was modelled after my own, and I was quite envious to see the way your long fingers caressed its apparent inertness into life. And when your dress fluttered up I could see that you wore no panties. I want you, Marlene. I had intended not to approach you once I had my little joke with you, but – I confess ulterior motives once I saw your nimble fingers at work. I could only think of having you do that to me. Here, please – coax my statue to life.'

Marlene backed away, careful not to slip over the sheer two-hundred-foot drop to the swirling waters below. She knew exactly what to do. There was no more fear, no trepidation – just the exhilaration of being in control.

'You want to fuck, fine. Let's fuck. I'd love to ride that long hard dong of yours all the way up to my throat, but let's not play silly mind-fuck games, OK? We fuck tonight, and that's it.

You don't owe me a thing, and more importantly, I don't owe you. If we enjoy it and want to fuck some more, that's fine too – but always on the same terms. Deal?'

Neil Waslinger, the master of negotiating the fortunes of superstars, was visibly shaken by Marlene's onslaught. He looked silly, standing there with his huge bulbous dick bobbing and twitching in the breeze.

'Is it a deal, Neil, or are you going to stand there like one of your statues on a cold day?'

Neil Waslinger seemed to regain some of his composure.

'Why, Marlene, I am impressed. You have fire – and you have my word on it. No favours – just fucking. Shall we shake on it?'

'But of course . . .'

And Neil offered his outstretched hand to Marlene who moved her own to accept his. Only just before contact she diverted her long fingers from his and wrapped them around the hardening shaft of Neil Waslinger's cock.

'I'd much rather shake this, just so you know that should you go back on your word as a gentleman I swear I'll tear this club right off at its root and feed it to you for breakfast at the fanciest restaurant in Hollywood.'

'And I shall willingly eat it should I break our agreement. Marlene – I love it when you talk so rough and dirty. Have no fear, fucking is first and foremost in my mind, and I won't interfere in your career one iota. It seems there is little I could do even if I wanted to. I must admit I underestimated you. You are every bit as good as they say.'

'They?'

'Around town you're reputed to be quite the iron lady when it comes to striking a deal. I thought the stories to be exaggerated when I met you in person, but now I see the real you. I like what I see.'

'Well, that's nice. Now are we going to fuck or pay each other compliments all night long? Pretty soon your guests are going to wonder where you are and I'd prefer not to have an audience – especially your wife.'

'Oh, don't worry. She's passed out drunk by now and no one else knows about this place but me. Let's fuck.'

Marlene marvelled at how the purple-headed monster in

her hands writhed and squirmed between the caress of her fingers.

'I have to admit, Neil, I much prefer the real thing to the statue. It throbs a lot better when I squeeze it – like this.'

Marlene reached down to Neil's cock with her other hand, joining the one she had used to shake the immense knob. With all of her fingers she hefted the trunklike shaft with a firm squeeze. The mere thought of fucking this incredibly attractive and assertive young woman had caused Neil to stiffen as he talked to her, but now that her warm and nimble fingers toyed with his shaft he became rock hard, just like the statue. Marlene stared into Neil's eyes and then at his straining penis and then back into his eyes – a wry smile building on her face. Neil looked up at the sky and then down at the ocean. He spoke softly, his voice mingling with the sea breeze.

'I hate to bring up practicalities, but I don't have even so much as a blanket for us to lie on. As I mentioned, I hadn't planned on being so lucky with you tonight.'

Marlene was not deterred. 'Not to worry, Neil, I was planning on being on top anyway. So why don't we fuck right here – right by the edge of the cliff.'

Neil spoke in staccato phrases as he anticipated the delights Marlene had to offer. 'How romantic – just like the movies. Moonlight, the ocean, the cliff, you – all we need is an orchestra. But wouldn't you prefer to make love a little bit further away from the edge of the cliff? What might happen if I get so turned on by that tight cunt of yours and thrust you over the side?'

'Then at least I'll die with a smile on my face. Please, please – lie down. No, no – don't take off your jacket, or any of your clothes. I've always wanted to fuck a man in a tuxedo – especially a man so well hung as you.'

'As you wish, Marlene.'

Neil Waslinger negotiated a small space amongst the sand and rocks where he lay on his back and held his mighty cock skyward, pointing it at Marlene. Marlene stepped back to admire the monument and in preparation for mounting the giant staff she dropped her small shoulder purse from her arm, careful to activate the small tape recorder she always kept with her so that she could dictate letters and briefs while stuck in LA traffic. She never dreamed it would be used in this situation, but she viewed it as just a little insurance to Neil's word as a 'gentleman'.

'So tell me, Mr Waslinger – now that you've brought me up here to this deserted spot, what do you want?'

As Marlene uttered the teasing words she swayed her hips from side to side, gradually raising her skirt. Slowly, tantalisingly, Marlene raised the hem of her black full skirt past her knees, continuing at an ever-slowing pace past her supremely erotic thighs to pause momentarily, hovering just slightly above the dark red reinforced band of her fishnet stockings. The delectable sight drew the desired response.

'You, Marlene. I want you – you know I want you.'

'But you have me, Neil. I'm your lawyer – I'm here to do whatever you want. And I do your bidding so well, don't I?'

The skirt rose ever higher. Marlene had decided against panties. After her late afternoon romp she had showered and felt the wantonness of her fucking glowing between her legs – panties would have been uncomfortable so she had selected a long full skirt and wore only stockings beneath it. The wanton mood had rapidly disappeared once Marlene had been isolated by Neil Waslinger, but now it had returned with a greater passion that the ocean breeze could not cool. Marlene was on fire with the idea that it was she, not Waslinger making the conquest. Her lusciously trim body silhouetted by the moonlight radiated sex. By the light of the moon Neil could make out the outlines of Marlene's pubic hair, the small tufts that descended from her cunt shining between her legs.

'Don't tease me, Marlene. Come, sit on my dick. Fuck me, fuck me now – before I knock you over the side of the cliff with the eruption of my load.'

Perfect, thought Marlene, perfect. She hoped the tape recorder caught every syllable of the implied threat. A good lawyer could do a lot with that – and Marlene was the best.

'Are you sure your wife won't bother us?'

'I've told you once – she's drunk, passed out and doesn't care. Now fuck me with that pussy, Marlene. Stop talking and fuck me.'

'Like this – is this pleasing to you?'

Marlene had positioned herself, legs astride, towering directly over Neil Waslinger's oozing dick. Like a parachute she lifted the hem of her skirt to its fullest extent and let it drop as she lowered herself swiftly to perch on the trunklike shaft of Neil's cock. Pausing slightly she let her hips gyrate to and fro, causing her pussy lips to slide around Neil's quivering cockhead. He moaned deeply as the sensitised tip of his dick slipped over the hills and valleys of Marlene's sex. Slowly, deliberately, with a distinguished sense of the occasion, Marlene lowered herself to her knees, sinking the swollen shaft deeply and deliciously within her. For the second time in one night she eased a mammoth cock inside of her. It was an exquisite feeling to be so full. She was still a little sore from her earlier exertions, but the size within her knew nothing of that – and the lust driving her brain couldn't have cared less about such a minor discomfort. Quickly she began to lubricate heavily, soaking her warm thighs with a moisture that quickly eased what little discomfort there may have been.

Marlene's full black skirt completely shrouded their lovemaking. Not even her trim ankles in their red fishnet stockings could be seen, and with Neil fully dressed in his tuxedo the whole scene took on a truly clandestine feeling for Marlene. It was as if they were at an expensive restaurant or perhaps the theatre, and the urge to fuck had overcome them. Without regard, fully clothed, they fucked with a wild passion made all the more intense by their formal dress.

Neil let Marlene do all the work and he just kept his magnificent maleness in its primed state – every so often slightly adjusting his ass on the hard ground to keep the other areas of his body awake. Marlene was the kind of woman that intrigued Neil Waslinger. He was amazed at the way she tossed her auburn curls back from her face and put her arms behind her head and rode him better than any high-priced whore he'd ever purchased. The starlets that he fucked, the friends' wives he'd had his way with, business associates he'd tangled with, his perpetually drunk and drugged wife who faked her orgasms – all seemed to want him, with his massive cock, to be the ultimate stud. To get on top and pummel away while they rolled and screamed, 'Oh God – oh God – you're so big.' He often felt like slapping them when they did and said that. Didn't they know he knew very well his size? He could tell Marlene wasn't like that. He admired the way that she had demanded the terms of their fucking as if she was negotiating a deal. And the way she fucked was even better. She enjoyed his sex for her sake, with little regard for anything else. With all the poseurs in Hollywood, Marlene Neumann was a breath of fresh air – the real thing.

Marlene used her legs to raise and lower herself along the full length of Neil's penis. Savouring every millimetre of skin, every small bump and ridge, every bulging vein – she could feel through her cunt walls every detail as the turgid member filled her to her capacity. With a squeeze of her downy thighs she could make Neil's cock twitch and pulse and every spasm of his dong – it seemed to fill her further – expanded her strained cunt beyond its already stretched capacity.

At the height of the stroke of her legs she felt her release start. It began like the breaking of the waves below – almost hanging in suspension before cresting on the shore. She stopped her movement and held herself impaled on the head of the twitching member. Feeling her thighs quiver she lifted her dress higher and higher, exposing her sex to Neil – exposing the overheating cunt to the night air. Higher and higher she lifted her skirt, pulling it into her mouth and holding it there with her teeth, stifling the scream she wanted to emit. Her hands tore at her hair as she plunged downward, plummeting like a rock falling to the ocean below, she descended the length of Neil's cock swiftly and mercilessly. Neil gasped with the slap of the violence of the impact of Marlene's thighs upon his body. The way the inside of her sex crashed into his cockhead, smashing the sensitive tip, brought Neil an agony he'd rarely felt. Marlene, lost to the throes of orgasm, was unaware of his discomfort. She ground her ass into Neil's thighs, willing his cock to penetrate her body. It was then that he came and the tip of his cock smashed tightly against the entrance to her womb, ground against her lust-engorged flesh in tiny smearing circles as she pressed her body into his. His orgasm had nowhere to go – it felt as if his mighty instrument would explode under the pressure that he felt. Slowly, with great relief, it found its way out of the compressed slit, oozing into every small nook and cranny of Marlene's cunt – few that there were, with his giant dick occupying her so fully. The effect was to prolong his release as it was to intensify hers.

They were disturbed in their respite from the exertions of furtive sex by the moans and screams of what sounded like a young woman. Neil, with his eyes closed, first thought that it might be Marlene, but upon opening them he realised that it was coming from the garden and the statue area. Marlene was still astride his cock, eyes closed – her skirt had fallen from her mouth – her hair was blown back, her arms were listless at her sides, she appeared asleep, held up purely by the remaining stiffness of Neil's cock inside of her.

Shortly, the wild screams emanating from the garden reached her sex-racked brain, disturbing her restful peace.

'It seems someone has found the statues.'

'Indeed. Shall we explore?'

'You go ahead – I want to stay here a while and compose myself. I'd like to enjoy the view.'

'By all means. Please take as much time as you like.'

Neil did his best to dust himself off and turned to leave the scene. He paused as if thinking of what to say.

'Marlene, I – I would like to make love to you again, on whatever terms you desire. No strings attached.'

'Certainly, Neil – certainly. No strings attached. It would be my pleasure.'

As he walked away Marlene turned off the tape recorder in her purse, reached for her hairbrush and sat staring out at the calming ocean, her shaky hands combing the tangles out of her hair. In the background she could still hear the screams of a young woman mingling with the sounds of the ocean, like some strange form of nocturnal seagull searching for scraps of food.

The source of the screams and moans was none other than Tawny Peters who had been led to Neil's party by Otto Verge. 'Led' was the appropriate term as they emerged from Otto's limousine – Otto first, followed by Tawny. Attached to the large brass ring hanging between her breasts was a six-foot length of chain which Otto held tightly. He was dressed in the stereotypical movie mogul garb of riding breeches, high leather boots, white silk shirt and a monocle firmly lodged in his left eye. Tawny was dressed as Otto had required earlier in the evening – except he had given her the dignity of a leather face mask from which her lovely mop of blonde hair fell in an arranged show of innocence.

They had caused quite a stir as they walked around, Otto greeting friends and business associates, Tawny always staying the full length of chain behind him, talking to no one – even when they fondled her exposed parts. Otto's instructions had been explicit. Acknowledge no one, even if they ask questions of you; let anyone I give my permission to do anything to you. This is your coming-out party, my dear Mistress Tawny – and tonight you will do a lot of coming.

Tawny played her part well, even when a couple – she thought she recognised the man from an old television show and the woman was an older, heavily made-up Beverly Hills tart who just might have been a transvestite – started sucking on Tawny's exposed nipples, much to Otto's glee. The 'odd couple' were quite inebriated and offered all manner of payments if they could borrow Tawny for a night. Otto pretended to consider the offer but much to Tawny's relief refused. It was after this encounter that Otto had promised her something special. It was the statues.

Otto had fondled one of the statue's cocks until it had hardened to its Neil-like length and girth. Still holding Tawny by the chain, he instructed her to remove her panties and mount the statue. It was by far the largest object Tawny had ever taken inside her young cunt and it hurt considerably to slide up and down the pole. Otto had Tawny wrap her legs around the statue, holding herself to it with her arms wrapped around its neck. For added support Otto used his not too small cock firmly placed up Tawny's bottom. Tugging backwards on the chain Otto fucked Tawny in the rear as she ground her sensitive cunt on to the fake stone penis of the fake statue. The hotter she got the harder the fake stone cock became until Tawny could not stand the dual entry any further. It was under such penetrations that she started to shake so violently with every thrust of Otto's dick up her arse.

'You are such a lucky girl, Mistress Tawny,' Otto hissed warmly in her ear. 'Twice in one night to be violated on such exquisite toys as the horse and Neil's virility statues.'

A scream was all Tawny could manage in reply.

It was then that Neil Waslinger, fresh from his own prurient pursuits, happened on to the scene.

'Otto Verge, what are you doing to that poor girl – and my statue?'

'What does it look like, Neil? I'm fucking her up the bottom while she grinds on your monuments to your ego. Would you care to sample Mistress Tawny's delights? She has the tightest boxes – in both directions – that I have ever sampled. Be my guest.'

'Oh, no thanks, Otto. I'd better get back to the party – I just wanted to see what all the commotion was about.'

Otto continued thrusting into Tawny's bottom. Tawny was completely oblivious to Neil Waslinger, content to ram her clitoris against the marble pubis of the fake statue. Otto conversed with Neil as if he were performing a menial task such as gardening or house cleaning.

'Suit yourself, but we must do lunch next week. I have to talk to you about my next picture.'

'OK, Otto, call me. We'll do lunch. Bye for now, Otto, Mistress Tawny.'

'Say *au revoir* to the nice Mr Waslinger, Tawny. I'm sure he'll want to meet you again sometime. Especially since you've got pussy slime all over his nice clean statue.'

It was all Tawny could do to scream an attempt at a farewell greeting to the retreating Neil Waslinger. The pain in her lower extremities was excruciating, but it seemed worse if she stopped, so she kept pumping as hard as she could. She wished for the statue to show some emotion – perhaps just a smile – to show a sign of recognition of her lustful craving. With this as a goal she banged her tender body hard against the stone, threatening to do herself and the statue considerable harm.

Marlene Neumann, from her vantage point behind the bushes, watched the scene in the garden grotto with a keen sense of amusement and fascination. Sex, she concluded, probably shouldn't be a spectator sport – especially the kind of sex that was unfolding before her eyes. It was almost too comical to watch, like two dogs maniacally fucking on a street corner, oblivious to all the passers-by doing their very best not to notice nature at work. The thought brought Marlene back to the reason why she was secluded behind the bushes. Before making her move back to the party, Marlene was waiting for the wet spot where she'd bitten through her skirt to dry. In the throes of rapture she'd torn a small hole in the expensive garment with her teeth but she was sure that in the state that most guests were in, no one would notice. Marlene was also sure she could sneak past the fornicating couple of Tawny and Otto without being noticed. They seemed somewhat preoccupied. It was important to Marlene not to be thought of as Neil Waslinger's mistress, so she wanted to avoid any chance of the fucking couple possibly putting two and two together and coming up with twelve inches of Neil's cock up her cunt.

Marlene need hardly have worried. Otto's eyes were riveted to the sight of his girth forcing wide Tawny's bottom and his thighs slapping into the creamy flesh of her leather-strapped buttocks. He watched the scene with the slow-motion detachment of a gifted movie director, ever watchful for the perfect angle for that sublimely surrealistic shot. Tawny's eyes were closed. She had long since stopped being aware of anything other than her clitoris. She had tried desperately to focus on that intense pleasure she felt there so as to avoid the pain that she felt in her cunt and in her ass. It helped to close her eyes and think of her little bud of flesh being pressed so tightly by her thrusts against the statue. To dream of nothing other than how her body was dissolving into her clitoris, slowly and surely – with every painful thrust one small iota of her being dripped from between her legs, around the surprisingly real dildo and down her long silky thighs to be absorbed by her stockings, as if she was melting with desire.

Otto began to come in her ass. She felt the warm liquid squirt upwards and inside her, jolting her body even more forward. Otto followed her form with an almighty shove of his stubby legs, as if he wished to push his orgasming weapon through her body and into the statue. The force of his thrust, combined with their body weights, overbalanced the statue. It teetered backwards and then forwards, threatening to fall on top of the still copulating couple, but one more of Otto's thrusts sent the statue reeling backwards once more. This time there was no stopping the statue's tumble as the combined sexual excess of Otto and Mistress Tawny sent it crashing to the ground with the couple still fucking as the statue hit the grass of the ornate garden.

Remarkably the statue didn't shatter, but the expandable penis was torn off by the force of the impact as Otto's fucking of Tawny caused their frenzied bodies to roll to the statue's side. The shaft remained stuck in Tawny's cunt, rapidly shrinking as it lost its hydraulic pressure. Otto remained up Tawny's ass, his cock doing a much better job of staying stiff under the taut constriction of the girl's anus. The statue lay on its back, a gaping hole in its pubis, shooting a fountain of hydraulic fluid skyward. From the corner of her eye Tawny watched the fountain spurt a few times and gradually subside to a slow trickle. Perhaps it was the fact that her face was pressed to the ground by Otto's body, thereby distorting her vision, but she was sure that the statue was finally smiling. Somehow, the thought pleased the subjugated Tawny immensely.

'Sydney Nats – how do you do? I thought you were on your way to England. And who do we have here?'

Neil Waslinger had started to address Sydney but had been riveted by Kimberly Duke's stunning presence. He was unabashedly leering at her tanned breasts and long legs that in her cowboy boots brought her eyes threateningly close to his own.

'Neil Waslinger – Kimberly Duke.'

'I'm charmed, Kimberly.'

'Mr Waslinger.'

'Please, call me Neil. Champagne?'

'Why, thank you.'

'I thought you'd like to meet Kimberly. She'll be signing with Rose Entertainment tomorrow. Modelling, dancing, acting exclusively, but I thought perhaps you'd like a crack at her before we signed. It came up all of a sudden so I had to cancel my flight. I hope you don't mind the intrusion at your party, but we just had to celebrate – and this is the place.'

Neil Waslinger hadn't taken his eyes off Kimberly Duke all through Sydney's speech. Neil's fucking by Marlene had primed his vulnerability for this stunning beauty. Her long blonde hair was tousled by the wind and her eyelids fluttered in a most come-hither manner. Something inside him told him that this was possibly the next Marilyn Monroe. He was damned if Rose was going to get her. Neil knew it was all a ploy by Sydney, but

133

he couldn't have cared less. He had to have her, in every possible way – carnally and professionally. Typical of the attention span of entertainment industry executives, all thought of his recent tryst with Marlene went right out of the ornate French windows as a new object of desire appeared before him.

'I don't mind at all – and yes, I'd like a crack at her. My dear, would you care to talk a little business?'

'Why, Mr Waslinger – Neil – I really don't know what to say.'

Sydney jumped in. 'I think we can say the standard plus ten . . .'

'Sydney – please stow it for a short while. I'd like to take Miss Duke on a tour of my estate – on her own – and get to know her. If I'm interested we can strike a deal tonight, terms to be discussed later. Is that acceptable to you, my dear?'

'Why, yes – Sydney?'

'Fine by me. Enjoy the tour.'

Neil Waslinger held his cocked arm out for Kimberly to take. She daintily accepted.

'Where shall we start? How about with the house? And then I'd love to show you my statues – they're from Greece, you know . . .'

Sydney smiled to himself as the two walked away. Things were going right according to his impromptu plan. He'd quickly schooled Kimberly in what would happen once he'd spun his fanciful yarn to the willing ears of Neil Waslinger. The investigations of Neil that Sydney had done in preparing for the week of negotiations had revealed Neil's weakness for emotionally strong, stunningly pretty women. It was common knowledge in Hollywood that Neil quickly grew tired of bimbos, so Sydney had rapidly prepared a plan for Kimberly and him to follow. It was not too hard to script. Once hooked by Kimberly's natural assets and the thought that another agency might snatch her up, Neil couldn't allow himself the chance of a missed opportunity. It would be just a matter of time before Waslinger would make a pass. Kimberly was to string him along, not to give in. She could kiss him, even let him fondle her a small amount. Then Sydney would find them, act somewhat indignant, play hardball and negotiate Kimberly a contract. Then she'd be on the road to the Big Time and could fuck whoever she wanted, and Sydney would make a quick and easy ten per cent. For all his power Neil Waslinger was very predictable – he always wanted badly what he couldn't have, and that made him quite an easy mark for someone of Sydney's capabilities.

Sydney's reverie was disturbed by an all-too-familiar voice.

'Mr Nats – I thought you couldn't make it?'

'Ms Neumann. Something urgent came up so I rescheduled my flight. You've torn your dress.'

Fuck, thought Marlene, trust him to notice right away. She thought fast. 'I went for a walk on the cliffs to look at the ocean and caught it on some brambles. Such a shame – but the view was worth it. But tell me – what could be so urgent that you'd miss your flight?'

Marlene fancied that attack was the best form of defence. Sydney was in no mood to tip his hand to Waslinger's attorney, so he decided to be coy.

'Oh, I just thought Neil might be interested in a new client of mine. He's giving her a tour of the place right now. Wants to sign her, I think.'

'Really? He didn't mention anything to me about a new signing.'

'Oh, it just came up – spur of the moment.'

'Where are they? I'd like to meet this client of yours.'

'Neil said he was going to show her some statues – do you know where they are?'

'Do I! Why don't we go and find them, Mr Nats. Follow me – I think the grotto is this way.'

Marlene kept telling herself she wasn't jealous. After all, it had been she that had insisted on the no-strings policy, but she was curious as to whether Neil was so insatiable as to want another woman just moments after he'd fucked her. Jealous, no – curious – most definitely yes. Sydney noticed her preoccupation and tried small talk to bring her back to the here and now.

'Call me Sydney, Marlene.'

'Sydney it is.'

Marlene didn't realise how true those last words were going to turn out to be as she and her Australian counterpart made their way past drunken, boring people droning on and on about their latest projects, through darkened rooms where drunken fornicating groups of arms, legs, buttocks and other body parts resembled something out of a movie about Roman decadence.

Finally they reached the grotto and the statues.

Marlene tried not to appear shocked.

Sydney had to work hard not to burst out laughing.

The grotto was a cornucopia of body parts, broken statues and lust gone wild. It seems that Neil had gotten quite angry about Otto's abuse of Neil's statues and a heated argument had ensued. This attracted quite a crowd who quickly discovered the anatomically correct nature of the objects and a frenzy of statue abuse had resulted. Kimberly had done her best to soothe Neil with her special talents, and in the process Neil had become thoroughly captivated by the tall Texas beauty. To be precise, the captivating occurred inside a small gazebo just out of sight of the grotto. Sydney and Marlene had stumbled on Neil and Kimberly quite by accident as they made their way past the orgy scene in the grotto. Marlene had been righteously huffed. Sydney was apparently indignant. Neil was overly apologetic. And Kimberly was justifiably pleased with herself.

After the obligatory exchange of words, Marlene and Sydney had wandered off thinking that perhaps they were the only sane people left in Los Angeles. They joked, arm in arm, about the weird lifestyles and bizarre characters they'd encountered. Much of the tension between them rapidly dissolved as they realised that they had much more in common than they could possibly have hoped for. For the past week Marlene and Sydney had been legal adversaries, and neither of them had given the slightest thought to the chemistry that had developed between them. They were ideal for each other, and like so many people in such situations, they had done their very best to ignore the obvious. It had taken the rolling waves and the windswept cliffs to make them realise that they were crazy about each other.

When all was said and done, Kimberly Duke had quite a lucrative contract and a permanent place to stay at the Waslinger Estate as a 'dance instructor' for the Waslinger brats; Otto Verge had promised to reimburse Neil Waslinger for his statues as long as Otto could buy several more as presents for Tawny and as long as Otto promised not to sue Neil for assault; Archie Steele had come in the hot tub, drunk himself silly and drowned amidst the bubbling waters, thereby assuring himself of legendary stardom status and substantial revenues for his ex-wives from the re-release of all of his old movies; and Marlene and Sydney had gone for a walk along the cliffs to look at the view – from behind the bushes – and Marlene had 'torn' her skirt again.

Just another party on just another night in the City of One-Night Stands . . .

1 a.m.

WEST LOS ANGELES: CIAO-BABY RESTAURANT

The empty vodka bottles littering the floor of Julia Majors' old VW reminded her uncomfortably of tombstones marking the death of her stillborn movie career.

'To Julia Majors, actress – RIP.'

The words were slurred and almost incomprehensible to anyone in the slightest bit sober. Since Julia was alone and blind drunk it didn't matter. The aspiring actress was in a funk of various colours – an altogether nasty, self-pitying, what's-the-point-of-living frame of mind. She toasted the empty bottles and proceeded to finish off another one so that it could join its compadres on the car floor. Julia Majors was roaring drunk, as if it were Christmas Day, Boxing Day, New Year's Eve, her birthday and a best friend's wedding day all rolled into one. Only the reason for her considerable alcohol consumption was not a festive one. She was drinking as if tonight were a wake, and the dear departed appeared to be her good fortune in general.

All night long as Julia attended to the rich and famous amidst the glitz, gloss and chrome of West Los Angeles' Ciao-Baby restaurant she had had one eye on the door to see if the erstwhile film producers, Xavier and Emilio, would come bursting in to announce her starring role in *Avenging Beauty*. As she robotically uncorked bottle after bottle of wine and recited in a bored tone 'this evening's specials', Julia had been fantasising about quitting Ciao-Baby as soon as she got the good news about being chosen as the Avenging Beauty. To say that she was a little distracted and didn't deliver the best of service wouldn't have been too severe a criticism. To make matters and her temperament worse there had been no entrance by Xavier or Emilio. Not even a phone call to announce that they were still deliberating.

138

As the evening had worn on, Julia began to realise that she had been taken, once more, quite literally, for a ride. She had been screwed – in more ways than one – and those creeps had the video to do with whatever they pleased. Would she never learn, she scolded herself? Someone only had to say 'starring role' and Julia lost all common sense and usually a lot more than her dignity. No matter how many times it happened, she never learned. There was always the chance . . .

As these thoughts preyed on her seething mind, Julia began to fume, and when a quite famous actress complained about the fettucine being too cold because Julia took far too long to bring it to the table, Julia lost her patience with the movie business in general and vented her anger on the actress in particular. With a sarcastic comment Julia dropped the overly cold fettucine into the actress's lap. A riotous scene ensued in which the maitre d' and the manager of Ciao-Baby did much grovelling and snivelling, and Julia was told to go somewhere and cool down and come back at closing time to 'discuss' her less than ideal behaviour. Julia knew she was going to be sacked so she took her tip money and bought as much imported Russian vodka as she could afford. Waiting for closing time to approach, she had already consumed one of them and was by now thoroughly pissed.

As the clock struck one and the lights in the restaurant were dimmed, there were but three cars in the parking lot of Ciao-Baby: Julia's VW, somebody's gold-plated Rolls-Royce Corniche convertible and the manager's Mercedes convertible. Everyone else had gone home, so at least she'd be spared the public humiliation of a lecture and a sacking in front of her friends – although she didn't quite see how she could feel any more humiliated than she already had been at the hands of Xavier and Emilio. With a deep breath Julia summoned up as much Dutch courage as a bottle of Russian vodka contained and stumbled across the parking lot to the restaurant entrance.

'Well, well, well – if it isn't our little actress babe come to finish her scene.'

The derisive words belong to Johnny, the manager's younger brother who tended bar at Ciao-Baby. He had refined sarcasm into a practised science.

'Lay off, Johnny – Mario wanted to see me. Where is he?'

'Hey, babe, calm down – I wouldn't be in such a rush. He is still primo upset with you. Care for a drink?'

'No, thanks. I've had plenty.'

Even though she said no, Julia moved towards the bar and her body language said pour me a stiff one.

'I can tell, babe. One more won't hurt, will it? What'll it be?'

'Stoli – straight up.'

Julia poured herself onto a barstool and let the chrome-plated bar support her alcohol-stunned body. She slammed the shot of vodka straight down. Without asking, Johnny poured her another.

'Bad night, uh?'

'The worst. I'm fucked, Johnny. Life's fucked. We're all fucked.'

'Hey – did somebody mention my favourite word?'

Mario had walked into the room and was standing at the end of the bar, surveying the scene.

Julia turned to face him and blurted out a volley of slurred words. 'Mario – I'm sorry. I know what I did was . . .'

Mario held up his hand to stop Julia's apologies. 'I will do the talking here, Julia. You – you can be quiet. Why don't you have another drink while you listen to what I have to say?'

Julia nodded at Mario in acknowledgement of his orders and Mario nodded at Johnny to pour Julia another drink. He did, and she slammed it. He poured her another which she nursed while she listened to Mario's lecture.

Mario began to pace the length of the bar, looking at Julia the way a cat might stare at a mouse that it had cornered but didn't want to eat just yet.

'Julia – your behaviour all evening, culminating in that most unfortunate display that I don't think I need to repeat the details of, was, shall I say – yes I think I will say it – fucking reprehensible. I have few options available to me. Thankfully, the table in question were understanding, and it seems we will get off with the tab for their meal and the cleaning bill for a rather expensive gown.'

'I'll pay for all of it . . .'

'Please be quiet, Julia, and I doubt you could afford it either.'

Julia hung her head. Mario was enjoying dishing out this punishment, and so was Johnny. Mario had a way of talking when he was disciplining an employee that was totally different than his normal LA speech. He adopted an authoritative, distinguished air, as if he were calculating the sting of every word. He learned this style from watching old black and white movies about oppressive headmasters and frightened schoolboys in Edwardian England. He never really understood the movies but he really liked the way the gruff dudes in the gowns got to beat up the little kids with these nasty-looking canes.

Mario and Johnny were the typical Los Angeles high-society restaurant males of vaguely Latin descent. They were probably from Rancho Cucamonga or San Bernadino or one of those other faceless inland towns that littered the Interstate 10 freeway to Las Vegas, but they deliberately cultivated a foreign image. It was good for business, it was good for picking up women. They both had long black hair pulled back into severe ponytails. They both wore expensive suits of pastel colours, collarless shirts buttoned tight against their olive skin, lizardskin shoes of incredibly bad taste, too much strong aftershave, and their tans were too rich and too dark for people who spent most of their time during the day asleep. They were too, too much of everything. The fact that they both constantly wore round gold-rimmed dark glasses gave both Mario and Johnny a faintly sinister air. Mario was older than Johnny and served as the role model for the younger. They were aptly described as 'nasty pieces of work'.

'So the question is: Julia – what is to be done with you?'

Julia kept her head low. It wasn't a conscious move – the vodka in her system required it. And besides, she was sure that Mario already had that question well and truly answered. She wished he'd get it over with and dole out her final check so she could split and finish the process of killing as many brain cells as possible.

'Look at me when I'm talking to you, Julia.'

Mario paused just a few feet away from her. With his outstretched arm he lifted Julia's head underneath her chin so that her gaze was directed at him. Julia did not resist.

'What do you think, Johnny? Any ideas on what should be done with Julia, eh?'

Johnny snickered. 'I sure can't think of anything that could even come close to making amends.'

'Perhaps Julia has some ideas, eh? Or is she too drunk to even care what happens to her, eh? Is that it, Julia? Too drunk, are you, eh? Perhaps I should beat you, eh? That is what we do to unruly women where I come from.'

And you can bloody well go back there too, thought Julia but did not say it aloud. There were other ways of getting back at Mario – and Julia was good at all of them.

Mario looked squarely at Julia. As he spoke he let his eyes wander over her attractive body. She was still dressed in her Ciao-Baby waitress uniform of short black miniskirt, tan tights (as if Julia's legs needed tan tights), white wingtip shirt, choker-style bow tie, black waistcoat that pushed Julia's breasts upwards against the crisp whiteness of the shirt, and black high-heeled spiked shoes. Her long blonde curls were dishevelled from her drinking bout, and her make-up had run down her cheeks. Still, in spite of these minor imperfections she was a woman of considerably striking beauty – especially since her miniskirt had ridden to the top of her thighs as she'd slumped on to the bar stool. Julia was sitting, her knees together, facing Mario. The skirt was tight and high enough on her legs for Mario to see clearly the white vee of Julia's panties through the sheer tan of her tights. Julia was in no mood to pull her skirt down – she couldn't have cared less about Mario being able to see her panties. Hundreds – thousands – would be able to see a whole lot more if ever Xavier and Emilio did anything with that tape. And to make matters worse, she hadn't even got paid for her trouble. What an idiot, Julia kept telling herself. What a fucking idiot.

Mario continued to devour Julia visually as Johnny watched in anticipation, casually drying the same glass over and over with a crisp clean bar towel.

'Cat got your tongue, Julia, eh?'

Julia looked up into Mario's eyes and said absolutely nothing. There was little point. It was clear what Mario and Johnny wanted.

'Pussy got your tongue has it, eh?'

Johnny laughed a sickly guffaw at his brother's pun.

'Perhaps I ought to loosen your tongue a little. Eh? We don't want it to get stuck in your pussy, do we?'

Mario leaned forward, all the while tilting Julia's head upwards to meet him. Something inside Julia said that she should object to this liberty, but a bottle of vodka and a general lack of self-esteem contributed to a couldn't-care-less malaise. She just kept looking at Mario's approaching visage with a zombielike lack of recognition. Mario pressed his lips against hers and kissed her lightly at first. Once he saw that he met with no resistance he slid his tongue between Julia's lips and ran the tip of it around her mouth. She toyed with the idea of biting his intruding body part, but decided that the path of least resistance was the best course of action. Gaining in confidence, Mario played with Julia's tongue, flicking it up and down and around and around, sucking the end of it into his throat as if it were a cock. Cocksucker, cocksucker, Mario's a cocksucker, Julia kept thinking to distract herself from his advances. His hand fell between her legs, forced them apart and roughly rubbed her nylon-covered crotch. After a few minutes of such stimulation he backed away, breathing heavily. Julia remained in the kissing position, her head cocked back, her eyes closed. It was Johnny who broke the silence.

'Viva la Tonguemaster Mario.'

Johnny and Mario both laughed in a back-slapping male-bonding manner. Julia looked at both of them in turn and turned to Johnny. She spoke very softly, almost subdued.

'I'd like another drink, please.'

Another vodka was poured. Julia slammed this one down quicker than any of the others. She was past caring – and feeling at this point. If she had to fuck this slime to keep her job, so fucking what. She'd fucked Emilio earlier in the evening while Xavier watched and had got nothing for her pains. Why worry about Mario and Johnny? They were just dicks. Hard dicks that would come and that would be that and whatever happened after that – who cared. Tomorrow's another fucked day in the continuing fucked life of Julia Majors and all that stuff. Somewhere in her confused brain Julia knew she was rationalising her self-pity into excuses for her actions, but the haze of vodka built a thick brick wall that sensibility found hard to penetrate. Mario, still breathing hard and fast, a lump building through his green pastel suit, continued his lecture, never taking his sunglass-covered eyes off Julia.

'I think it best if we perhaps retire to Johnny's apartment to continue this discussion. I'm sure we can come to some permanent arrangement that insures your continued employment with us here at Ciao-Baby.'

'OK.'

Johnny was ebullient at his brother's ability to get his way with women.

'Yeah. I've got lots of vodka and a big water bed.'

'Johnny, why don't you take Julia over to your place in Sir Justin's Rolls-Royce. That way you can return it to him tomorrow morning as planned without having to come back here to get it. I'll follow in my car and then go home to Elena afterwards.'

'Cool. We'll wait for you in the parking lot.'

Johnny practically winked at his brother.

'Julia, go with Johnny while I lock up the restaurant. Wait in the parking lot for me.'

Julia was ushered bodily by an attentive Johnny out to the gold-plated Rolls-Royce. With his arm around her he supported her stumbling form, careful to feel as much breast as he possibly could. After a few fumbles he opened the door and tumbled Julia into the passenger seat. Her purse fell from her shoulder, spilling all of its contents. She struggled to pick up everything, during which her skirt rode completely up her buttocks, exposing all of her tights-covered thighs, ass and panties to Johnny. He just loved the way he could distinguish the nice round bulge of her cuntlips pouting beneath her white panties, straining underneath the tension of the tan nylon, showing every imaginable detail to his eager view. It was all he could do to stop himself from diving on top of her seductively drunken form and taking her there, in this expensive car, on the soft leather of the passenger seat.

Complimenting himself on his restraint he opened the driver's side door and sat down. Julia had made no effort to pull down her skirt. She just reclined in the seat, her lingerie in full view in the dim parking lot lights.

'So whose car is this?'

Julia's words were mumbled and slurred. Johnny, ever the skilled bartender, was used to the verbal meanderings of drunks, and was easily able to decipher their intent.

'It's this English dude's. Sir Justin Ponceford-Smythe or something like that. He's a regular customer. Mario knows him well. Mario gets him whores – pretty kinky stuff. Anyway he always gets real drunk at the restaurant, so Mario sends him home in a taxi with a girl and returns his car to him in the morning. The Sir dude lets Mario use the car for the night – it's kind of an understanding they have.'

'Oh.' Julia was not in a conversational mood. She just lounged in the seat, unconsciously rubbing her thighs together out of what might have been termed sheer drunken boredom. The crackling noise that the static charged nylon made as her superbly proportioned thighs rubbed together in the dry hot air of the Los Angeles summer night focused Johnny's raging libido on Julia's legs and the delicious sight that the taut muscles rubbing together created. Each little rustle was like a cattle-prod shock to his brain. It was too much for him to endure. He pounced on Julia, forcing his lips on to hers and his body against every one of her private places.

'Oh, Julia – oh, Julia,' he slobbered. 'I've wanted you this way for so long, babe. Ever since you started to work here I've wanted to fuck you good. And I know you like it. I've seen you wiggle your ass at me.'

As he breathed the explanation of his actions he somehow felt obligated to deliver, Johnny tore at Julia's wingtip shirt, popping the small white buttons off. Roughly his hands probed inside her black lace bra and found Julia's nipples. He writhed on top of her, rubbing his sex against her nylon-covered mound, squeezing her titties in a frenzied motion of unrestrained lust.

Johnny was not refined in his fumblings. He clawed and fought for leverage on Julia's inert form as if he were a mountain climber grasping at a sheer cliff-face for hand holds. At one point his whole weight was concentrated on Julia's stomach. It was not a polite thing to do to someone who had consumed many litres of Russian vodka. Julia gagged and coughed as she retched. She was able to mumble a brief warning.

145

'I'm going to be sick . . .'

It was something that a worldly bartender was used to hearing. It brought him back to the reality of the situation better than a brisk slap on the face.

'Oh, no – not in Sir Justin's Rolls.'

He clasped his hand over Julia's mouth and forced open the door. Johnny veritably kicked Julia out of the car where she stumbled to the back of the prestigious automobile and was violently ill in the ornamental bushes of the Ciao-Baby restaurant.

'Shit – shit – shit – shit – fuck.'

Johnny couldn't believe his bad luck so he took out his frustration by thumping the leather steering wheel of the Rolls-Royce while he yelled the appropriate profanities. Once his fists were sufficiently sore, he got out of the car and stood by the radiator grill of the Rolls, trying not to hear the crude noises being made by the boot.

'Hey – where's the chick?'

It was Mario, fresh from closing the restaurant and full of anticipation of the sex to come.

'Throwin' up – too much vodka.'

'Shit. I should have canned her earlier in the evening, but she looked like such a good piece of pussy. I hope this is worth it. I had to try – you know what I mean, Johnny? I've always fancied this babe. Well, who cares if she's sick? We can still fuck her, just as long as she doesn't throw up all over us. It'd be tough to explain to Elena how I got pussy juice and throw-up all over me.'

'Yeah. Real tough – but your wife would believe anything you told her, Mario.'

'Yeah – I got a way with the chicks, that's for sure.'

'Well, then, prove it.'

Mario and Johnny whirled around to come face to face with five foot three inches of Julia Majors. She was sweating profusely and her tanned complexion was ghostly pale. Her lovely strawberry-blonde shoulder-length hair was tangled and messy. Her black high heels were scuffed and dirty from her brief ordeal in the bushes.

And she was naked except for the high heels. In the dim light of the parking lot the two males were able to clearly see that

Julia's pubic mound was covered with a soft golden down that matched the unruly curls on her head.

Mario was the first to respond. Johnny was still trying to blink his eyes at a rapid pace to make sure he got the best view he could get in the poor light.

'Jesus Christ – are you crazy?'

'No. I'm drunk and I'm randy and I want to get fucked – now. So let's do it here – OK? I've always wanted to be fucked on the hood of a Rolls-Royce.' And with that pronouncement Julia climbed on to the bonnet of the gold-plated car and lay spread-eagled, the cold metal against her sweating skin, her head propped up on the windshield, her legs wide astride and her cunt directly in line with the Rolls-Royce bonnet emblem – the arched wings of the small gold statue exactly mirroring the angle of Julia's thighs.

'Jesus – don't scratch the car with your heels.'

'Then take them off me, boys . . .'

She dragged out the 'boys' as if she were Marlene Dietrich holding forth in a dingy western saloon in some old black and white movie. To show she really did mean business – serious business – Julia began to finger her cunt playfully. She forced her pussy lips apart, the stickiness making faint noises as her folds of soft flesh gradually separated and her opening began to moisten. She lifted her legs off of the bonnet and seductively dangled her black high heels from her toes. Mario and Johnny snatched at the shoes and hurled them into the bushes in a juvenile demonstration of anger.

'We ain't gonna fuck here. Now get in the car or . . .'

'Or what? You'll beat me up. You'll rape me. There's nothing you two can do that hasn't already been done – and worse. And I'm not going to anybody's apartment until I get fucked here, on this car. It's a fantasy of mine, so indulge me – OK? I've had a bad evening. You guys have wanted my pussy ever since I started working at Ciao-Baby, so here it is. Listen, it's all wet for you.' Julia fingered herself once more making as much noise as possible, careful this time to slide her fingers all the way inside, thereby coating her hand with her musky sourness. She licked her fingers slowly, deliberately, arching her long lovely neck backwards, delightfully shaking her full mop of blonde hair.

'Hmmm, tasty. My pussy is getting cold, boys. Are you going to fuck me or do I start screaming and run down the street yelling sexual harassment in the workplace to the first policeman I meet?'

Mario and Johnny looked at each other in amazement and with a shrug of their shoulders they both reached in perfect synchronisation to the zippers of their expensive suit trousers.

'Now, that's better. I was beginning to wonder whether you boys really did like girls.'

Julia laughed as she rotated her body so that her head was at the radiator grill and her legs were pointed at the windscreen, thereby assuming the most versatile position she could think of. She lay perfectly prone on the bonnet, her head to one side of the Rolls-Royce winged statue and her legs spread as wide as the bonnet would allow. She felt like one of those sleazy calendar girls that all the petrol stations have pictures of up in their backrooms. In some small way she was beginning to feel like a star again. Throwing up had done her a world of good – it had cleared her head, emptied her stomach and given her the semblance of a plan of how to handle Mario and Johnny. Julia laughed to herself – there was something to be said after all for the so-called 'Beverly Hills diet' of eating, drinking and throwing up so as not to gain any unsightly pounds of flesh.

Mario was the first to mount the Rolls-Royce. He hadn't disrobed but merely pulled his pecker out of his trousers. Johnny stood by the wheel, watching and waiting. Mario was uncomfortable on his knees – the hard metal not being the most supple of beds. He felt as if he might fall off the car at any instant. Julia reached between his legs and held his cock in her hands, assessing its prowess. Mario's dick was nothing to write home about, but it rapidly assumed an acceptable hardness under Julia's expert touch.

'Well, come on, Mario – teach me not to be such a bad waitress. Teach me to be good, big boy – teach me with that nice big prick of yours.'

Julia finished her cajoling with a seductive laugh that inflamed Mario's macho sensibilities. He lunged at her and plowed his cock into her moist furrow.

'Take that, bitch . . .'

'Oh, that's so much better, Mario. I hope it feels good to teach me such a strong lesson with that big nasty dick of yours. I promise to be a good little girl from now on.'

'You'd better – cause if you don't put out whenever we want it, you're fired.'

Julia silently laughed at the threat as Mario's dick plunged into her. Did he really think that this stinking job meant that much to her? She let him think it did as she told herself she couldn't care less. Inwardly she was enjoying manipulating Mario's macho male ego. A few minutes ago she was passive, literally willing to do whatever she had to do to save her job, and now that she was doing it she felt invigorated and in command. She bucked harder against Mario's thrusting form, creating the impression that he was really sticking it to her good whereas in reality it was she that was setting the sexual pace.

'Oh, what a weapon you've got, Mario. What a firm stick.'

As they fucked so energetically Julia and Mario bounced up and down a few inches off the gold-plated metal of the car's bonnet. It was as they shook so violently that Julia had a naughty idea. She turned her head to see Johnny gawking at his brother's fully clothed body fucking her nakedness.

'Johnny – Johnny – start the car engine. I want to feel it vibrate under me. I want it to shake my ass until I come. Start it, please – start it now, and I'll do something special for you.'

Johnny didn't wait for Mario to nod his ascent, but immediately reached in to the car and started the engine. The Rolls-Royce purred into life, the warm vibrations of eight pumping cylinders perfectly matching the quivering of Julia's ass and thighs. It was an ecstatic charge to feel such unbridled power underneath her body, coaxing more urgent thrusts of her thighs. She wrapped her long silky legs around Mario's ass and goaded him into a more forceful motion by bending her knees towards her chest so that her breasts rubbed against the soft material of his suit. Her nipples hardened under the friction of wool on tender flesh and the taut skin of her bottom shuddered from the pulsing of the engine.

'Oh, oh – that's wonderful Johnny – you sure know how to turn a girl on.'

'Hey – you're fucking me, not him.'

'Oh, don't complain, Mario – there's plenty to go around. Come here, Johnny. Bring your dick over here.'

Johnny hesitated and then advanced to the side of the car not to far from Julia's head. She reached out and grabbed his cock and worked it up and down with her hand, pulling back its foreskin with her long nails. It was all Johnny could do to stand still under Julia's caress. He rocked backwards and forwards, lost in the intoxication of her touch. She pulled him to her with her fingers until the swollen purple head was just inches away from her mouth. At its fullest erection, Johnny's cock was quite thin, but it felt remarkably nimble and agile, twitching animatedly in her palm. Julia couldn't wait to feel the younger man's dick leap in her mouth under the teasing touch of her equally nimble tongue. Playfully she looked up at the younger brother and blew kisses at his cock, confirming his hopeful suspicions that she was actually going to suck him off, not just wank him into release.

Julia was in no mood to wait for Johnny to take the initiative and put his dick in her mouth. Using her hand as a guide she pulled Johnny by the dick towards her so that his body was pressed tight against the car. Julia closed her eyes and let the velvetlike skin of Johnny's cock penetrate her supple lips. His dick was warm and comforting in its urgent hardness. Julia opened her eyes to look at the younger brother. He was staring at her, amazed at how his organ seemed so perfectly at home between her lips. Much like the calm before the storm, he seemed to Julia to be thoroughly contented, happy in the fact that his cock was finally nestled into her warm alcohol-soaked mouth. With her hand she reached between his legs and cradled his ass, her arm rubbing against his balls, all the while pulling him into her so that she could suck his length again and again, as slowly or as quickly as she desired while his brother fucked her exceedingly wet cunt.

Neither one of the brothers dared look at each other, although it was difficult for Mario not to see his younger brother's cock sliding in and out of Julia's mouth. Mario closed his eyes in the classic grimace of someone about to come, although he was still many more thrusts away from his orgasm. Through half-closed eyes he stole views of Julia's fellatio capabilities. She was good, she knew how to suck cock – he could tell by the way his brother's dick made a bulge in her cheek. She was rubbing the sensitive part of his dick on the ridges and crevices of her mouth, making him squirm with delight. Oh, she was good, thought Mario – as good as the stars of those porno movies he made his wife watch with him. Next time Johnny and he fucked this babe, he wanted the blow job.

Julia released Johnny from her mouth and continued the pressure on his small cock with her clenched fist, the wetness of her saliva providing a continued lubrication for her hand motions. She looked up at Mario and pouted, her tits heaving for breath, her lips wet from sucking Johnny's dick.

'Do you like the view, Mario? Do you like fucking a woman while she sucks another guy off? Does it make you really hard? Harder than you've ever been? Is it like watching a porno movie? Is it like being in a dirty film? Do you fantasise about another man fucking your wife while you watch, wanking off as some guy's tool bangs your wife's box black and blue?'

'Aahhhh – ohhhhh – ahhhhh . . .'

'Come on, Mario. Unload that load in me. All of it – fill me full.'

'Uh – uh – uh – uh . . .' Mario kept grunting as he continued his spent thrusts into Julia's cunt. She wrapped her legs tighter around his body like some perverted wrestling hold and squeezed his hips firmly, waving his body from side to side, creating a deliciously filling sensation in her cunt. Mario slumped forward, nestling his head between Julia's firm globular breasts. The purr and the warmth of the Rolls' engine, combined with Julia's enveloping flesh, lulled the satiated Mario into a quiescent state of bliss.

Julia turned her head to continue her oral ministrations to Johnny's cock. Her jerking hand motions had clearly primed his shaft to bursting point. It wouldn't be long.

'Come on, Johnny, come on. We can't let big brother have all the fun now, can we?'

Johnny's answer came in the form of a pelvic thrust aimed right at Julia's face.

'Impatient – that's what I like. Hmmmmm . . .'

Julia made a deep throaty noise that matched the vibration of the idling luxury car as she swallowed Johnny's penis between her lips. The thin shaft was hard and rhythmically pulsing with every lash of her tongue. Johnny had developed a momentun of his own, no longer needing Julia's guiding hand. He slapped his body towards her tilted head, his balls banging against the grille of the car. The heat of the engine fairly stung as he made contact with the metal, forcing him to momentarily jump away only to do a pendulumlike reverse of his swing and fall like a skydiver back into Julia's invitingly tight mouth. The lusty sensations battering his body fought each other for dominance until the swelling of his balls won out, ordering the lingering sperm immediately to escape from the thrusting cock.

Julia felt the orgasm rise from deep within Johnny's balls and was tempted to pull her lips away and let the hot sperm fly all over Mario, but she decided she couldn't be quite that bad – and besides, she had now developed a plan that would require the total complacency of her fucking partners. Julia quite rightfully concluded that a load of sperm in the face wouldn't have resulted in a happy Mario. Instead she swallowed the fountain of come quite easily, Johnny not having a tremendously large capacity. It felt unusually good as the warm stream trickled down her throat, a small amount leaking down her chin in a rebellious fashion.

Johnny was whimpering in delight, but Julia was not about to let him go. So that she could drain every last drop of Johnny's semen she increased the pressure of her suction, forcing her tongue into the sensitive slit at the end of his dick. He began to whine as the sensations became too much to bear. His legs buckled and he was held aloft purely by Julia's mouth. With an almightly slap his stretched cock sprang forth and Johnny collapsed to the ground, eyes closed, dead to the world – happy at having been well and truly sucked into oblivion.

Mario had been lulled asleep by the vibrations of the engine, Julia's cushionlike breasts and the draining effect of his own release. He was snoring loudly and didn't bat so much as an eyelid as Julia eased herself from underneath him. She was still a little tipsy, even though she had only rented most of the alcohol. The majority of it was now moonlighting as weedkiller amongst Ciao-Baby's ornamental bushes. After a few teetering steps she was soon able to gain her balance. Stepping carefully over the passed-out Johnny she stealthily opened the door of the Rolls and settled herself into the comfortable leather of the seat. It felt luxurious against her sweating bottom. She hadn't come – perhaps she really didn't want to come. She really didn't care – it would have been too much of a compliment to Mario and Johnny to let her limbs fly with the frenzied release of her musky nectar. She had enjoyed them for what they were. She had better things in mind – it was payback time. Julia drew in a deep breath and put her plan into effect.

And still Mario slept, his floppy dick dangling out of his expensive suit trousers, plainly in view of Julia in her position behind the steering wheel. Delicately she placed the car into gear and slowly manoeuvred the Rolls out of Ciao-Baby's parking lot and on to Fairfax Avenue.

And still Mario slept, oblivious to the strange looks he was getting from the late-night traffic of West Los Angeles. It was after they had gone about a mile that Julia decided enough was enough.

'Three, two, one – blastoff!'

And she hit the horn as hard as she could. The Rolls-Royce boasted a deep, guttural horn blast that sounded something like the QE2 on a bad foggy day.

Mario leapt vertically in the air as if he'd been shot. He was completely disoriented. The last thing he remembered was that he was fucking in Ciao-Baby's parking lot, and now – and now he was standing on top of a car's hood in the middle of Los Angeles with his dick hanging out. His confused brain concluded it was a nasty nightmare but his brain didn't cooperate. The nightmare got worse – a grinning Julia gave him a small wave and sped the car away, causing him to jump off the bonnet to the safety of the road. As she turned the corner on to Olympic Avenue Mario still hadn't put two and two together. He was standing in the road, his bright red shrunken dick hanging out of his expensive pastel-coloured trousers, much to the amusement of the motorists who had to swerve to avoid him.

Looking in her rear-view mirror at the dazed figure, Julia blew Mario a kiss and a wave.

'Ciao-Baby,' she muttered under her alcohol-tainted breath.

She wasn't sure what she was going to do now, but she felt a

153

whole lot better than a few hours ago, so she pressed the convertible release, let the top down and let the warm night air blow over her naked skin. She laughed hysterically at the crazy city around her. It was a fine night for driving, so she pointed the nose of the Rolls towards the ocean and let the wind blow back her strawberry-blonde curls.

She would have to find another job, but she didn't want to think of that mundane detail now. The only thing that could have made her feel any better at this point was if she happened to come across Xavier and Emilio crossing one of the dimly lit roads carrying a bunch of video tapes to a furtive location.

She knew it was a slim chance, but the thought of bearing down on those sleazy bastards in this gold-plated Rolls-Royce, naked – with fire in her eyes – thrilled Julia immensely. I'd give them an Avenging Beauty, she thought. She laughed hysterically once more, again hoping desperately that she would get the chance to even the score.

This was after all Los Angeles – the City of One-Night Stands – where dreams and nightmares all too easily come true.

2 a.m.

A HOLLYWOOD MOTEL

The Liberace Suite of the Tropicana Motel on Vine Street was thick with smoke of various kinds. Half-smoked cigarettes burned to grey embers in ashtrays filled with half-eaten chewing gum as the room's occupants turned to other more potent vices. The stray shard of a broken mirror was passed from person to person with an almost religious reverence. Ice cubes melted in the close atmosphere of the room further diluting mixtures of Jack Daniel's best with a little of this and a little of that. Conversation had lulled – or perhaps it had never really started? Occasional laughter fought with the strain of the worn-out air conditioner for the dominant background sound. Pretty girls giggled and long-haired sweaty men winked knowingly. It was a typical after-show party for England's latest rock export to America, Momma's Nails.

Most of Momma's Nails members' members were anticipating a thoroughly good night of bonking. It had been a real groovy show with lots of in-your-face rock and roll and hundreds of screaming young girls jiggling their boobies in the front row. The best of the willing had been selected for the band by the road crew and the leftovers were right around now opening their legs for the roadies – Nobby, Harry and Jimmie – in a cheaper room on a lower floor.

It had been quite a night for Jimmie. He'd known the elation of his indoctrination into band sex at the experienced hands of Cassandra, and within a few hours he'd known the terrible disappointment of rejection as she'd turned her attentions to the stars. Cassandra had been nice about it, even pausing to acknowledge the young roadie, but she had maintained her distance when Jimmie had become too friendly in front of the

155

band. It took Jimmie but a few moments to turn disappointment into juvenile revenge between the tender white thighs of an eager fan, no older than he.

In the Liberace Suite the pretty young damsels chosen to service the stars were undergoing what coarsely went for the niceties of getting to know the band. Unlike the roadies, the band did at least make the effort to socialise with their prizes prior to fucking them. It was good for the image and likewise good for record sales to be nice to the tarts, or at least that's what Slick – the band's manager – told them. Slick worked hard to keep the four young Englishmen from Birmingham on the mainline to stardom and megadollars. His fifteen per cent cut helped him put up with the bullshit of baby-sitting four overgrown kids who had up until a year ago been on the dole. They fought constantly, not having the maturity to handle the ravages of stardom. If they survived this tour it would be a miracle.

The bass player, Bov Ril, the guitarist, Spickle, and the drummer, Clod Hopper, were united in their jealousy of Axle Greeser – the band's screeching lead singer who had attracted what had to be the prettiest rock-and-roll groupie any of the band had ever seen. It was Cassandra – and she'd put her hard-earned backstage pass to good use. She was Axle's for the night, and more importantly, he was hers. And the rest of the band was jealous. They always shared the 'slags', but Axle never shared his. He usually coveted the girl in his room and no one ever saw her again, and the fact that she was always the prettiest of the night's selection was starting to irritate the other three members of the band.

Unknown to these band members, one member of one of the members of Momma's Nails wasn't really looking forward to a good night's bonking. It was rather afraid of it all, but did its best to keep up appearances of being a real sex pistol. It belonged to frontman Axle. Axle's cock wasn't too happy because it was having a little difficulty coming to attention – which wasn't doing the egotistical rock star's confidence, or stage presence, that much good.

Cassandra was unaware of this predicament and was thus totally unprepared for what happened after Axle had led her into his room adjacent to the smoky suite.

156

'Here's five hundred dollars – please leave out the back door and don't come back and don't say anything about this to anyone.'

Cassandra was shocked. She had worn her most stunning outfit and wasn't prepared for rejection. 'What?'

'You heard me. Take the money and leave.'

'Let me get this straight. You want to pay me five hundred quid to sneak out of here and keep my mouth shut about us not fucking?'

'Yeah. Easy money.'

Cassandra plopped her long lean form down on the bed. 'I'm sorry, I can't just leave. This is Cassandra – I have a reputation to uphold.'

'So do I – and no one will know. I won't bleedin' well tell the sodding papers.'

'But I know.'

'Oh please go – most of the girls are happy for the money.'

Cassandra was shocked by this admission. The idea that a normal red-blooded male didn't find her worthy of a good bedding was completely unacceptable to her ego. 'Most – so it isn't me? It isn't just tonight?'

'Nah.'

'You're not gay, are you?'

'No – not at all. I'm no faggot.'

Well, what is it? Have you got the clap?'

'Nah – clean as a whistle.'

'AIDS?'

'Nah – I give blood regularly.'

'So what the fuck is it?'

'Curse my bloody luck to get the inquisitive one. Look, my dear – I don't want to talk about it, so get on yer bike and leave me alone. Look – I'll make it a thousand.'

Axle held out a bundle of twenty-dollar bills, fanned invitingly. Sensing a more valuable prey, Cassandra was not impressed.

'You can't get it up, can you?'

'Leave . . .'

Cassandra had slept with hundreds – possibly thousands – of men. She was expert at reading their body language. It was always what they didn't say that spoke volumes. 'Is that it?'

Axle stood at the end of the bed clenching his fists looking angrily at Cassandra, who was sitting cross-legged on the bed nodding knowingly. Axle spun around, his back to her, looking at the floor, continually clenching his fists much more rapidly than before. His reply was muted, mumbled into his chest. 'Yeah.'

'Is that all?'

Axle spun around, his stringy blond hair sticking to his face, obscuring his twisted expression.

'Is that bleedin' all? It's a bleedin' enough, let me tell you.' Axle looked incredibly vulnerable, like a little boy lost in a big bad world. It was all Cassandra could do not to rush over to him and give him a reassuring hug.

'Oh, Axle – keep your money. Let me show you the best night you've ever had.'

It was time for contact. Cassandra walked over on her knees to the edge of the mattress. She was just below Axle's eye level. She swept his hair from his face and looked directly at him. 'It doesn't matter if this doesn't get hard. You have this and these, and most important, this. We can use all those things, and who knows what might pop up in the process.'

As she spoke Cassandra had touched Axle's crotch, and then his mouth, his fingers and his head. She pulled him to her and planted a kiss on his lips. He was not responsive and pulled away.

'It's no fucking use. I ain't in the mood. You're a nice girl – just leave now before I get angry and clobber you. Let me break up the hotel room in peace.'

'I'm not going. Threats won't scare me. Just let me have my way with you. Let me do what I do best, and you just sit back and do exactly what I say. I am the best fuck you'll ever have. And what have you got to lose? Just a few sleepless hours . . .'

Her spiky black hair and pale face radiated a determination that Axle had never faced in a woman. This could be good material for a song, he reasoned, so he decided to play along. Coincidentally, Axle hadn't been able to write much worth a damn lately either. She was the most beautiful bird he'd ever seen. If anybody could stir his pecker it would be her.

'All right. You win.'

'I always do. Now turn out the light and come undress me.'

The diffuse glow of neon from the Tropicana's garish sign illuminated the darkness of the room with a surreal red and blue cast. Cassandra stepped off of the bed and stood with her back to the window. She seemed aglow with the phosphorescence of the sign. Sparks could have easily shot from her black spiky hair and Axle would not have been surprised.

'Sparks fly – sparks fly . . .' the lyric swam through Axle's brain.

'Neon light – hot night – sparks fly – sparks fly,' he mumbled under his cigarette and alcohol tainted breath. Axle could feel the pounding bass and the thud of the drums. Four-four time – nothing fancy – no guitar just yet, just that pounding rhythm and his own screeching vocals delivered in a throaty subdued manner until the song really kicked into gear.

He walked over to Cassandra humming the tune inside his head. This could be a winner, he told himself. Platinum material.

Cassandra was the first to speak, her hands lying gently, palm down, on the singer's skinny chest, stroking his nipples through the thin fabric of his 'Led Zeppelin Will Never Die' tee-shirt.

'I'll undress you, you undress me. Slowly – slowly.'

Not bad, thought Axle. That makes a good second line. In his head he recited the beginnings of the song . . .

Neon light – hot night – sparks fly – sparks fly
I'll undress you – you undress me – slowly – slowly.

He'd raise his voice a few octaves on the last word as the guitar kicked in with a wailing power chord. Then the song would break loose with a thunderous wall of sound.

Cassandra, oblivious to the inspiration her words and skilled actions were having on Axle, continued her impromptu plan to arouse the lead singer. Through the flimsy material of the well-worn shirt she made small circles with her long fingers on Axle's nipples, raising tiny points of hardness that burned through the thin cotton. With ever increasing circular motions she forced the tee-shirt out of the waistband of Axle's torn jeans and worked it up to his neck. His chest, hairless and white, beckoned her lips to it like footprints in a pristine drift of fresh snow on a crisp winter's morning. She planted red figure-of-eight lipstick marks on his body, gradually working her way to the hardness of his nipples. With her hands she forced the tee-shirt over his head – Axle lifted his arms skyward so that the garment could be freed from his body. It fluttered to the ground – he kept his arms held high as Cassandra worked her lips on his chest.

She used her tongue to inscribe small ever-tightening circles around the small bud, playfully nipping at the hardness with her teeth. First one, and then the other – she alternated her attentions to ensure that all the nerve sensors in Axle's body received as much stimulation as possible. It was her plan to avoid all contact with his cock until she had titillated every other part of his body. By that time he would be on fire with a raging hardness he'd find hard to contain. From his nipples she eased her tongue up his chest to his neck, where she nibbled intently on his throat. Her hands traveled slowly up his raised arms until her fingers met his. She pulled herself level with Axle's face and planted her lips firmly on his. This time he responded. Their hands entwined and gripped each other's tightly as their tongues did likewise. Slipping and sliding, exploring the newness of each other's intimacy.

> Neon light – hot night – sparks fly – sparks fly
>   I'll undress you – you undress me – slowly – slowly
> Flesh on flesh – wet on wet – sparks fly – sparks fly

The song was rapidly taking shape in Axle's mind. Line after line formed in his subconscious, mingling with the music he could hear from deep within, every sensation giving new direction to the song's meaning, even the distant traffic noise on the Hollywood Freeway and the occasional police siren. He'd call the song 'Sparks Fly' and dedicate it to Cassandra and Los Angeles. He could even begin to imagine what the video would look like. They'd even shoot it in this hotel room.

Cassandra pirouetted around on her high heels offering her back to Axle – at first he wasn't sure whether to bite her neck or feel her ass, but then he saw the glistening of the zipper to her dress and remembered her instructions to undress her. In the darkness he fumbled with the catch until he was able to release it and pull the fastener all the way down from Cassandra's neck to the hem of her dress, just below the slight curve of her bottom. Cassandra let her arms drop forward and the lace garment fell from her shoulders and to the floor. She stepped out of it and placed it on a nearby chair. It was her favourite dress. She'd found it in a small store on Melrose Avenue – one of those that have only a few clothes, but the few they have cost thousands of dollars. The moment she'd tried the dress on she knew it was for her, but the price was prohibitive. It fitted her long skinny body well, giving an illusion of voluptuousness by virtue of the shadows its semi-transparent construction created. It was made of a see-through black lace that gathered in a ruffle high around the neck. The dress then flared out substantially in a capelike fashion to a length that revealed more than it obscured. Ribs of a thicker, decidedly opaque, material added structure to the dress creating an overall spider's web effect. Her arms were encased in full sleeves of matching lace that billowed around her thin limbs, adding to the impression of the shortness of the skirt and the desirability of its contents. She'd stood in front of the mirror in the store admiring how the black lace matched the black of her hair, and how the paleness of her skin contrasted through the diaphanous material. Under the fluorescent light of the shop her small breasts had been clearly visible and her sex was covered by the merest of panties. She'd known she had to have the dress, and she'd also known she wasn't the only one admiring how well it suited her. The shop owner had been amenable to a trade situation, and she'd walked out of the store with her prize after a few minutes in the changing room doing the owner.

Tonight she'd planned her undergarments carefully, knowing that all would be visible through the spider-web black lace material. Cassandra had chosen a white satin corset with matching white satin suspender straps. Her small breasts were completely visible through the lace when one of the darker web lines moved to one side or the other. To contrast with the lace of the dress she'd worn white stockings with black seams. Her panties were black satin with a white satin vee embossed in a strategic location. She'd completed the outfit with black patent high heels. Against her white skin and black hair the outfit was merely an extension of her own sensuality, a second skin that was easily shed.

Standing with her back to Axle she turned to see him once more with his arms raised skyward as if being held up at gunpoint. He seemed mesmerised, almost in a trance. He was a tempting target – she felt her juices stir as she inched closer to his body and began to nibble at his neck, and then his ear and then they locked in another kiss, her hands around his neck teasing his long blond hair. Finally he let his hands fall down from their sky-high position to rest on Cassandra's shoulders. The whiteness of her skin was soft and cool in the heat of the room. He could feel the points of her tits touching his chest and deep within he felt the stirrings of lust he'd thought long gone.

Cassandra sensed it too. There were no overt signs but she could sense the increased urgency in his kiss, the quickening of his pulse, the way his body was no longer rigid and unresponding. She let her hands drop to the buttons of his jeans where she deftly undid them one by one. Cassandra used both her hands to force the tight denim over his hips, pulling his skimpy underpants down with them. She released Axle from her grasp so he could kick off his high-top sneakers and his jeans from around his ankles. He stood there naked in front of her, their bodies only inches apart. Even in the dim light Cassandra could see that Axle lived up to his name. He was hung like the proverbial bull – no wonder he had difficulty getting an erection. He just didn't have enough blood in his body to get that monster hard without fainting, Cassandra mused as she tried hard not to stare at Axle's large cock. Skinny white boys from England weren't supposed to have dicks this big, thought Cassandra. Now more than ever she felt the need to rise to the occasion and succeed in bringing the slumbering giant to life where so many others had failed – had not even tried. A cock this big deserved special treatment, and Cassandra was expert in such manoeuvres.

She lay back on the bed and opened her legs. 'Untie my panties.'

Entranced by the sight of Cassandra's pale flesh, complemented perfectly by the white of her lingerie, Axle undid the bows that held the satin panties to her slender hips. She raised her bottom off the bed so he could pull the garment from underneath her. He was about to discard them by the side of the bed when Cassandra spoke. The darkness of the room made her words all the more filthy. 'Taste them – smell them. Put them in your mouth, Axle. Eat my satin panties. You're starving for the taste of cunt, you're ravenous for a feeding and I'm willing to let you gorge yourself on my sweet juices.'

Axle acted tentatively at first until the pungent odour of Cassandra's satin sex-soaked panties permeated his nostrils, then like a starving beast, he began to chew on the dainty garment until just the straps dangled from his mouth.

'Does it taste good?'

Axle could only nod affirmatively.

'Good. Now rub my soaked satin panties on my cunt, Axle. Rub your spit into my hole – get me wet with your wetness.'

Cassandra reached for one of the ties to her panties that dangled from Axle's mouth. With her long fingers she pulled the sopping garment free and draped it on her sex. Axle then showed some initiative. He bent down and placed his head between Cassandra's legs and used his mouth to rub Cassandra's panties on her cunt. The sopping black and white satin felt like velvet gliding over her clitoris with Axle's tongue and teeth providing the firmest pressure to guide the garment into all the right places. Cassandra squeezed her stocking-covered thighs against Axle's head and pulled his body into her by his long stringy hair. She used his hair like the reins of a horse, guiding his head to and fro between her legs, directing his tongue to push her panties from side to side and up and around her swollen bud.

With Cassandra's thighs squeezing his head Axle could hear very little but her soft moans and the static-charged nylon crackling of her stockings rubbing against his head. Visions of sparks flying in the night air brought back to his consciousness the song Cassandra's seduction had inspired. As he licked away at the writhing woman's cunt more lines sprang into his supercharged mind ...

Neon light – hot night – sparks fly – sparks fly
    I'll undress you – you undress me – slowly – slowly
Flesh on flesh – wet on wet – sparks fly – sparks fly
    I'll caress you – you'll entice me – warmly – warmly
Nylon stockings – thighs on fire – sparks fly – sparks fly

Over and over Axle recited what would become the chorus of the song in his mind, all the while humming the tune as he sucked on Cassandra's sex. His lips vibrated softly to the imaginary music titillating her cunt like a battery-powered sex toy. The muskiness of her juices soaked through the satin panties mixing well with Axle's saliva. He tasted the material and Cassandra's telltale signature deep in his throat as he probed his tongue into her quivering hole. She arched her back and pushed one of the pillows from the bed under her ass so that Axle's tongue could penetrate further into her cunt. With his tongue he pushed the soaked panties deep inside Cassandra's cunt and withdrew his tongue to dart it over her naked clitoris. Free from any protective covering, the sensitive flesh erupted with lustful energy sending wave after wave of shockwaves up from her cunt all through her body. Cassandra's lean form undulated on the bed, rippling like an ocean wave as the intensity from her clitoris burst through her. Axle continued his gnawing at her sex, charged to excess by the way Cassandra's black patent high heels dug into the white flesh of his back. The tugging on his hair hurt tremendously, but the feelings of lust circulating through his once dormant cock dared not interfere with the chemistry of this bizarre situation. All the pain, all the excitement he channelled into his song. As he licked and probed he conjured up the first verse, mumbling the words as he nibbled on the soft white flesh of Cassandra's thighs. Her moans provided the background music – he wished he had a digital sampler so that he could include the real thing on the recording, but perhaps there would be other times . . .

> There is no place that I can hide
>> Deeper and deeper you want me inside
> I'm lost in your crush – a mortal spell
>> Agony and ecstasy – you're heaven and hell
> Cry into the night as the walls break down
>> Making my head spin round and round
> Stare at the flesh of your velvet thigh
>> As lust takes over – makes sparks fly . . .

Cassandra felt her cunt begin to quiver with the impending burst of her orgasm. She was beyond words at this point in their frenzied lovemaking so she chose to stimulate herself rather than ask Axle. He was doing just fine between her legs and she felt no desire to distract him from his oral endeavours. It was always better that way – most men just didn't know how to touch a woman in these places, especially when she was coming. Releasing Axle's long blond hair from her grip she guided one of her hands to take hold of her nipple and the other she pushed underneath the pillow so that she could penetrate her anus.

The white corset caused her small breasts to lift slightly and throughout the evening had rubbed her tiny nipples into a state of high-intensity sensitivity. The merest touch sent electrical shocks streaking around her body, and here was Cassandra twisting the little red bud feverishly. The long black fingernails of her other hand toyed with her anus, guiding the dripping lubrication of her cunt around the tight opening. Once sufficiently wet she forced one finger into her bottom and flexed it inside herself. Whether it was this intrusion, or the twisting of her nipple, or Axle's continued sucking of her cunt was a purely academic matter, for at the precise moment when all three sensations collided, Cassandra heaved her body into a nerve-wracking, thigh-melting, heart-stopping orgasm. She bucked violently on the bed, threatening to crush Axle's head between her thighs as she fought hard to let his lickings continue. Part of her wanted to pull him away, but her downy thighs gripped him tight and refused his release. He was a prisoner of her cunt, and the only way he could possibly gain his freedom was to continue sucking until her thighs could grip no more.

With a tiny attractive squeal Cassandra gradually subsided in her lust-induced seizure. Her thighs lost their grip and Axle found that he could hear once more. With a final lick of his tongue he sent one more salvo of shivers cascading through Cassandra's body. She wasted no time in recovering her composure. She was determined to overcome Axle's difficulty, and in the depths of her own orgasm she'd had the inspiration on how best to do it.

'Axle, come here. Lie down on the bed.'

Cassandra got up and stood by the side of the small bed while Axle reclined on it. His face was covered with a thin film of Cassandra's juices which he wiped on his forearm. The musky odour of sex hung heavy in the stillness of the room.

'Close your eyes.'

'Why?'

'Just close them. I'm going to do something to you, but I want you to feel it before you see it.'

Axle stuck the pillow over his head. It was the one that had been under Cassandra's bottom while he'd being eating her. It too bore the telltale trademark of a woman's release. Covering his face with the scent reminded him of what he had just done and how eating Cassandra had stimulated his desire. He felt the faint stirrings of an erection that were not unnoticed by Cassandra's vigilant eyes.

'Now keep your eyes covered.'

'I will – I will, I tell you.'

Axle's reply was muffled by the pillow. So too was his hearing. He heard what he thought was the sound of furniture being moved and then he felt fingers on his cock and something wet and warm, soft and silky, was wrapped around his cock. Then the fingers went away and nothing could be heard or felt – except for the strange covering. It felt as if a velvet glove, filled with something warm and sticky, had been placed around his cock. The sensation was strange and unusual. He struggled to figure out what it could be, and in the process found his dick starting to grow. His mind toyed with the possibilities of all manner of perversions stirring his slumbering cock into life.

'Keep your eyes covered. The best is yet to come . . .'

Axle wanted to scream with the joy of his refound sexuality, but was interrupted by another strange sensation. Cassandra was right. This was the best – and he could certainly see himself coming if whatever Cassandra was doing was kept up. It felt as if two warm and sticky pads of something firm, yet covered in some kind of silk, had been placed on either side of his cock, compressing whatever had been wrapped around his dick – and were now wanking him off in long slow up-and-down motions. The firm pads seem to have individual extensions that could grip his dick in numerous places, applying pressure at just the right moment. Within seconds his dick was fully erect. It was his first true hard-on in almost a year, and he wanted to lean out the window and tell the world. In a way he would once he finished writing 'Sparks Fly', but now he couldn't think of anything but the sensations rippling through his large staff. At ten inches tall it stood proud and red, glowing like a beacon under the neon light.

'You can look now.'

It took a short while for the words to sink in through the muskiness of the pillow.

'I said you can look now.'

Axle tossed the pillow aside and was greeted by what he would later describe as the most brilliant erotic sight he'd ever clapped eyes on. His dick was back to its full hardness and the head was red and exceedingly angry. Cassandra's come-soaked panties had been wrapped around the girth of his cock and tied to his shaft by the black satin straps. But it was what was doing the rubbing that pressed all Axle's buttons. Clasped against the side of his cock were Cassandra's stocking-covered feet. Soaked by the moisture of her panties, they gripped every small nuance of Axle's cock, and in the dim light of the room he could see those long white stocking-covered legs flexing as she jerked off his cock with her feet. She sat in a chair staring at his erection, admiring her work the way an artist might appreciate a painting. It was then that Axle decided that he might possibly have a foot fetish, and how really incredible it was of Cassandra to suss this out. He was glad she hadn't taken the five hundred dollars and split.

'Do you like it?'

'It's brilliant. I've never felt anything like this.'

In response Cassandra flexed her toes upwards and downwards, jerking Axle's mushrooming cockhead to its full extent.

Reclining on the bed, Cassandra's feet wrapped around his cock, Axle had a perfect view of the young woman's charms. He marveled at the flatness of her belly, constrained by the gauntlet of her white corset, her childishly small tits lifted upwards and to the side in a most perverted manner by the same virginally white garment. The way the darkness between her legs stuck out like the spiky hair on her head. How she was able to arch her legs so graphically, opening them wide in a huge bow that was focused on his cock, the thin muscles taut and tensioned, primed for sex, underneath the intoxicating sheath of white nylon. The way the black seam of the nylons ran all the way down her thighs, her calves, and to her ankles, stopping at the darker, reinforced white nylon of her heels. In the dim light of the neon sign he could distinguish the intricate patterns manifested by her soaked stockings as the black seams twisted and turned and she rubbed his cock up and down with her feet. Never still for the slightest moment, her stocking-covered legs performed an enticing dance of delicate white nylon wrinkles on pale flesh, portraying a tempting vista of erotic imperfection. Every few strokes of those delicious gams Cassandra would remove one foot and heft Axle's balls with her toes, flicking them playfully, balancing the swollen sacs on the skinniness of her toes as if measuring their weight before launching them into space.

After several repetitions of such wanton abuse, Axle couldn't control his teased manhood much longer. He was drunk with the perversion of the moment – living a year's worth of failed memories in a glorious instant of pure, uncompromised sex.

'I think – I think I'm going to come.'

'Please do – please come all over my feet – soak my white stockings with that lovely jism. I want to feel its warmth on my toes, mixing with my own come-soaked panties wrapped around your dick. Shoot it all out – vent your cock on my feet – come – come . . .'

Cassandra continued talking as Axle orgasmed. She coaxed his long-delayed release with provocative phrases, encouraging moans and exquisitely soft sighs. When Axle came his ejaculation didn't shoot skyward as one might expect, but oozed out like a slow erupting volcano. The milky liquid squished between Cassandra's toes, soaking first the toe and then the heel-reinforced portions of her white stockings. The sensations that emanated from her feet were complex and unexpected. They were strange and exotic feelings; unnatural, sophisticated and perfectly decadent in their aberrations. And yet there was something basic and primal – almost childish – in the way it made her feel. It was like running her toes through the sand on the beach when she was younger and innocent. It was as if it was she who had orgasmed over Axle's toes, the way the warmth of the oozing sperm drained the life from her legs. It was this thought that prompted Cassandra to make a mental note to bring herself off with her hand the next time she used her feet on a cock. If she could time her release for the moment when that hot jism oozed on to her toes, it would be an unbelievable high.

Cassandra continued playing footsy with Axle's cock as his orgasm subsided, the young woman enjoying his release as much as he. Now was when his dick would be the most sensitive, so Cassandra wickedly stretched her toes as far apart as possible and attempted to use Axle's throbbing dick to force the soaked stocking between her toes. In doing so she pinched the tender shaft tightly between the slippery stocking material, causing Axle violently to jerk his racked body completely off the bed. He lay sprawled half on and half off the cheap bed covers, muttering something about having died and seeing sparks fly. Cassandra recognised the male delirium that a mind-squashing orgasm induces and let the lead singer return to earth in his own good time. She went to the bathroom, removed her soaked lingerie and wiped her body dry with a towel. Deep inside she knew a welcome satisfaction at getting Axle off with her feet – as if there were no part of her body that could not be used for sex. And if that wasn't enough of a reward, oh how soft her feet felt after giving that slippery dick a massaging.

Cassandra and Axle exchanged the obligatory cigarette with their post-coital musings. They both sat naked, leaning on the rickety headboard of the bed, talking. Their conversation punctuated by the occasional giggle, slap or yell from one of the other rooms.

'So for the last year you've paid off girls and then what – just sit in your room all night contemplating your navel? I mean, there's no way you could sleep after all that coke.'

'Yeah, I know, dun I. I'd try and write songs mostly – watch television. But you know what's strange? I couldn't even write a decent song, so I'd smash up the room – that is until tonight. And you changed all that. As we were fucking I thought of a great new song – I'm going to dedicate it to you.'

Cassandra was truly flattered. 'Neat – sing it to me.'

'Nah – I haven't finished it yet. Which means we'll have to fuck some more. I think I need some inspiration.'

Cassandra playfully thumped Axle on the shoulder. 'Well, before any more inspiring I need a drink.'

Cassandra donned Axle's tee-shirt and popped into the suite's lounge to get a drink. Axle immediately began scribbling the words to 'Sparks Fly' on a Tropicana Hotel bedside notepad. It amazed him how vividly the words stuck in his memory. He could hear himself singing the chorus – screaming out 'Sparks Fly.'

Screaming? Screaming? Disturbing his writing Axle heard the unmistakable noise of a woman's high-pitched scream. The bansheelike wail was coming from the lounge suite! In a flash he leapt from the bed and flung open the door. The room was in darkness, but the light switch was right by the door. Without thinking he turned on the lights to the lounge, momentarily blinding himself. When his eyes adjusted he was met with a sight that made his blood boil. Clod Hopper and Bov Ril were frozen over Cassandra. She'd been pushed over the back of a sofa and Clod was holding down her arms and head at the front and Bov Ril was about to enter her from the rear. She was screeching every curse imaginable at them. Clod and Bov looked at Axle with all the innocence of children caught breaking a window. Axle glared back with eyes that spelled murder.

'You fucking bastards.'

'Steady on Ax, old son. We wuz just having a little fun.'

'Yeah – we just wandered in for a beer and there she was bending down looking in the fridge, her snatch all inviting, like, sticking out from between her legs. So we thought – you know. Well, she is a fucking groupie, Axle. You know what that means. We're a fucking group, aren't we. We should share the slags, not keep 'em to ourselves.'

If Clod had hoped to pacify Axle with this diatribe he failed. Failed miserably.

Axle swung the nearest loose object, which happened to be a large table lamp and shade, at Clod. It hit him right between the eyes, knocking him back over the sofa. Bov Ril released Cassandra from his grip; she lashed out with her hand, scratching him across the face, drawing blood in long gouges across his cheeks.

'You bitch-cunt.'

Bov motioned to hit Cassandra, but was interrupted by the breaking of a chair over his back by Axle. Bov crumpled to the ground in agony. Axle took Cassandra's hand and they both backed towards the bedroom door. Clod, disentangling himself from the lampshade, began to stir menacingly towards them. Axle picked up a half-empty bottle of Jack Daniel's and smashed it on the table, holding the jagged edge towards Clod. Axle was crystal clear in his warning.

'Don't even think of it, Clod, or I'll ruin you for life. I swear it, I will.'

'I'll get you, Axle, for this.'

'You shouldn't have done that, Clod – shouldn't have. 'Cause we ain't a band no more. I quit. I'm through. This is the end for Momma's Nails. Go get yourself another lead singer.'

Axle and Cassandra slammed the door to the room and Axle stood guard as Clod and Bov shouted insults through the relatively thin wood. Presently Axle heard the calming voice of Slick the manager. He was no doubt unsurprised by the incident – almost expecting it. Axle figured Slick was already calculating the extra dollars he would make by having two separate entities to manage. Cassandra stood close to Axle. Their breathing was forced and heavy.

'You didn't have to do that for me.'

'I did it for me – and you.'

'Well, thank you. No one has ever looked out for me except me. It's a funny feeling.'

'Well, I've never looked out for anyone but me – so the feeling is mutual.'

Their bodies pressed up against the door, Axle and Cassandra kissed long and urgently. Somewhere during the intense embrace they felt a strange sense of fate. When their lips parted very little explanation was required.

'If we leave now we can be in Las Vegas by the early morning.'

'Why Las Vegas?'

'Because they have drive-in wedding chapels where we can be married by an Elvis impersonator. I saw hundreds of them as we drove through after playing there a couple of weeks ago.'

'Is this a proposal?'

'Yeah.'

'But I don't have a car.'

'You must be the only person in Los Angeles that doesn't. Not to worry – we'll take a cab.'

'A cab – you know how much that'll cost? We could fly for cheaper.'

'Yeah, but I need inspiration, don't I? And I think the smelly backseat of a taxi going to Las Vegas will be more inspirational than an airline seat and a stewardess who keeps wiggling her ass and telling us to buckle up. And not to worry – I've got the thousand dollars you didn't accept.'

'Then I accept now.'

'The money?'

'No, your proposal, bozo. And I can even wear my black lace dress with my white lingerie underneath. Sort of a fitting wedding dress, don't you think?'

'Yeah. And I'll rent a tuxedo from the chapel – and the taxi driver can drive us through the drive-in chapel, and then he can take us to the ritziest hotel in Vegas where we'll spend our honeymoon. I'll charge it to the record company.'

And they cemented their deal with another long kiss that caused a noticeably visible reaction from Axle's penis.

'I think you're getting inspired.'

'We'd better go find a taxi – quick.'

Hurriedly they threw their sparse belongings together and quietly evacuated the hotel room. Down on Vine Street they found a yellow cab parked with the driver asleep behind the wheel.

'Say what?' The cab driver obviously thought he was dreaming.

'Five hundred – cash – to take us to Las Vegas and to a drive-in wedding chapel.'

'Is this *Candid Camera*?'

'We aren't kidding. We want to go to Las Vegas *now*, so we can get married.'

'Shit – that's a four-hour drive. You could fly. I'll take you to the airport. Thirty bucks.'

Cassandra could see that they were getting nowhere fast. It was time to use her not so subtle charms.

'OK. Seven hundred and fifty – cash – final offer and it's for real. And if you like you can watch us while we fuck in your back seat all the way there. Just don't get in an accident, OK?'

172

'Hop right in, folks.'

They had no sooner turned on the Interstate 10 freeway towards the desert than Axle and Cassandra were engaged in some serious inspiration.

Axle had a song to finish and a solo album to begin . . .

3 a.m.

NEAR THE MANHATTAN BEACH PIER

It is a peculiar convenience of the summer weather in Los Angeles that on most evenings following a baking hot day a particularly heavy cooling fog rolls into the Southern California coastal towns, providing a thick blanket of mist under which to hide a multitude of sins.

Around the witching hour of two a.m., all the beachside bars, with names like The Red Onion, Hennessey's, The Lighthouse, The Poopdeck and Chillers, regurgitate their patrons into the all-consuming fog. In the moments that follow closing time a large percentage of the inebriated find their way to the beach to continue their partying. Those fortunate to have formed a temporary liaison for the evening most probably will fornicate on the sand, blanketed by the fog and their own alcohol-induced bravado. A few regular 'steady' relationships in need of that much sought-after variety will dare to bare all and have sex on the beach, and then there are always the special occasions – birthdays, anniversaries, weddings, divorces – the traumas of modern life that spawn a crop of night-time fucking by the sea.

And all the furtive fornicating is made possible by the sense of secrecy that the fog gives these brave souls. Oftimes couples making love will be but a few feet apart, totally oblivious to the proximity of other human beings, hidden by the undulating beach and the enveloping fog. The desperate moans and lustful cries of sex on the beach travel haphazardly through the thick night fog, occasionally bursting above the background roar of the ocean. The fog confuses all sense of direction, making it near impossible for the wistful voyeur to pinpoint the entangling of limbs and the stroking of genitals that may have produced such erotic emanations. The late-night, early morning period on the beach is an anonymous orgy of copulating couples unaware of each other's presence. And as can be expected, the fog also makes a perfect cover for the hasty retreat from a less than ideal fuck by someone who, as they sober up in the cool night air, suddenly realises that there is no truth in the old bartender's saying that 'no one is ugly when the bars close'.

And on this August night it had been so warm in the San Fernando Valley that a fog to rival the thickest London peasouper had been sucked in from the Pacific Ocean by the inviting warmth of the land. Visibility was cut down to a few feet, making it quite difficult for Nancy Thorne to find Andrew Benjamin and vice versa.

After disturbing several heavily engrossed couples by walking into their passionate embraces like bulls in a china shop, Nancy and Andrew literally collided with each other at the end of the pier. The identifying white carnation worn by Andrew was crushed in the process. Over small talk and nervous laughter, he and Nancy plucked the remaining petals and let them fall over the side of the pier into the ocean, the fog obscuring the carnation's fall into the gently rolling surf below.

Or so they thought. In fact the petals never made it directly into the sea. They were accidentally intercepted by the naked body and surfboard of Moose, the legendary night-time nude surfer of Manhattan Beach. Moose had spent the night, as he did every night, getting pleasantly pissed at one of the many surfbars. And regular as clockwork, right around three a.m. he'd carried his beloved surfboard down to the water, stripped bare-ass naked, and prepared to surf *sans* clothes until sunrise spoiled his cover, at which point he'd usually find an alley in which to sleep through the day to prepare for another night of storytelling and drinking. He had no money, and he needed none. He lived on the beach, a blanket the only roof he ever needed. He never had to buy a drink – people waited in line to buy him drinks – and there was always some gullible babe willing to buy him dinner. Moose was a living legend whom aspiring beach bums, wannabe surfer dudes and buxom beach chicks all gladly patronised.

Moose looked like the stereotypical surfer dude. He was skinny and tanned a deep golden brown. His stringy shoulder-length hair was bleached whiter than white. He seemed to own few clothes – tee-shirts of surfpunk bands he'd supposedly been in, a pair of torn jeans – and he never wore shoes. Moose's speech was peppered with the *lingua franca* of surfing, but unlike many of the poseurs who littered the surfbars, Moose had earned the right to speak the speak, walk the walk and talk the talk.

Surfing for Moose was a religious experience, and by surfing naked he felt he communed with his 'godhead'. Isolated by the fog, in total darkness, he felt like a foetus in the womb. And as he crashed on to the beach it was like being reborn all over again. Many times he would get sexually excited by the exhilaration of riding a wave. Sporting a hard-on of moose-like proportions, he would jack himslf off as he surfed, attempting to climax as the wave crashed, leaving him momentarily suspended in midair, ejaculating into the night. When Moose talked of 'hanging ten' everyone around the beach knew it didn't mean the usual boast of standing up on the board with one's feet hanging over the edge.

And so, when white carnation petals landed on his body and his surfboard, he took this as an indication that it was going to be a very special night – and the carnation petals must be a type of manna from heaven sent by the godhead of surfing. So like any good surfer with no money, he ate what was offered to him, said 'thanks dude', burped, and paddled offshore to wait for a really big one to come along – and he wasn't just thinking wave size.

Up on the end of the pier conversation was still somewhat stilted. Such difficulty was understandable and predictable – after all, what can you say to someone who you've never met but have masturbated over the phone with? They both avoided mentioning their recent phone-sex conversation concentrating instead on such universally innocuous subjects as the weather and careers. For obvious reasons Nancy and Andrew talked quite a bit about the fog – how it had been particularly thick this year – and then about their respective jobs. And since Nancy worked for one of those big computer manufacturers whose products Andrew used all the time at his aerospace company, they talked about computers. And then they stopped talking and looked out to where the ocean meets the sky – if they could have seen that far through the opaque grey shroud that hung heavy around them.

They both knew they'd come here to fuck, but like some difficult-to-start chemical reaction, they needed a catalyst – and talking about computers just wasn't going to get cunts wet and dicks hard. As was the case, befitting their proximity to Hollywood, inspiration came from the movies.

'Being by the beach always reminds me of *From Here to Eternity*. I just love the scene with Burt Lancaster and Deborah Kerr making love on the beach, in the waves. I see movies like that and it just makes me want to write and write and write.'

'They certainly don't make them like that any more, do they?'

'I hope someday I'll be able to write a movie screenplay as good as that.'

'I'm sure you will. You have a tremendous imagination and a real feel for words.'

'So do you – perhaps you should take up writing or phone sex. You'd do pretty good.'

Andrew laughed, his chubby face turning red – even in the dense fog his reaction was clearly visible to Nancy.

'I'm sorry. Did I embarrass you?'

'No, no – not at all. Well, yes – a little. I embarrass easily. Especially around women.'

'You have nothing to be shy about, Andrew. You have a rare talent, and I should know.'

'Yes, but . . . it is so much easier on the phone. In person I never get past the first few sentences before I trip over my tongue and then they laugh at me. On the phone I never have to see their faces. I can just imagine.'

'Don't you think it's been the same for me? I've heard enough harpoon jokes to last me a lifetime. I'm not laughing at you. Not at all. I'm just wondering when you're going to kiss me.'

Andrew raised his eyebrows and realised that it was time for action – the hell with words and hang-ups, small-talk time was over. Andrew placed his hands on Nancy's broad shoulders and pulled her body towards his own in a very deliberate action. Bending his neck and closing his eyes he placed his lips on hers and held them there, quite immobile, as they stood for several seconds, awaiting each other's next move. It was involuntarily

Andrew's. His cock grew hard under the feel of Nancy's warmth pressed close against his own. It was impossible for him to hide his stand, since their bodies were pressed tightly together. Their lips parted and Nancy acknowledged the feel of Andrew's erection.

'Finally, a harpoon I can enjoy.'

'Didn't I tell you – my favourite movie is *Moby Dick*.'

This time their laughter wasn't nervous at all – it was natural and expectant.

'Would you make love to me on the beach – with the waves crashing around us like in *From Here to Eternity*?'

'It would be my pleasure.'

Andrew offered Nancy his outstretched arm, which she took in a very ladylike manner. As he led the way from the pier to the beach, she was reminded of their recent phone-sex conversation.

'I must say that I have never enjoyed a phone call as much as ours tonight.'

'It was something special, wasn't it?'

'I've never actually played with myself before during a call. It has always been so businesslike. The clients rarely show any imagination. With you tonight it was different.'

'And I hope reality will be every bit as enjoyable for you as was our fantasy.'

'It already has been.'

'You are too kind . . .'

Before they knew it they were standing before the waves, watching entranced the foaming white effervescence bubbling out of the grey panorama. It was a mystical sight. As if inspired into a religious fervour, Nancy dropped to her knees. Andrew was about to do the same, but Nancy halted his descent.

'No, no, Andrew. Stand here with your back to the waves.'

Andrew complied, realising quite quickly what Nancy had in mind. Her trembling fingers fumbled with his belt and the catch of his trousers. His fly zipper persisted in being difficult, requiring a final persuasive tug from Nancy's grasp. Her hands pulled his trousers down to his ankles and he stood before her, a noticeable bulge among bulges inviting her to pull down his standard department-store issue big white underwear. Those, too, quickly joined his trousers around his ankles. To some the sight may have been grotesque – Andrew was not in the best of shape. His belly hung down over his hardened cock, giving his lower body with his cock sticking out the appearance of a turtle with its head reluctantly peering out of its shell. Nancy saw nothing of the kind. To her it was a vision of pure ecstasy. Pushing his weight aside she buried her face in his sex, rubbing his cock all round her cheeks, cupping his tight balls with her hands, blowing her hot breath into his nest of pubic hair.

'I want to suck you off, just like you imagined I would when you talked to me on the phone.'

'Hmmmm – I had hoped you would, my dear Nancy.'

Over the roar of the crashing waves Andrew could hear Nancy's mouth slipping over his dick. She was devouring his cock as if it were a lollipop on a hot day, sucking down every sweet drop before the sun melted it away. Nancy was not expert in the fine art of cocksucking and neither was Andrew an expert cocksuckee. Nancy had sucked off one guy in high school in a most regrettable incident, and Andrew had once paid a whore to give him a blow job. It too was quite regrettable – she did more hand jerking than mouth sucking, and he had lost his load after a few brief licks. It wasn't worth the hundred dollars.

On the other hand, this blow job was priceless. Nancy, for all her inexperience, was doing a most thorough job. What she lacked in technique she made up for in enthusiasm, and she'd read enough of *those* kind of books to know a majority of the tricks. All those lonely nights, all those anonymous phone calls in which she'd described exactly how she would suck the caller's dick, making him come with just her words. Now she was going to enjoy the real thing, but to guide her motions she was reciting in her head what she should do, as if she were giving a phone-sex fantasy . . .

'I've got my hand wrapped tightly around your throbbing shaft and I'm jerking it for you as I lick its long length. Whhhooah – you like that, don't you? I can tell by the way your prick twitches when I stop, as if it's begging for more – a thin sliver of my spit dangling from the tip. Your long length arches and jerks, its angry purple head jutting proudly out like a king cobra snake poised to strike.'

She knew to use her hand as a companion to her mouth to compress Andrew's dick with her hand as she withdrew her lips, adding just that extra bit of pressure which helped so much to intensify the suction. And she knew from her reading that men had many special places that they liked to be touched during oral sex.

'Now I'm going to make you want to come so bad. All I have to do is run my tongue across that sticky little slit of your big bad cock, and you won't be able to stop shaking. You'll beg me to make you come. Especially if I use my little finger to stroke you right here, in that soft, hidden place between your balls and your ass.'

She knew to use the tip of her tongue to probe across the sensitive flesh of the tip of Andrew's cock. It was as she was doing just this that Andrew staggered under her lickings and she was forced to use her hands to grasp his ass and pull him to her, to stop him from falling over on to the wet sand of Manhattan Beach. It was a really nasty thing to do, she felt, gripping his fleshy buttocks and forcing him to grind his weight into her face. In her mind she visualised Andrew as if he were a huge fat dildo, a plaything for her to use to pleasure herself in any lewd way she wanted. In pulling Andrew so close to her she was able to let her breasts rub on Andrew's thighs. She'd worn no bra underneath her long sweater dress and so her ample titties swung free in a lascivious manner. Instead of just rubbing them on Andrew's quivering legs she slapped her body across his thighs, rejoicing in the feel of her breasts swinging so freely against her body, against Andrew's thighs, making that lewd slapping sound that she tried to echo with the slurping noises her mouth made on his cock. Underneath her dress she could feel her large nipples harden under the pummelling they were receiving – and as that hardness grew she could feel the moistening begin to flow between her thighs. The effect was to spur her on to a more vigorous sucking motion that had Andrew in severe doubt as to whether he would ever walk again.

If it hadn't been for the fact that Andrew had come twice just a few hours earlier as he'd talked to Nancy on the phone, he would have orgasmed almost immediately into her warm mouth.

As it was, his release took quite a while to build, allowing him the double-edged pleasure of a prolonged sucking. On the one hand, he relished the sensation of Nancy's warm mouth on his penis, the way her tongue seemed to encapsulate his cock, the way her fleshy hand with her pudgy fingers kneaded his balls – it was a feast of sensations beyond his wildest wet dreams. And yet he longed for it to cease – he desired his orgasm as if it was all he had ever wanted from life. He wanted to fill Nancy's mouth with his warm load of milky fluid – and his legs could then collapse and he could enjoy the pleasant afterglow that sexual release brings.

As these thoughts racked his brain he thought of the many fantasy calls Nancy must have done in her phone-sex career. He visualised the men she'd tantalised with her words and how he was the one – the one that she'd chosen to meet. The thought made his cock grow rigid as he thought of Nancy, some night in the not-too-distant future, describing to some hard-up guy the sex she'd had on the beach with him, Andrew – shy Andrew who never scored with girls. Nancy would be describing how she'd sucked him off and the hard-up guy on the other end of the phone would wank himself off thinking it was all a fantasy and dreaming of having it off with Nancy just like the way he, Andrew, was doing. And the hard-up guy would come in a big shooting fountain all over the phone, come in a big stream of hot warm spunk, just the way he – Andrew – was. Coming, coming, coming – filling Nancy's mouth with his orgasm. Pulling her head tight against his sex, grinding her face into his pubic nest, feeling her throat swallow the end of his cock, trying hard to take all the fluid down inside her as he fell backwards into the sand, her mouth locked on his dick, drinking hard, draining every last drop of his relief.

They rested for a short while. Nancy kept her mouth around Andrew's cock until the turgid member started to lose some of its rigidity. As it did so Nancy rolled the shaft around her mouth, luxuriating in the feel of the hardness growing soft. She promised herself that she would do the reverse next time – it would be wonderful to put a totally flaccid dick inside her mouth, take all of it down her throat, teasing its soft length with her tongue, revelling in the way it magically grew hard inside her mouth,

181

filling the warmth and wetness within to its capacity. Hmmmm – that was something to look forward to.

Andrew, although exhausted, realised that it would not do for him to roll over and fall asleep, assuming that his snores would be compliment enough for Nancy's ministrations. No, he knew better than that, but he was realistic enough to know that he needed a short break. He was going to suggest perhaps a walk along the beach. It would wake him up and give him the breather he needed to resume their lovemaking.

'Would you like to . . .'

Nancy was one step ahead of him. 'Ssshhh, don't speak – let's just rest for a short while. Hold me here, on the beach, in your arms.'

Thousands of phone-sex calls had schooled Nancy well into the post-orgasm blues that most men suffer once their pent-up release had burst forth. A short rest would do them both good, and she knew exactly how she wanted Andrew to fuck her. But the time would have to be just right.

Out in the fog of the ocean Moose was not having much luck. The waves were just not cooperating and he'd barely managed to get his cock hard the few times he'd caught the crest of a few small shore breaks. There seemed a strange something – something he couldn't quite define – in the water and the fog. Something full of anticipation, something like a deadly calm before the storm. A sense of foreboding filled his body as he paddled once more out into the greyness of the night. There was something out there watching – waiting – and he had a nasty feeling it had his name on it. He kept thinking of the white carnations, wishing now that he hadn't eaten them.

Revived by the short respite, Nancy was getting her toes wet in the ocean as Andrew lay on the beach toying slyly with his cock, hoping to get it hard once more. Out of the corner of his eye he watched Nancy dabbling with the waves, lifting the hem of her long ankle-length black dress out of the water. Occasionally a heavier wave would crash, catching her unawares, getting the soft black sweater material soaking wet. Once one larger wave soaked her to the waist. She squealed delightfully and ran playfully away from the water. The wet dress clung to her ample figure, outlining the voluptuousness of her frame. Andrew felt his dick stir in his hand as he watched her large thighs rub against each other as she ran away from the ocean, and he grew noticeably hard as she turned and walked back down to the waves, her large buttocks rippling underneath the soaked material. He wanted her with a lust that surprised him with its intensity. In a classical sense Nancy was not a true beauty but there was something exceedingly erotic about the way her ample flesh was displayed by the wetness of her dress. He wanted to fuck her, plain and simple. And he wanted her quickly. He wanted to plough into her like the crashing waves just like Burt Lancaster did to Deborah Kerr in the movie. Nancy had said it was her favourite old film. How poetic then, thought Andrew, to fuck here on the beach, amidst the crashing waves – just like *From Here to Eternity.*

He stripped naked and followed Nancy into the water. He stroked his dick to keep it hard. The water was quite cold and was definitely not conducive to maintaining a throbbing erection, but he kept his senses firmly concentrated on Nancy's soaked form just a few feet away. Just as he reached her she turned around to face him, having heard the splash of his approach over the roar of the ocean. The black sweater dress was now completely soaked and her breasts were easily visible through the cloth. Andrew reached out and grabbed her tits, pulling her towards him by the nipples.

'I want to fuck you here – in the water.'

'Oh god – yes, yes.'

Once more Andrew had succeeded in pleasing Nancy's sexually charged mind. He'd done it on the phone – sensing her love of ballet – and now he'd fulfilled her need to be fucked amidst the rolling waves. Eagerly anticipating the pleasure of his cock between her plump thighs, Nancy reached down to the sopping hem of her dress and pulled it up above her round belly. The dress clung persistently to her legs in a slinky, sleazy fashion, revealing inches of flesh in a slowly tantalising striptease as she pulled the hem higher, and the sopping material subsequently slid reluctantly upwards. She'd worn no underwear under the smooth material of the sweater dress because she really didn't own any frilly little panties that she considered sexy enough for the moment that she'd hoped would happen and was now fast approaching. Consequently, the splashing waves had soaked her mound with the cooling saltiness of the ocean, as if the pounding surf had sensed that inside her pussy she was boiling with lust. Nancy felt consumed by a hunger for sex that moistened her profusely as she eagerly thought of surrounding Andrew's dick with the fleshy folds of her cunt.

Sensing Nancy's abandonment to the pleasures of the flesh, Andrew advanced on her inviting form, putting his arms on her waist, holding her as firmly as possible by her swelling buttocks. Fighting to keep his balance under the irregular onslaught of the ebbing tide, he bent his legs slightly so that he could enter the rotund woman's sex. It was a difficult manoeuvre, requiring Nancy to guide Andrew's throbbing cock with one hand while opening her cuntlips with the other at the precise moment that Andrew straightened his legs. It took several frustrating tries until the timing was perfected and Andrew was able to feel the sensuous glide of warm pussy over his cold, hard, salt-water-splashed cock. In celebration of his achievement Andrew wasted no time in thrusting repeatedly into Nancy's moist opening as they stood ankle deep in the icy cold Pacific Ocean, the waves slapping against their legs as he thrust into her wetness. The bulkiness of their bodies made it near impossible for them to stay vertically coupled, and in their lust-charged frenzy to have sex amidst the rolling waves they toppled first one way and then another. The sand shifting beneath their feet made it difficult to stay fixed in any one location, and inevitably the rush of a crashing wave took their legs from underneath them and they fell into the cascading waters. Andrew fell on top of Nancy, the water cushioning their heavy fall slightly.

'Oh yes, yes, yes . . . it's just like in the movies. It feels so good.'

Nancy squealed with enthusiastic praise for the scene that she and Andrew portrayed. Nancy may not have been Deborah Kerr, and Andrew certainly wasn't Burt Lancaster, and Manhattan Beach wasn't Honolulu – and the Pacific Ocean in Los Angeles was a darn sight colder than the waters in Hawaii – but it didn't matter. Nancy and Andrew's embraces were the real, urgent and glorious glowing Technicolor embodiments of that classic old black-and-white movie fantasy. It was true that the ocean water battering their bodies was icy cold, and that they shivered with each tortuous splash, but their passion could not be damped by such a minor detail. It made their actions that much more crazed and frenzied.

Grabbing Andrew's hard cock with her hands, Nancy pulled the salt-water-soaked member towards her humping thighs and launched her groin at Andrew's cock. Aided by the buoyancy given their bodies by the ebb and flow of the waves they were able to float together, at which point Nancy locked her legs around Andrew's lower body and thrust her cunt at his groin with all her might. The crashing waves buffeted their fucking bodies to and fro, adding that much more energy to their already fever-pitched lovemaking. Underneath his thrusting form Andrew could see Nancy's head turning and twisting from side to side as his cock buried itself deep inside her quivering cunt. Fucking in the ocean was difficult because the salt water removed every trace of their natural lubrication the moment their thrustings produced that deliciously musky nectar. Each long stab of his shaft hurt immensely as the salt water stung their grinding flesh, but there was no stopping the rhythm of their bodies. The very discomfort they felt drove them on to new heights of sexual excess, for to stop would have been even more painful.

Nancy moaned loudly, almost screaming with every searing thrust of Andrew's cock. She looked the very essence of depraved sexuality, writhing underneath his heaving body. In her long black sweater dress, soaked through and pushed up around her waist, she was totally abandoned to the emotions of raw, unrefined, primitive sex. Andrew was mesmerised by the apparent erotic seizure which had taken charge of her body. Her screams hypnotised his body so much so that he became a fucking robot, thrusting into her writhing body with the detachment of a medical student watching an autopsy. It was the closest thing to a state of physical shock his body and mind had ever endured. Fittingly, it was Nancy that shook him out of his lustful trance.

'Andrew, Andrew – bite my tits. Quickly, quickly – bite them.'
Nancy's breasts were large and lacking in firmness. With her

lying on her back they had fallen to her sides, pressed close against her body by the weight of her soaked dress. To Andrew it was an intensely erotic sight to see such mammoth sacks of soft flesh rippling and shaking underneath his thrusts in a way that a woman of a much smaller frame and firmer body could never do. He gladly fed on her mammaries, biting hard and roughly on jiggling flesh. The salt-water-soaked black material covering Nancy's tits intoxicated Andrew with its taste, as if he were feasting on some rare form of caviar or other aphrodiasiac. He was able to balance his thrusting weight on Nancy's round belly, thereby freeing his hands from supporting himself so that he could gather up Nancy's sagging breasts and push them together so that they met in one huge mountain of titflesh in the centre of her chest. He buried his face deeply into the soaking mass of contrasts – hot flesh, cold water, hard nipples, soft material – and enjoyed a feast worthy of a condemned man's last meal.

'Oh, don't stop – don't stop. Plunge me deeply, make me come in waves like the waves . . . make me come . . .'

Andrew found it difficult to speak as he bounced up and down, thrusting his battered penis in and out of Nancy's sex. Instead he concentrated on devouring her tits – kneading, pinching, moulding, distorting, abusing them in a devout rapture that the usually mild-mannered aerospace executive had never known.

Nancy began to scream with a passion that frightened Andrew, as though he were possibly hurting her in some manner. He began to slow his motions, only to be slapped on the back by her arms and kicked by her legs.

'Don't slow down – don't . . .'

The words were screamed as if they were the last words she would ever speak. As soon as Andrew had resumed his momentum he felt Nancy's hand underneath his crotch fondling roughly his balls. She squeezed the distended sacks the way he'd manhandled her breasts. It was agony – and ecstasy – and he too began to moan as the fingers milked his orgasm from him.

Fate then dealt its mysterious hand. Deep within the earth's crust, miles below their fucking bodies, layers of rock, perhaps sensing in some hereto unfathomable manner the release of sexual tension above it, began to slide, releasing years of pent-up energy.

By most seismic standards it produced a small earthquake, the kind California feels almost every month, but in its application and its ramifications it could not have been better targeted.

Seismologists at the California Institute of Technology in nearby Pasadena eventually pinpointed the epicentre of the quake as being just slightly offshore of the Manhattan Beach pier. This served to minimise the effects on land, but as a result, the shifting of the sub-oceanic sands caused a rather large wave to erupt where previously only small bathtub-sized disturbances had been. As Fate would have it, the earthquake occurred just as Moose was beginning another run. He was quite convinced that tonight's surfing was a lost cause when the ocean seemed to fall from beneath him and he was lofted skyward on a thin wall of water.

This was going to be the ride of his life, and immediately his erection grew to its normal mammoth mooselike proportions, and he stroked the swollen flesh as he plummeted towards the beach. He had been right earlier, this was going to be a very special night. When this wave broke he would be airborne, flying – he would come as he crashed back down into the water to be bashed around in the seething foam of the ocean, his jism mingling with the ocean he so dearly loved.

'*Awesome* . . .' he yelled into the foggy night, relishing every moment of this once-in-a-lifetime ride.

In their orgasming frenzy neither Andrew nor Nancy felt the earthquake, heard Moose's cry of exhilaration nor even saw the onrushing wave with the long-haired blond denizen perched precariously on the crest, on top of a fluorescent pink surfboard, sporting a monster of an erection, bearing unwittingly down upon them.

As the wave crashed around Nancy and Andrew they were lost in the throes of their release, screaming at full pitch the kinds of things that people coming amongst crashing, icy cold waves do. Guided by some mysterious force, Moose crashed towards the beach, his cock in hand, desperately pumping away to achieve his own orgasm, oblivious to the passionate couple that writhed in his way. Like an automated homing missile he zeroed in on the copulating couple, his statuesquely hard penis pointing the way, his brain completely unaware of the target before him.

Upon reflection neither Moose, Andrew nor Nancy had any idea what happened, and perhaps more pointedly, why it had happened. Neither did the residents of Manhattan, Hermosa or Redondo Beaches who years later still talked of the bloodcurdling yells that ripped through their half-sleep shortly after the earthquake had disturbed their slumber that foggy August night a long, long time ago.

The whole act lasted but a few instants, but to the participants it seemed to take an eternity. It was poetry in motion, an ethereal ballet, choreographed by some obscenely wicked director. Moose – ten-inch hard-on in hand – fell on top of Nancy and Andrew's writhing forms as the wave crashed on top of them, depositing Moose with some force upon their lovemaking. With a grim precision the crashing minitidal wave threw Moose headlong into Andrew's thrusting bottom at precisely the moment Andrew was sticking his snow-white buttocks in the air, preparing to thrust mightily into Nancy's shaking body. Moose hit Andrew hard, with Moose's swollen member penetrating Andrew's humping bottom with one perfectly targeted bull's-eye of a shot. Moose screamed as he orgasmed, his cock suddenly swallowed into the tight constriction of Andrew's asshole. In unison Andrew screamed as he was violated, adding to the primal rush he felt as he orgasmed inside Nancy – and the shocked woman screamed a bansheelike wail that deafened the two others as Andrew pushed harder into her than any single human could – quite probably because he was propelled forward by the onrushing momentum of Moose's wipeout.

Locked in this bizarre coupling they remained, being washed around the beach like a huge piece of seaweed or other debris. It was quite some time later that they were able to disentangle their bodies, introduce themselves and piece together the improbable series of events that had brought them together. Like people who had survived natural disasters or other trying moments, the chance coupling of their bodies forged a bond between them that was going to withstand the strongest test of time.

It was daylight before they could even walk again, and then with some great difficulty. Gingerly – Andrew, understandably, the most ginger of all – they all retired, arm in arm, supporting each other to the close-by safety of Andrew's house in Hermosa Beach. Over the next few months they forged an unusual *menage à trois* from which Nancy acquired many ideas for screenplays and phone calls. Moose got a place to stay and learned all about safe sex, and Andrew learned he could go both ways. And as much as anyone in the City of One-Night Stands ever does, they all lived happily ever after – in their own bizarre manner.

4 a.m.

THE STREETS OF CENTURY CITY

The horrible tearing sound of a vast chunk of expensive metal being ripped violently from its place of rest by another, faster moving, but equally expensive chunk of metal echoed through the deserted streets and the towering high rises of early Sunday morning Century City. Perhaps a few residents turned uncomfortably in their well-protected sleep, but ultimately no one stirred from behind their concrete and glass fortresses to discover the sound of the disturbance.

Otto Verge's Mercedes limousine screeched to a rubber-burning halt as he watched the gold-plated door of Sir Justin Ponceford-Smythe's Rolls-Royce go bouncing disconsolately down the empty street. His attention was drawn from the bouncing golden door to the bouncing golden breasts of the naked young lady who was running after the amputated door. He looked back into the rear compartment of the limousine at Mistress Tawny, who had remained calm throughout the ordeal, and ordered her to stay put. She could hardly do anything else as she was restrained into the backseat of the Mercedes by numerous leather straps that completely immobilised all but the slightest movement of her hands. By rocking her arms to and fro she was able to move backwards and forwards in a most provocative manner a rather immense steel dildo that had been positioned with surgical accuracy between her legs, a motion she continued in great earnest, apparently unconcerned with the reason for the limousine's sudden stoppage.

'Young lady, young lady – Miss, please . . .' Otto shouted after Julia Majors who was rapidly closing on the careening door. As the hunk of metal came to rest Julia reached the mess of tangled metal and stared at it in disbelief. Otto hurried to her side, not so much out of concern for the naked young woman's safety, but because she did have quite a nice side, front and back too.

'Are you all right?'

'The door is dead . . .'

'I could not avoid it – you opened it right in my path . . .'

'The door is dead – you killed it.' Julia was suffering from the illogical aftereffects of too much alcohol and the shock of nearly being killed. After launching Mario into near earth orbit she'd driven to Santa Monica beach where a few drunken surfers had been more than willing to give a naked babe with a gold Rolls-Royce as much beer as she could consume. She wasn't quite sure how she'd gotten from the beach to Century City, but she did remember thinking she shouldn't be driving in her condition, so she just stopped the car and took a quick nap on a relatively quiet tree-lined street. She'd stirred uncomfortably, feeling the urgent need to pee, and was in the process of opening the car door when it had been ripped out of her hand rather rudely by Otto's Mercedes. The shock of the sudden impact had caused her to wet the stately leather seats of the Rolls-Royce, but she had little time to ponder her accident-provoked incontinence. Without consciously making a decision to get out of the car, she'd done just that, and the next thing she knew she was running naked down the street insanely pursuing the careening door, yelling at it to stop its getaway.

Otto, on the other hand, could not use excessive alcohol consumption as an excuse. He was quite sober as he drove himself and Tawny home to his Beverly Hills mansion from Neil Waslinger's rather eventful party. Otto had strapped Tawny in the back seat and was enjoying watching her slide the steel dildo in and out of her pussy by using the straps of the harness to move her hands to and fro as she arched her body. It was an example of erotic poetry in motion that Otto thought should not be disturbed by taking the quick way home. He meandered through the streets of Century City watching Tawny auto-masturbate herself, understandably paying more attention to the supple writhings of the girl than the boring details of the quiet streets. The first he knew of the open car door was when he

191

heard the impact, stamped on the brake, looked up and saw the golden hunk of metal go flying down the street followed by a rather attractive, naked young woman.

The first Julia knew of the approaching Mercedes was when the door flew out of her hand. They were, to quote the legal vernacular of the insurance companies, who would no doubt enjoy hearing about the circumstances surrounding this accident, equally at fault, both distracted by matters completely under their respective control.

Surveying the decimated door Otto offered Julia his coat. 'Would you like to cover yourself?'

'Oh, yeah – thanks.'

Otto was a little surprised that this obviously inebriated young woman offered him no explanation for her nakedness. It would have been the usual thing to do. Considering the situation quickly, Otto decided to do a little enquiring. He felt that by introducing himself he could impress the attractive woman into revealing more about her intriguing story. Otto was a legend in the movie business, and like most living legends he knew the power of his name.

'I am Otto Verge, the movie director.'

'I am Julia Majors, the stupid fool.'

'Yes, it was rather careless of you to open the car door right in front of me.'

'No, not that. Someone just has to offer me a movie role and I do stupid things – fuck assholes – and then I get screwed, and then I get drunk, and then I fuck more assholes – and then I go for a drive in someone's else's car and some asshole runs into my door. That's why I'm Julia, the stupid fool.'

'Ah, I see. Is Sir Justin close by?'

'Who?'

'Sir Justin – unless I'm very much mistaken this door belongs, or should I say used to belong, to his car. I'd recognise it anywhere. He lives next door to me.'

'No.'

'I'm afraid he does – I talked to him only yesterday.'

Julia laughed the silly laugh that drunks emit when they have to deal with sober people. 'No, silly, he isn't close by.'

'Well, where is he, and why do you have his car?'

'I just told you – I got screwed. Oh hell, it's a long story and you killed the door.'

Otto mistakenly thought he was beginning to get some sort of clue as to the nature of the events that had led up to the impact of his car with the open door of Sir Justin's gold-plated Rolls. He knew that Sir Justin was a bit of a lad, and this young woman was quite a lot of woman. Obviously Sir Justin had committed some manner of indiscretion with the young woman, and the cheap tawdry affair had not turned out as planned. In true Hollywood fashion Otto decided that by helping to cover up this potentially embarrassing situation, Sir Justin would be in Otto's debt. And such credits could be useful in the dog-eat-dog world of movie-making. And further, in equally true Hollywood fashion, the appealing young woman standing just a few inches before him appeared to be easy prey for Otto's skilled predatory talents. Trying to effect an air of superiority, Otto spoke to Julia like a father trying to calm a distraught child, frightened by a nasty nightmare.

'Yes, yes – it seems I did rather damage it some, so why don't I put it back with the car, and we'll return the car and the dead door to Sir Justin in the morning so he can bury it. In the meantime, my car is relatively unscathed – can I offer you a ride somewhere? Or perhaps you might care to come back to my mansion, since I live next door to Sir Justin. In the morning we can explain everything to him. I'm sure he'll be understanding, and if I know Sir Justin he'll not be in any condition right now to talk any more coherently than you.'

Otto's naughty mind was working overtime. He dared to think that fate had dealt him a winning hand. This little mishap might yet bear him forth bountiful fruit. He eyed Julia's full breasts and downy thighs through the opening of his unbuttoned jacket draped over her shoulders. His thoughts returned to the restrained Tawny in the back seat of the Mercedes and the possibilities of a bondage *menage à trois* began to stir his loins.

'Why don't you come with me . . .' Otto put his arm around the drunken Julia and steered her to the passenger side of the Mercedes. She put up little resistance, showing more concern for the torn-off door.

'The dead door – we've got to bury it.' Suddenly, Julia's tone changed as the proverbial penny dropped. 'Hey, I know you – you're the movie director. I saw your last movie – *Wives, Daughters, Sons and Lovers*. Weird.'

'Indeed. If things weird appeal to you, perhaps you'd like to see some of my private collection? Would you like that? I'm sure you would. Why don't I take care of the door, and you just rest in my limousine? It will be much better this way.'

'OK.'

Julia plopped down into the passenger side seat and Otto quickly closed the door behind her and locked it. He was confident in her drunken stupor that she'd not be able to find the lock in the short time it would take to remove the door from the road and put it with the Rolls. He needn't have worried – Julia was quite intrigued with the possibilities of getting to know Otto Verge. After all the poseurs and fakes she'd dealt with, it was somewhat encouraging to meet the real thing. Perhaps, perhaps, perhaps . . . but she was not about to get tricked again. The memory of Emilio and Xavier boiled within her and she felt the need to vomit. Sitting quite passively on the front seat of the Rolls-Royce, Julia struggled to regain her composure, still unaware of Mistress Tawny in the back seat.

With the door safely stowed in the boot of the Rolls, Otto put the keys to the gold-plated car in his pocket and turned hopefully to his Mercedes. The impact with the open door had smashed the headlight, but there appeared to be little other damage to his limousine. At least the car was driveable, and it was only a few more miles to his mansion in Beverly Hills. Within minutes he would be home, and then he could take Julia and Tawny down into his study. In anticipation of the permutations and combinations of one cock, two cunts, four tits, three arses, three mouths, thirty fingers and three brains, Otto's penis was firmly erect by the time he opened the limousine's door and sat down behind the leather-covered steering wheel. Otto put the limousine in drive and pulled slowly away from the curb. He noticed that Julia was staring, mouth agog, at Mistress Tawny's masturbatory endeavours.

'Ah, I see you two have met. I'm so glad. Julia, this is Mistress Tawny – Tawny, this is Julia. Now that the formalities are over, why don't we retire to the sanctity of my study?'

'Jesus. You are as weird as your movies.'

'More so – there are censors in the movie business. In real life I have no such restrictions. Would you be so kind as to remove the gag from Tawny's mouth so that she may join in our conversation?'

'Sure.'

Julia leaned over the seat and undid the straps that held the small rubber ball inside Tawny's mouth. As the long-legged blonde struggled with Tawny's restraining straps, Otto enjoyed the view of Julia's bare bottom sticking out from underneath his jacket. The desire to enter Julia's rearmost orifice ached in the pit of his stomach. Finally, the gag came free and Julia sat down, examining the object with a morbid curiosity. Otto pretended to be concentrating on driving, whereas in reality the only driving he was thinking about was the directing of his aching cock up Julia's ass while she rabidly licked Tawny's breasts.

As if cognizant of Otto's libidinous thoughts, Tawny spoke softly, almost in a worshipping manner: 'Otto is an artist of immense talent.'

'I bet he is.'

'Miss Majors, may I say . . .'

'Look, please – Otto, Tawny – it has been a very long night for me, and I don't need anymore bullshit. I've had enough promises and threats to last me a lifetime. Now I've had a little too much to drink, and I'm in no mood to have my heart broken one more time by somebody in the movie business. I'm practically naked, she's trussed up like a turkey at Christmas and you're hard enough to do the stuffing. It doesn't take a rocket scientist to figure out what's going to happen next, now does it? So let's not beat around the bush, if you'll pardon the expression. We're all going to have sex, aren't we? So if we want to fuck, great, let's do it – but don't try to get me to sit on her face for you with the promise of a part in your next movie, OK? Let's not even mention the movie business, OK? Let's just fuck. That is what you want, isn't it? It's what she wants. It's what I want. It's all there is left to do.'

'Well, such honesty is indeed very refreshing, I must say. And the answer is a forthright yes. We would be honoured to feast upon your body. Would we not, Mistress Tawny?'

'As you wish, Otto, but may I remind you that I must be back in Burbank in a little over two or three hours. That leaves us precious little time.'

'Then stop the car and let's fuck here. There's so much room back there that we could invite in the Lakers and still have space left over for the Rams.'

'A capital idea, Mistress Julia. Why wait indeed?'

Otto pulled the car into one of the side streets that acted as a service road for one of Century City's tallest buildings. On a Sunday morning there would be no traffic to disturb their fornication, and the tinted windows of the Mercedes would be completely opaque to even the most curious of early-morning joggers. With the press of a button the front seats reclined and Otto and Julia were able to crawl into the spacious backseat area where Tawny was held captive by the leather harness.

'Would you fondle Mistress Tawny for me, Mistress Julia?'

'Yes, Mistress Julia – please touch my body for Otto. I've always wanted to feel such a caress. Your long fingernails, your long fingers – they are so appealing. I have been staring at them, imagining your touch on my most private parts.'

Julia stared at the scene before her. Otto was reclining on the flattened driver's seat, stroking the bulge in his jodhpurs. Mistress Tawny was swinging in her harness, beckoning Julia to fondle her pretty body as the steel dildo slid in and out of her soft cunt. For all her bravado Julia was a little nervous. The effects of the alcohol were lessening and so too was her damn-the-torpedoes attitude. Julia had never had sex with a woman before, and really wasn't quite sure what to do. She'd read lots of books and saw lots of movies, but that was about as much help as reading about sky-diving just before jumping out of the plane. She thought it best to pretend that she was just playing with her own body and see what happened.

'Here, let me do this for you.' Julia started by grasping the steel dildo and sliding the glistening metal cock in and out of Tawny's already soaked cunt. The metal was warm and comfortable from its recent journeys. With her other hand Julia untied Tawny's arms, leaving her legs and her shoulders strapped to brass hooks in the limousine's ceiling.

'You are a very pretty woman, Tawny.'

Julia forced herself to say 'woman'. She guessed that Tawny was no more than twenty – most possibly younger – but the use of any other term in the position she was in would have been incorrect. Sexually, Tawny was a woman.

'May I touch you?'

'Please – please do.'

Julia let Otto's coat slip to the floor. Her full breasts were round and heaving. Her pink nipples were taut and stiff. Tawny let her hands fall across them as gently as a cool night breeze. Julia marvelled at how soft and tender Tawny's skin was – how it felt like the smoothest of silks floating across her sensitive buds. She closed her eyes and softly sighed. The feel of Tawny's hands across her breasts aroused a desire in Julia that begged to be fulfilled. More than anything she wanted to kiss those apparently innocent lips – so perfect, so fresh, so tempting in the dim light of the limousine. Julia bent foward and placed a slight kiss on Tawny's forehead. Slowly, in small halting movements, she continued her kisses down Tawny's nose until she met her lips. To Julia the contrast was palpable. Here were her own lips – she thought of what they had experienced tonight – and how used up they must feel. And she thought of Tawny's silky flesh and how alive and fresh her lips felt – almost virginally innocent. Harder, Julia pressed her lips against Tawny's, Julia's tongue sliding over every small undulation and curve as if she wished to assimilate the younger woman's innocence to renew her own.

And the irony was that Tawny's lips were no more innocent than Julia's. Like everything in Los Angeles, the image was more important than the reality of the situation. Tawny may have spent as equally sordid an evening as Julia, but Tawny looked and felt like Julia wished she did. It created an intense attraction for Julia that burned with a fire she'd never felt for any man before. She forgot completely about the eager eyes of Otto Verge enjoying her vampiress activities.

Otto was very willing to sink into the background. He had removed his clothes and was stroking his erect cock, admiring the view of the two women exploring the newness of each other's respective bodies. He was perfectly content to be a spectator throughout this enticing encounter, it being a long-standing fantasy of his to watch his beloved Tawny being consumed by another woman. When he'd planned to take Tawny to the party – her first exposure in public as his sex slave, her coming-out party, so to speak – he'd dared to think of the possibilities that might arise. The sensuous scene unfolding before him was more than he had hoped for. And this newcomer that fate had brought to him, this Julia Majors – such a contradiction, such a beauty, such an anger, such a great pair of tits, such an ass ... In his photographically driven mind Otto vacillated between poetry and pornography as he enjoyed the abandon with which Tawny and Julia oozed over each other.

'Your lips are so soft, Tawny, like silk against mine, like a baby's skin. I kiss you and I feel myself falling inside you.'

'My nether lips are softer, and you can fall inside me through them.'

Julia marvelled at Tawny's worldliness. The fact that she had called her labia 'nether lips' was extremely erotic – much more so than if she'd have used a more vulgar term. It was a classically erotic term that spoke of a sophistication surprising for one so apparently young and modern. Any doubts about Tawny's depth of experience were completely eradicated from Julia's mind as she descended between Tawny's soft thighs. Julia let her hair cascade down over her head as she bent her neck to taste Tawny's lustful fountain. Julia's blonde curls flowed over Tawny's silken thighs as Julia let her cheeks linger on the warm and tender flesh of Tawny's inner legs. Julia was about to kiss the tufty patch of light brown curls when Tawny interrupted her with a polite request.

'Please, Julia – straddle my body so that I may kiss your sex as you kiss mine.'

Julia complied eagerly. It took a certain hurried agility to hook her legs through the harness that held Tawny suspended over the plush seat of the Mercedes limousine and position her hands to the side of Tawny's widespread thighs. It was a perfect compromise of positions. Tawny was held open and freely accessible by the hammocklike harness that allowed Julia to prey above her, balanced on her hands and knees, her face just moments away from Tawny's sweet prize. As Julia bent her head and lowered her face between Tawny's thighs she felt the young woman arch her neck and place small wet kisses on the inside of the aspiring actress's legs. As if tasting a rare and possibly dangerous tropical fruit, Tawny was restrained in her licking until Julia lowered her body closer to Tawny's face. Freed from the leather harness, her hands were easily able to grip Julia's buttocks and add just the right amount of direction and pressure to that of Julia's own movements. She had been consumed by men many times, but Tawny's exploring forays sent lascivious lightning shocks of lust through her body as if she were being touched there, in that way, for the first time. And in some way she was. No man had lips as soft and as tender as Tawny's, and no man knew the intimate details of a woman's anatomy as could another woman, whose inquiring hand had explored those precious confines many times in the dark of night.

And Tawny was right. Her 'nether lips', as she had so quaintly called them, were every bit as soft and as silken as those upper ones which were locked with a youthful enthusiasm on Julia's cunt. Julia let her tongue pry open the musky labia to slide gently into Tawny's tight cavern. The unmistakable signature of a male's cock informed Julia that the young woman had played host to a dick – or possibly several – quite recently. And then Julia realised that Tawny must also be able to sense the same of her, and somehow she felt a strange kinship – almost like a sisterhood with the shackled young woman – and she pressed her tongue deeper, sliding the wet probe around Tawny's intriguing sex, drinking intently the contrasts she contained. In her mind she imagined that her tongue was able to slide completely through Tawny's undulating body and emerge inside her own juicing box. With eyes closed and lips apart, Julia felt as if she were tonguing her own cunt, as if it were her own nimble instrument that was flicking lightly across the sensuous terrain of her vagina, teasing and probing, sucking and kissing, even biting at that small swollen bud that was usually the sacred domain of her thumb and finger.

As if choreographed by the finest of dancers, Tawny and Julia's bodies undulated together, rippling like oscillating electronic waves in perfect phase. As Tawny arched her slender hips upwards, thereby thrusting her sultry sex deep into Julia's face, Julia would pull her head slightly away from the dripping target, forcing her firm stomach down towards Tawny's flat belly. In this position Julia's pussy would slide up Tawny's throat, leaving a musky trail of feminine odour until the young woman's lips were able to latch on to Julia's swollen labia, and during the apex of the undulation cycle, Tawny's outstretched tongue was able to penetrate deeply, as if it were searching for Julia's tongue so that the two women could intimately kiss each other, entwining their tongues as their bodies did likewise.

On her hands and knees, her head bowed between Tawny's thighs, Julia's full breasts hung low from her body, swinging across the leather straps of Tawny's harness. With each stroke of their mutual licking, Julia's breasts slid, sometimes hard, sometimes soft, across Tawny's belly, titillating her hanging nipples on the roughness of the leather. Julia didn't comprehend the effect her motions were having on Tawny, who revelled in the luxurious feel of hard nipples sliding across her stomach. It was a sensation that no man could provide her, and it made Tawny long for further discoveries of the joys of making love to another woman.

With each probing thrust of Julia's tongue deep inside her pulsing quim, Tawny gained in the confidence to experiment. Tightly she gripped Julia's trim waist and held Julia's buttocks spread before her, solidly against her breasts. Holding her tongue firm and hard, like a small and rigid cock, Tawny let slide her slippery instrument from Julia's taut cunt, causing a moan to escape from her otherwise occupied mouth. Gently Tawny blew a cooling breeze across Julia's exposed orifices, gradually guiding her breath more and more towards Julia's anus. Zeroing in on the tight little button, Tawny licked clear across Julia's ass, spreading a thin film of saliva from tan line to tan line of Julia's bottom, circumnavigating the dark, pouting centre. Curling her tongue into a rock-hard point, Tawny slowly forced her tongue deep into Julia's bottom. Julia felt Tawny's tongue wriggle inside her as if something alive had hatched within her. She broke away from her own ministrations at Tawny's nether lips and moaned, her tousled blonde hair falling seductively around her face as she grimaced in delight as her bottom was tongued. Julia slapped her breasts across Tawny's belly, unable to move her lower extremities, so hard was the younger woman's grip. At once Tawny removed her tongue and pushed the rigid instrument against Julia's swollen and sensitive clitoris. Tawny's aim was understandably perfect, and the prod that Julia felt ignited a bubbling orgasm that welled simultaneously from the pit of her stomach, the depths of her thighs, the tightness of her bottom and the warmth of her cunt. Julia collapsed on to Tawny, causing the hammocklike harness to rock violently from side to side in perfect time with the ebb and flow of her rolling orgasm.

Both women strained for air in the closed confines of the limousine, their heaving breasts beating a fast rhythm against each other's quivering form. The rocking of the hammocklike harness lulled Julia into an orgasm-induced coma. She felt as if she were encased in a cloud of cotton wool where all sounds and sensations were dulled into a background noise much like the distant faint roar of the rolling Pacific Ocean or the constant rumble of the jets taking off from LAX. Of all the orgasms she had experienced in many degrading situations, this one was somehow different. It had been more of everything, perhaps because there had been no promise of a movie role, no not-so-hidden agenda to which to script her sexual favours. And there had been no man to try to take advantage of her.

'Miss Majors – Julia – I have for you one of Mistress Tawny's favourite toys.'

The voice breaking through her enjoyable haze was that of a man, reminding Julia of Otto's presence. His interruption irritated her. She tried to ignore him, but Otto was persistent.

'Julia, Julia – Mistress Tawny must leave soon and dawn is fast approaching. There is not much time. For Mistress Tawny's sake, please wake up.'

Men, thought Julia. Always ready with an excuse for more sex. She lifted her racked body off Tawny and was greeted by the sight of Otto Verge, naked and erect, holding in his sweaty hands a surprisingly lifelike phallus of more than normal proportions, replete with two oversized balls covered in tiny rubber spikes. Emanating from the shaft were several leather straps and an electronic cord which led to a small control device.

'Here. Strap this around your waist so that it covers your sex. If you like you can take the balls and insert them up into your pussy. As you fuck Tawny with the dildo you can adjust the vibrations of the cock with the controller. It even makes the balls pulsate – hence my suggestion. This is Tawny's favourite toy. She has used it on me many times. She particularly likes the balls up her cunt, but she has never had it used on her since I have my own apparatus. I'm sure she would be thrilled if you would oblige her, Mistress Julia.'

Tawny stirred and added her encouragement, betraying some of her youthfulness with her giggles.

'Oh yes – please strap on the dick, Julia, and do, do insert the balls inside you. I promise you will not regret it. I have had the most awesome orgasms with those spiky things inside of me.'

Julia eased herself off Tawny and complied with the odd couple's request. The leather straps bit slightly into her tender thigh flesh as she pulled the connector tight behind her back – it was not a totally uncomfortable feeling – to feel leather constrict her skin. She began to understand Tawny's apparent enjoyment of bondage, but it would be a cold day in hell before Julia would let herself be that vulnerable around a man ever again. After all her bitter experiences Julia was convinced that men, in general, could not be trusted. Now, Tawny was a different matter ... Julia could easily see herself getting lost in those thighs, and doing things that she wouldn't willingly do with a man.

With the surrogate cock and balls securely fastened around her waist, Julia kneeled on the limousine seat, stretching her body as high as the confines of the plush Mercedes limousine would allow. With the huge extension jutting out from her pristine flatness Julia felt strangely out of balance, the way a man might if he suddenly woke up with thirty-eight-inch breasts. She felt awkward with the artificial penis sticking out from her pubic mound, being more used to cocks being pointed in the other direction. With that thought in mind Julia turned her attentions to the open cunt that was eagerly writhing before her in anticipation of what was to be inserted in its well-lubricated passage.

'Spread wide your nether lips, my Tawny. I shall fuck you like no man could ever hope to.'

Julia was in the mood of the moment, and drawing on her skills as a wannabe actress, she began to play the part of a dominatrix.

'I know you worship my big staff, and you have pleased me

202

well tonight with the magnificent use of your mouth on my nether lips. Now it is time to sacrifice your sex to me.'

Out of the corner of her eye she could see Otto almost applauding with joy. Maybe she would get a movie role out of this after all. Wouldn't that be ironic, she mused. After all the men she'd fucked who had promised her the moon and ended up giving her nothing but the shaft, here she was, fucking just for fucking's sake, at her own request, with no movie strings attached. And in the back of Julia's mind the distinct possibility existed that the world-famous director and producer Otto Verge might be persuaded to show his thanks by getting Julia a role. Julia decided to continue with her dominatrix act.

'With my mighty instrument we need no man to satisfy our base urges. We are superior, you and I, with perfect bodies we make men crawl to us, begging to us to be receptacles for their nasty fluid, but you and I mock them and send them away. We need not their puny tools, their silly little cocks – not when we have this . . .'

Julia, straining hard not to laugh at what she'd just said, knelt between Tawny's legs and inserted the cold tip of the instrument between the younger woman's cuntlips. Tawny gasped at the feel of the dildo. In a voice struggling to escape between heavy forced breaths she urged Julia not to forget her own pleasure.

'Do not forget to put the balls inside you before turning on the machine. I have had the most extraordinary orgasms from it. You will die – you really will, Julia.'

Julia reached under her cunt from behind her and forced the dimpled plastic orbs inside of her one by one. It took considerable effort to force open her lips and insert the large objects. Once inside she felt heavy, bloated, and strangely unnatural. Slipping out of her dominatrix role she added in a whisper to Tawny a slight comment aimed at adding a little levity to the situation. Already there was developing between the two women a strong bond of more than friendship.

'I feel like I should make a countdown or something.'

'Oh no, Julia. Surprise me – flick the switch without warning me.'

Julia stared at the rubber length poking out from her body and watched as she excruciatingly inched the dildo into Mistress

Tawny's sopping cunt. Julia paused with the shaft fully embedded into Tawny. Her eyes were closed and she rolled her head from side to side in that way that people in intense pain or ecstasy do. For the dildo to be fully inserted inside her small tight cunt it must have coiled itself against Tawny's tender insides, causing the young woman to shake, every movement of her body sending violent ripples of sexual release as her supercharged cunt rubbed against the dildo's flexible surface.

Behind Tawny's head crouched Otto with his firm erection peering above Tawny's blonde curls. Ever the director he was motioning with his hand for Julia to start the device. She tried to ignore him but found her desire to feel the vibrating balls too curious to ignore. Holding the control behind her back she flicked the on switch and the confines of the limousine were filled with a dull humming.

It took but an instant for the sensation to hit Julia. So sudden, so violent, so unusual was the intensity of the shock that she almost passed out. It was like being kicked repeatedly in the stomach. Each one of the rubber balls inside her seemed to be swelling to fill her moist cavity as they slid over one another and rotated around inside her, like some bizarre caterpillar-tracked vehicle attempting to negotiate a steep and rocky hill. Julia had never sensed such convulsions within her, the result being that she bucked the shaft of the dildo into Mistress Tawny as hard as she could.

Julia's head had rocked back as she tried to maintain her stance as her legs buckled from the punches she was receiving inside her. She flung her head forward and immediately noticed that the shaft of the dildo was undulating up and down as she thrust in and out. Like some rolling wave or fleeing snake the dildo held its firmness as it rippled in a grand s-like shape. No man could ever wield his unit with such agility, and Julia wondered why Tawny was not screeching with delight at the torrid sensations this malleable device must be causing throughout her restrained body. The moment Julia looked up to view Tawny's face it became obvious why she was so silent. A few muffled moans escaped, but no major cries could emanate from Tawny's mouth, as her lips were clamped tightly around Otto's balls. He had crouched behind her and she had arched her head backwards so that he could dangle his testicles into her open mouth as if he were feeding her grapes in the classically decadent Roman fashion. His shaft protruded forward, pointing at Julia as she slid the fake cock in and out of the young girl. It was indeed a scene worthy of Caligula.

Otto stroked his shaft as his eyes remained riveted upon Julia's surrogate male actions. He held his cock fixed at roughly the same level such that, as Tawny shook her head from side to side under Julia's thrustings, his scrotum was pulled rather painfully to its extremes by Tawny's mouth. At full stretch she would bite the thin fleshy walls of the sacs between her teeth, causing Otto to grimace in pain.

'Ahhh – I love having my balls chewed, Julia. Perhaps someday you might be persuaded . . .?'

'I can be persuaded of most things, Otto.'

'Ahhh – I can imagine stroking my penis as you suck my sacs dry.'

'I can imagine much more. Much, much more . . .'

'Ahhhh.'

Tawny participated in this verbal sparing between Otto and Julia by increasing or decreasing the pressure on Otto's balls. It was an incredibly effective means of communication. Julia watched in fascination the shaking of Tawny's body, the way her firm tanned breasts, criss-crossed with leather straps, shuddered under Julia's onslaught. There was a fearful symmetry to the strange scene. Julia had the fake balls inside her cunt, and Tawny held Otto's swollen testicles in her mouth. As before, when Tawny and Julia had eaten each other's cunts, it seemed as if the two women were connected through the fusing of their sexually charged bodies.

The fake balls seemed to be lodged somewhere in the back of Julia's brain. The vibrations they caused seemed no longer to be coming from her pussy but from throughout her entire lovely form. Every pulse, every ripple, seemed to send extremely dirty thoughts and desires ricocheting to and from every sweating sinew. She thought of past fucks, she dwelled on the sordid scene before her, and surprisingly she thought of the fucks to come. She dreamed of sliding the long rubber cock up Otto's ass and watching him play with his purple shaft as she slid the dick in and out of his tight asshole. All the while the expanding balls within her stripped away any inhibition she might have, causing more lewd thoughts to be generated. Permeating all the erotic visions, Julia thought of making love to Tawny – naked feminine flesh on flesh, no leather straps or devices, just their silky bodies touching in every conceivable place.

In her delirium Julia flicked the control switch of the electric dildo on to full mondo vibrations. It felt as if all fuses had blown and the instrument had gone wild. She saw her flat stomach bulge and strain under the explosions that seemed to be taking place inside her dripping cunt. The shaft was no longer undulating inside Tawny but was whipping to and fro, tossing Tawny's slender frame around like a rag doll.

Otto was the first to release his orgasm into the foray. It erupted with such force and violence that it easily traversed the steamy space of Tawny's wracked body and splattered on Julia's breasts. With huge rivulets of come dripping from the swollen head of his cock Otto continued to milk his throbbing penis, sending blobs of semen down on to Tawny's neck and breasts. To his credit he maintained his self-control. Keeping his balls locked inside Tawny's mouth, she toying with the instruments – rolling them around inside her as he orgasmed above her. It was a sensation that reminded Otto of earlier in the evening when Tawny had pissed on his orgasming cock. The all-enveloping warmth, the darting pressures all held something primal about them.

The warm splat of sperm on her chest made Julia think that she was orgasming inside Tawny, as if the throbbing extension of her body had somehow become real. She felt as if she were literally melting inside the girl as Julia's second orgasm drained from her thighs. She fell forward on to Tawny, narrowly missing Otto's still-hard cock. Slumped on the younger woman, she continued to thrust as the balls inside her danced on, completely unaware in their mechanical way that perhaps it was time to slow down.

Tawny had majestically delayed her release as long as possible. With Julia slumping on top of her she felt the slap of those firm breasts on her leather-strapped flesh, she felt Julia's strawberry-blonde hair mingle with Otto's semen on her throat, she felt the huge artificial cock inside her burrow deeper, as if it wanted to be sucked off by her expert mouth. Under all of the impulses she was being inundated with, Tawny's body went rigid as if she'd died and rigor mortis had set in. Nothing could have been further from the truth. She was very much alive as the stiffness of her limbs was melted by the acidlike onrush of her orgasm. Her body arched, her legs kicked, and deep within her body streams of electrical signals flowed from nerve endings to nerve endings, culminating in one huge explosion inside her cunt. With an energy that such a small body could never contain she blew Otto's balls out of her mouth, she repulsed the artificial dick from her cunt, thereby causing the vibrating balls to slide out of Julia's distended opening, and in the same motion she tore the leather restraints from the ceiling of the Mercedes. Locking her arms and legs around Julia she held the other woman tightly against her as the rush of moisture fled from her body. Only later did she realise that throughout this time she had been screaming at fever pitch.

Julia was a passive observer at this point, content to be held by Tawny's writhing form. In all of the bucking and writhing the strap holding the surrogate dick and balls had come undone, and the object had fallen to the floor. Out of the corner of her eye she caught sight of the still-activated electric dildo and balls squirming across the plush carpet of the limousine like a chicken with its head cut off running around a farmyard. It was the last thing she remembered seeing before she fell into a deep sleep. There was something about the sight that was both poetic and prophetic. She fell asleep thinking that perhaps she no longer needed men, their promises, their cocks, to help her succeed. She had herself, her self-confidence, and she had Mistress Tawny, and somehow everything was going to work out just fine.

Otto slid off the seat and struggled to regain his composure. His balls ached from the biting they'd received, and he found the continued din of the unmuffled vibrations of the dildo annoying. In his dulled state it was difficult to apprehend the wriggling device and cease its incessant chatter. After several futile grabs he snared the rude instrument. Finally, the inside of the limousine was quiet except for the gentle breathing of the two women slumped together in a passionate embrace.

With great effort Otto slid naked into the driver's seat and turned on the engine, put the limousine into drive and slowly pulled away from the streets of Century City. He wasn't sure who said it, but from deep in the back seat, amidst a few schoolgirl like giggles, came the forced sound of a fake haughty English upper-class accent.

'Home, James . . .'

5 a.m.

A Downtown Penthouse

'I'm starving.'

'Me too. The food they serve at those entertainment business parties does leave one a mite peckish.'

'Do you eat meat?'

'Yes – and I know you do.'

Marlene Neumann playfully punched Sydney Nats on the shoulder, smiling at his not-so-oblique reference to her fellatio talents. 'Good – you are in for a treat that no tourist ever sees.'

'And what may that be? It can't be the picturesque sight of the moon, framed by your widespread legs, setting over the rolling Pacific Ocean. I've already seen that, so what more could there be?'

'Jay's JayBurger.'

'Whose what burger?'

'The best burgers in Los Angeles, and Jay's stays open all night on weekends. It's not in the best part of town, and the accommodation is somewhat spartan, but the burgers are to die for. It's not the kind of place that tour guides on the way to Disneyland stop off at, but your trip to Los Angles just wouldn't be complete without a visit to Jay's.'

Marlene steered her BMW off of the Hollywood freeway just before the downtown area. After a few turns past graffiti-blasted walls and armour-plated stores they arrived at the intersection of Virgil and Santa Monica Boulevards. It was quite a contrast from Neil Waslinger's palatial Malibu Beach estate which they had just left. Upon hearing of Marlene and Sydney's tryst Neil had been quite gracious, even offering to have one of his servants drive Sydney's rental car back to the airport so he wouldn't have to worry about it. Sydney thanked Neil for his hospitality and turned to get in Marlene's BMW. He didn't see Neil wink at Marlene, and her smile back, all the while maintaining her cool composure. Sydney missed all the winking because he was busy giving a furtive smile to Kimberly, who responded with an extremely attractive raising of her eyebrows. As they drove out of the sprawling rounds Sydney reflected upon how life had a strange way of resolving situations for the best. Kimberly was better off with Neil, and Marlene and he seemed the perfect match – finally, he had hit it off with someone who wasn't a waitress, a bartender or a dancer.

Far in the distance Sydney could see the lights of the airplanes taking off from LAX. It reminded him of the delay that had made him so angry and set him on the Saturday-night-Sunday-morning odyssey that had eventually led him to the passenger seat of Marlene Neumann's BMW. He said a silent prayer of thanks to British Airways and tried not to think of his upcoming departure.

'Well – here we are.'

The intersection of Virgil and Santa Monica Boulevards played home to several run-down Mexican bars, an all-night convenience store, whose parking lot was home to a clan of mean-looking derelicts, and Marlene's early-morning eating Holy Grail, Jay's JayBurger. Marlene had been more than right, thought Sydney, but he was too much of a gentleman to question whether Marlene had taken leave of her senses in bringing them to this rather threatening location. Jay's JayBurger was a small corner stand with no indoor seating – just a few stools positioned under the cover of a garish red awning. In the relatively cool morning air, clouds of grease-laden steam issued from the grill. Various nefarious-looking night characters ate their burgers slowly, deliberately, without daring to look at each other, making their one meal last as long as possible. Marlene ignored them all, marched up to the counter and placed her order with the Mexican cooks.

'Two single JayBurgers with egg – no onion – and two lemonades.'

Sydney and Marlene sat on stools close by the car so they could keep an eye on the BMW. Marlene tucked her long black pleated skirt underneath her to prevent it from fluttering up and revealing her lack of underwear.

'How the heck do you know about this place? It doesn't seem the kind of establishment that a prominent and sexy LA lawyer goes on dates to or takes clients to.'

'It depends on the clients.'

'Ah, I see.'

'Too bad about Archie – after all those negotiations.'

'Well, he had a good innings, and his ex-wives are going to do well off of the re-runs – as will your client, I might say.'

'Those are the breaks, Sydney. At least he went with a smile on his face.'

'And a boner to be proud of. Did you see the size of that thing when the paramedics fished him out of the spa?'

Their hysterical laughter was interrupted by the cook.

'Your burgers.'

Sydney stared at the huge thing in his hand.

'Don't look at it – just put it in your mouth and enjoy it.'

'Sounds like good advice. I bet all the boys say that to you.'

Marlene was busy devouring the delectable burger and didn't bother to reply to Sydney's dry humour.

'Well, here goes.'

Sydney became an immediate convert. The combination of spicy chili, fried egg, tomato, pickles, mustard and of course – hamburger – all between two soft buns was quite simply the most amazing burger he had ever tasted. It took a remarkably short time for both Jays to be consumed. Over lemonade he complimented Marlene on her choice.

'You were right – that was the best burger I've ever had.'

'They are great, aren't they? Just the ideal thing to soak up alcohol after a long night's drinking, and oh, by the way – after one of those you'll be able to fuck for days.'

'Perhaps we should order a couple more?'

'Sydney – have you forgotten? You have a plane to catch today.'

'Oh, it was just wishful thinking . . .'

And with that they headed back to the BMW, arm in arm, Sydney occasionally squeezing Marlene's firm bottom through the thin material of her skirt. Within minutes they were in the very centre of Los Angeles and entering the elevator of Down-Town Towers to take them to Marlene's plush penthouse apartment. Ever the polite gentleman, Sydney asked Marlene which storey she lived on so he could push the appropriate floor button. 'Thirty,' she replied, but before he could hit the thirtieth-floor button, Marlene deflected his aim and hit the twenty-eighth-floor button.

Puzzled, Sydney decided to go along with whatever game Marlene was playing. As the elevator passed 23, 24, 25, 26, Sydney decided that whatever was on the twenty-eight floor must be dessert, the final course to their scrumptious Jay's JayBurgers. Reaching the selected floor, the doors opened, revealing not some latenight café, but rather the DownTown Towers Athletic Club, founded 1982.

'Clients of mine,' Marlene responded to Sydney's unasked question.

'Business this time of night, tonight of all nights?' queried the still randy male solicitor.

'No, not at all. The club is closed, but I have a key. I often come here when there's no one around. It is the best thing after a night like we've had. Some good old-fashioned exercise – you know, lift some weights, sweat, clear out the cobwebs in your brain, burn off those JayBurger calories.'

Sydney was about to add that he knew of a much better way to burn off some calories on the thirtieth floor, but thought better of it. 'Exercise? You're kidding, right? I didn't take you for one of those steroid-popping weightlifters.'

'Look, Sydney, there's nothing wrong with keeping your body in shape. Not that you look half bad or anything. Just humour me for now, OK?'

Marlene finished her plea with one of her famous winks. Sydney gave in, accepted the towel Marlene offered him and made his way through the door marked 'Men's', found a locker and stripped down to his birthday suit. It was then that he realised he had nothing to wear but that very same towel. Oh well, Sydney thought, there was no one here to see him, and besides, he'd only be a few minutes before he talked Marlene out of her odd mood and into her cosy penthouse for some more meaning-ful exercise.

As Sydney emerged from the locker room Marlene was already hard at work. It was difficult for him to maintain his composure as he watched her sweat away on the bench press machine. She wore a pair of skin-tight Lycra white shorts. The top of the shorts had straps that led up over the breasts, over her shoulders and down her slim back to connect with the back of her shorts. Under the exercise shorts she wore a tight peach-coloured sleeveless top, with a round neckline that showed her tits off admirably. To complete the outfit she had on peach socks and white tennis shoes – LA Gear, of course. Sydney thought she looked the epitome of the fit California woman, the kind men dream about meeting in a gym.

Still wearing just a towel that strained to hide the burgeoning erection he was sporting, Sydney walked up to Marlene, admiring her flexing chest and arm muscles as she strained under the weight of the bench press. With a supremely sexy gasp that Sydney thought best belonged in the throes of orgasm, Marlene finished her repetitions and turned her attention to the Australian lawyer.

'Good, you're ready. What do you want to start on?'

'I must say I'm really not into the indoor exercise craze. I much prefer a game of cricket or tennis, so I'm nor familiar with these perverse contraptions.'

'Well, you must know some of the old time machines that they probably had at school when you were younger. What about the rowing machine? Try that, I'm sure you'll like it.'

Marlene seemed so serious, yet so friendly, that Sydney, though feeling self-conscious dressed in barely nothing, could hardly say no. Off he went across the room to the rowing machine. He sat down in the ancient device, positioned his legs, grabbed the pull bar, and promptly his towel fell down to his sides. Trying a different strategy in athletic club decorum, Sydney removed the towel and placed it on top of his still hard cock, although he was unsure who he was hiding it from. Still, modesty won the day and Sydney began grunting away, pretending he was rowing down the Cherwell with Marlene, and only a towel to cover his male pride.

Deep in such thoughts, Sydney failed to hear Marlene walk up to his side. In fact, with his eyes closed he failed to see her

213

squatting next to him. He did not fail, however, to feel her hand peel away his towel, stroking his momentarily softening penis, which immediately became rock hard again under her able touch. Expecting that Marlene had finally lost the silly notion that this was a good time for exercise, Sydney stopped his rowing, preparing for a more pleasurable sport. But Marlene would have none of it.

'Keep going, Sydney – it's more fun this way.'

As his body slid up and down the length of the rowing device, Marlene's grip pulled the skin of Sydney's cock up and down its length. Sydney began to get the picture. Under the combined sweat of Marlene's hand and Sydney's dick, Marlene administered a smooth, hot hand job. At first it was a little rough for Sydney's tastes, but by controlling his pulling action he was able to stabilise her pulling action.

Sydney's breathing, already short and laboured from the rowing workout, became punctuated with a series of gasps, moans, groans, squeals and other involuntary sounds of delight from Marlene's attentions as his personal fitness trainer.

'Pull, pull, pull,' coached Marlene, seemingly talking not just to Sydney, but to herself as well.

In response, Sydney's legs began to tingle with that wiggly sort of feeling that overstimulated muscles get. As much as Sydney desperately wanted to stop what he was doing and have Marlene continue in peace, another part of him knew she would stop if he gave in. There was no choice, then, but to do what Marlene said – Pull, pull, pull.

Marlene eased the wear and tear on Sydney's throbbing oar by applying to it a liberal amount of weightlifter's chalk. The chalk was soft, like talcum powder, and made Marlene's hand slide effortlessly up and down Sydney's shaft despite the stickiness of the accumulating sweat. The smoothness of Marlene's touch, her grip varying from tight to loose, loose to tight, and the tiredness of Sydney's entire body from their combined exertions began to wear down Sydney until he resolved to give in to his body's urgings.

Like a man overboard, Sydney became drenched in a torrent of liquid as legs and cock gave out at the same moment.

It was several minutes of gasping and hard breathing before

Sydney could talk, during which time he imagined what it must feel like to be a world champion sculler crossing the finish line after a gruelling competition against the arch-rival team. He envisioned himself as the boatsman collapsing after his victory, gliding down the river past hordes of cheering, adoring fans.

Sydney's reverie was broken by Marlene's soft voice.

'Come on, Sydney, get up on your jelly legs and let's go take a steam.'

Zombielike, sweat dripping from his face, his back, his legs, his crotch, Sydney let Marlene lead him into the steam room. Once inside she sat Sydney down and disappeared into the billowing clouds of superheated water with an 'I'll be right back.'

Moments later the steam door reopened and Marlene, stark raving naked, slinked in. Taking a seat across the room from Sydney, she leaned against the wall, legs stretched out in front of her, sighing with pleasure at the feeling of hot steam droplets on her freshly energized body.

'Sydney, are you feeling better now?'

'Ripper! This was a brilliant idea. And you?'

'I couldn't be more relaxed. There's something about a steam room that gives me the most erotic thoughts. Usually, though, I have to keep my thoughts to myself – I mean, you can't exactly carry out your wildest fantasies in a public steam room, can you?'

'I think I see what you're getting at,' said the ever-perceptive Sydney. 'Tell me about these erotic thoughts of yours, if you don't mind.'

'Oh you know, just the normal thing. I would just love to have a steamroom orgasm, just once. It's sort of like how the sun makes me incredibly randy. Whenever I'm at the beach, lying there in the warm sand, I wish the whole world would go away so I could put my hand between my legs, and play and play and play. Do you ever feel that way, Sydney?'

As Sydney pondered her question, Marlene readjusted herself. She was now lying flat on her back, arms stretched over her head, knees bent as though she was about to do sit-ups – which, needless to say, was not on her mind at this moment.

'Yes, I know exactly what you mean, Marlene.' Sydney had moved to the stop directly above Marlene, lying on his side, head propped up by his arm. He reached down with his other hand, lightly touching the steam-covered body of Marlene, fingers drawing a path amongst the sweat droplets coating her skin. He began making small circles over her flat stomach, circumnavigating her belly-button, then expanded his repertoire into figure-of-eights around her breasts. He put his index finger on her chin, slowly ran it down her neck, down her chest, down her belly, to the soft, wet area of her pubic mound, entangling in the sweat-soaked hair, pulling and twisting, stimulating her lower senses into a mild frenzy.

Quiet sighs emanated from Marlene's mouth, her head rocking slowly back and forth, her mind gliding over thoughts of how she'd always wanted to feel like this in a steam room. She liked the way Sydney knew better than to break the silence at this point, letting her privately run through her fantasy in the solitary domain of her sensual psyche.

He continued stroking her pussy hair, occasionally letting his middle finger sweep down between her lips, where the moisture of the steam intermingled with the wetness of her cunt. He slid his finger up inside her vagina, and upon pulling the soaked digit out, he trailed her juices along her upraised inner thigh, feminine nectar mixing again with sweat, running in rivulets back down to its origin.

Marlene was lost in the tactile sensations created by Sydney, and he was similarly wrapped up in his explorations. This was better than shower sex, or bath sex, he thought, where water washed away all traces of slithery body fluids. Not only was there cunt wetness to slide fingers around in, but there was also the added stimulation of the extra moisture caused by the renewing bursts of steam spewing from valves in the walls.

Through the heavy fog of the steam room Sydney heard Marlene whisper to herself.

'Everyone's moving so slowly, like in a dream. It's so dirty to have all these people watching – you can tell they really like what they see.'

Marlene's eyes were closed as if her fantasy was taking her farther and farther away into never-never land of erotic wonderment.

'Yes, Marlene, they love to see your legs spreading open, my hand playing with your cunt.'

'Mmmmmmmmmmmm,' was all Marlene managed to get out in response, so Sydney resumed his quiet meanderings around the dreamy woman's body.

With the image in his head of people watching the lovely Marlene wriggle beneath his touch, Sydney now concentrated solely on Marlene's box, challenging himself to coax out more pussy juice for the onlooking fantasy audience. He rhythmically ran one finger up Marlene's cunt, sliding it out and up and over her clitoris, back and forth, back and forth, always feeling the wetness of the steam and the distinct slippery wetness of her come. As he sensed Marlene's increasing insistence of her hips rocking up and down, urging his hand to move faster, Sydney plunged two fingers up her cunt, then three, spreading the musky fluids over her swollen bud, over her pubic mound, over her belly and thighs. Giving in to temptation, he allowed one finger to overshoot on its quest for her quim and enter her bottom, the unexpected sensation urging Marlene into further agitated rocking motions.

As Sydney's hand once again reached her desiring clitoris, Marlene reached down and held his fingers there, telling him through body language to engage his efforts on that one particular, very small portion of her stimulated body. Sydney, in response, ran his finger in slow circles over and around her clit, enjoying the smoothness her come created between his skin and hers. As Marlene's sweat-drenched legs spread wider and wider for Sydney, her moaning became more audible, her head nodded back and forth in her delirium and her hips thrust up and down under Sydney's hand.

'Marlene, they all want you to come. They're waiting for you to come all over your thighs. You can practically feel their breath on your cunt, can't you? You can feel their eyes staring at the pinkness between your legs. They're all starting to touch themselves, imagining they're touching you. Come for them, Marlene, come as if you're coming for them all. Feel the hot jets of steam, imagine it's shooting all over your pussy, and everyone can barely see you through the hot fog, but they know just what you're doing. Come for them, Marlene.'

Sydney's fingers probed and slid endlessly around her clitoris, her juices flowing faster and faster, her hips thrusting fast, then slow, slow and deliberate, searching for the exact sensation that would make her come. Marlene's dreamy imagination raced, thinking of the fantasy audience watching in mute anticipation of the Event. She was performing for them, their peering eyes, their lurid thoughts, their fondling hands. Marlene breathed louder and louder, moans turned into breathless screams, and she came at last in torrents, hot, steam-engulfed torrents. As her orgasm subsided, fresh steam poured into the room, wrapping her inert form in a comforting blanket of sex-induced sleep.

Sydney allowed Marlene but a few minutes rest, then revived her to get themselves out of the now stifling steam. Marlene appeared understandably disoriented, but quickly regained her senses once her eyes focused on the wall clock.

'Wow – we'd better get out of here. The morning health-club crew will be here soon.'

'I'll get your clothes.'

Sydney dived first into the men's changing rooms to collect his clothes and then into the empty woman's changing room and gathered up Marlene's garments.

'Let's go.'

'But we're naked . . .'

'So? It's only two floors. There'll be nobody in the elevator.'

'OK – after you.'

Nude, dripping wet, laughing and giggling from an excess of adrenalin, Sydney and Marlene bundled into the elevator and made the two-storey journey almost hoping that they'd bump into someone, just so they could act as if there was absolutely nothing wrong with being stark, sweat and steam-soaked naked in the DownTown Towers elevator on a Sunday morning.

After a few fumblings with uncooperative keys Marlene threw open the door to her penthouse apartment and led Sydney at breakneck pace into her bedroom, where the first vestiges of morning sunlight were illuminating the room. Sydney was momentarily stunned at the sprawling vista of Los Angeles spread before him through the looking glass of the penthouse floor-to-ceiling windows.

'Wow – what a view . . .'

It seemed such a tritely predictable thing to say that Sydney immediately regretted uttering the comment. There was no need to worry, he looked at Marlene who strutted over to the sheer glass and pressed her soaking body against the windows.

'Yes, isn't it.'

Sydney joined her there, pressing his body tightly against hers, crushing Marlene against the cool plate glass. They kissed long, hard and deep, wet flesh against wet flesh, the City of One-Night Stands sprawling below, slowly awakening on another new day in Paradise Lost. At this moment Marlene and Sydney cared nothing for the normal Los Angeles cynicism that pervaded the streets, the beaches, the high rises and the homes of the second largest city in America. Marlene and Sydney were alive, fresh, exhilarated with each other's bodies. All things seemed possible – deep inside they hoped, they knew that the passion that burned fiercely at this priceless moment in time would not cool with the passage of time. This would not be just another one-night stand in the City of One-Night Stands.

Still laughing with the recent freedom of being naked in a public place, Marlene pulled Sydney from the window and tumbled him on to the bed. They rolled in each other's arms, the sheets soaking up the dampness of their bodies. Out of breath, her breasts heaving, Marlene rolled on top of Sydney and mounted his hardening penis with surprising ease. The fullness within her expanded luxuriously to fill her beckoning cavity. She felt like she wanted to proclaim how good she felt, but both she and Sydney were past coherence – any words they attempted to utter being forced out of their sex-racked bodies with every gasping breath.

'Ohh, ohh – I want you, I want you bad.'

'Take me – then take me, take all of me, Marlene.'

She held his arms down on the bed and kissed his salty lips, forcing open his mouth with her tongue, probing in perfect synchronicity with the motions of his now stiff cock, in and out of her quivering sex . . .

'Stick it up me Sydney. Stick it to me good.'

Marlene was in a whorelike frenzy of passion, bouncing off the bed on her knees. Her shoulder-length auburn hair was soaked through, spraying a constant cooling rain of moisture on their fucking. The sheets were wet with the dripping remnants of their steam-room antics, causing the silky material to stick to their bodies as they rolled over and over, traversing backwards and forwards the expanse of Marlene's king-sized bed. With every thrust of their pounding bodies they continued to roll to and fro, as if one or another were fighting for supremacy. The wet sheets stuck to their bodies, getting caught up in the rolling motion, forming a restrictive cocoon around their sexual excess.

In the frenetic violence of their lovemaking, each bodily contact stung like an electric shock. Poised above Sydney, Marlene slid up and down his shaft, her breasts slapping against his chest, colliding with his face, battering his mind with the urgency of their coupled bodies. Marlene's nipples, hard and wet, teased Sydney like fingers dancing over his body, even a momentary passing contact speaking volumes of erotica.

They were completely enshrouded with wet sheets as their orgasms erupted. Sydney felt his penis explode into Marlene's cunt, feeling as if he was going to thrust her off of his body, but the constriction of the sheet held her tightly against his stomach. The convulsion inside her rent her release at almost the same moment, causing her to squeeze her thighs tightly against Sydney's cock, threatening to devour the orgasming penis into submission. Marlene's cunt pulsed in time to the spurts of come from Sydney's cock that rained deliciously inside her. Her breathing, matching Sydney's gasps, locked on to the undulating rhythm of their sex, hypnotising their exhausted forms into a deep oblivion of new-found love.

It was hours later when Marlene rolled over and out of the damp sheets and looked at the clock. If Sydney was going to make his flight they would have to get moving quickly. Reluctantly, she shook Sydney who was happily recovering from their sexual marathon. Secretly she'd wished that she hadn't woken up, and that they'd slept through the flight's departure, but she didn't want Sydney to blame her for missing his obligations in England.

'Sydney, Sydney – wake up. If you're going to catch your plane we'd better get on the road.'

'Hmmmm.'

'Sydney – wake up. It's at least forty-five minutes to the airport, and we both need a shower.'

Sydney thought of the prospects of catching his flight and

being in court the next day. He thought of Marlene's silky thighs, and it took him but a short time to reach a decision. He'd already missed the final test match and he could easily justify an extended stay in Los Angeles to take care of poor old Archie's affairs. And Carruthers could easily handle the court session for him. Sydney rolled over and straddled a surprised Marlene, holding her arms down he bent to kiss that tender spot just below the ear lobe. After a little nibbling he whispered the words she wanted to hear.

'Does Jay's JayBurger deliver?'

Epilogue

After several more JayBurgers, Sydney stayed in Los Angeles to marry Marlene Neumann. Together they started their own law firm, Neumann and Nats, and today they have a burgeoning list of top entertainment-industry clients.

Tawny Peters and Julia Majors moved into Otto Verge's mansion where they live together in a small attached guest cottage. Otto enjoys the occasional services of both women, although Julia is quite busy these days starring in numerous movies. Otto gave Julia her big break in a movie mysteriously called *Home, James* ...

Andrew Benjamin quit the aerospace industry and opened a surfing shop with Moose in Manhattan Beach. Nancy Thorne never got her screenplay published, but she now runs her own pre-recorded phone fantasy service, Digital Dating, for which she scripts and records most of the calls. They all live together in Hermosa Beach, still relatively happy. Moose is teaching Andrew to surf – nude.

'Sparks Fly' went to number one with a bullet and stayed there for almost a year. As a result of the success, Axle Greeser and Cassandra moved to Bel Air estates where they purchased Rod Stewart's old house. Mrs Greeser is currently pregnant, and Axle has refused to tour until the baby is old enough to accompany them both.

After a brief affair with Neil Waslinger, Kimberly Duke went back to Austin, Texas where she opened a dance studio. It is speculated that Neil had a little something to do with the finances of establishing the business.

Largely because of the Kimberly Duke affair, Neil Waslinger's wife filed for divorce, prompting one of the messiest, dirtiest and costliest divorce cases in US legal history. The result was surprising – Neil's wife was awarded co-ownership of Neil's entertainment agency and the largest cash settlement ever awarded.

The law firm of Neumann and Nats represented Mrs Waslinger.

HELP US TO PLAN THE FUTURE OF EROTIC FICTION –

– and no stamp required!

The Nexus Library is Britain's largest and fastest-growing collection of erotic fiction. We'd like your help to make it even bigger and better.

Like many of our books, the questionnaire below is completely anonymous, so don't feel shy about telling us what you really think. We want to know what kind of people our readers are – we want to know what you like about Nexus books, what you dislike, and what changes you'd like to see.

Just answer the questions on the following pages in the spaces provided; if more than one person would like to take part, please feel free to photocopy the questionnaire. Then tear the pages from the book and send them in an envelope to the address at the end of the questionnaire. No stamp is required.

THE NEXUS QUESTIONNAIRE

SECTION ONE: ABOUT YOU

1.1 Sex *(yes, of course, but try to be serious for just a moment)*
Male ☐ Female ☐

1.2 Age

under 21	☐	21 – 30	☐
31 – 40	☐	41 – 50	☐
51 – 60	☐	over 60	☐

1.3 At what age did you leave full-time education?
still in education ☐ 16 or younger ☐
17 – 19 ☐ 20 or older ☐

1.4 Occupation _____

1.5 Annual household income

under £10,000	☐	£10–£20,000	☐
£20–£30,000	☐	£30–£40,000	☐
over £40,000	☐		

1.6 Where do you live?
Please write in the county in which you live (for example Hampshire), or the city if you live in a large metropolitan area (for example Manchester) _____

SECTION TWO : ABOUT BUYING NEXUS BOOKS

2.1 How did you acquire this book?

I bought it myself ☐   My partner bought it ☐
I borrowed it/found it ☐

2.2 If this book was bought ...

... in which town or city? _____

... in what sort of shop: High Street bookshop ☐
local newsagent ☐
at a railway station ☐
at an airport ☐
at motorway services ☐

other: _____

2.3 Have you ever had difficulty finding Nexus books on sale?

Yes ☐   No ☐

If you have had difficulty in buying Nexus books, where would you like to be able to buy them?

... in which town or city _____

... in what sort of shop from
list in previous question _____

2.4 Have you ever been reluctant to buy a Nexus book because of the sexual nature of the cover picture?

Yes ☐   No ☐

2.5 Please tick which of the following statements you agree with:

I find some Nexus cover pictures offensive/
too blatant ☐

I would be less embarassed about buying Nexus
books if the cover pictures were less blatant ☐

I think that in general the pictures on Nexus books
are about right ☐

I think Nexus cover pictures should be as sexy
as possible ☐

SECTION THREE: ABOUT NEXUS BOOKS

3.1 How many Nexus books do you own? _____

3.2 Roughly how many Nexus books have you read? _____

3.3 What are your three favourite Nexus books?
    First choice   _____
    Second Choice _____
    Third Choice   _____

3.4 What are your three favourite Nexus cover pictures?
    First choice   _____
    Second choice _____
    Third choice   _____

SECTION FOUR: ABOUT YOUR IDEAL EROTIC NOVEL

We want to publish books you want to read – so this is your chance
to tell us exactly what your ideal erotic novel would be like.

4.1 Using a scale of 1 to 5 (1 = no interest at all, 5 = your
ideal), please rate the following possible settings for an
erotic novel:
    Medieval/barbarian/sword 'n' sorcery ☐
    Renaissance/Elizabethan/Restoration ☐
    Victorian/Edwardian ☐
    1920s & 1930s – the Jazz Age ☐
    Present day ☐
    Future/Science Fiction ☐

4.2 Using the same scale of 1 to 5, please rate the following
styles in which an erotic novel could be written:
    Realistic, down to earth, set in real life ☐
    Escapist fantasy, but just about believable ☐
    Completely unreal, impressionistic, dreamlike ☐

4.3 Would you prefer your ideal erotic novel to be written from
the viewpoint of the main male characters or the main
female characters?
    Male   ☐   Female   ☐

4.4 Is there one particular setting or subject matter that your
ideal erotic novel would contain?
_____

SECTION FIVE: LAST WORDS

5.1   What do you like best about Nexus books?

_____

_____

5.2   What do you most dislike about Nexus books?

_____

_____

5.3   In what way, if any, would you like to change Nexus covers?

_____

_____

5.4   Here's a space for any other comments:

_____

_____

_____

_____

_____

_____

_____

_____

_____

_____

_____

Thank you for completing this questionnaire. Now tear it out of the book – carefully! – put it in an envelope and send it to:

Nexus Books
FREEPOST
London
W10 5BR

No stamp is required.

Japan Answers

cooking service

(Epot 4/4 21)

man well

R 30
lodges

THE BEST IN EROTIC READING – BY POST

The Nexus Library of Erotica – over a hundred volumes – is available from many booksellers and newsagents. If you have any difficulty obtaining the books you require, you can order them by post. Photocopy the list below, or tear the list out of the book; then tick the titles you want and fill in the form at the end of the list. Titles marked 1992 are not yet available: please do not try to order them – just look out for them in the shops!

EDWARDIAN, VICTORIAN & OLDER EROTICA

ADVENTURES OF A SCHOOLBOY	Anonymous	£3.99	
THE AUTOBIOGRAPHY OF A FLEA	Anonymous	£2.99	
BEATRICE	Anonymous	£3.99	
THE BOUDOIR	Anonymous	£3.99	
THE DIARY OF A CHAMBERMAID	Mirabeau	£2.99	
THE LIFTED CURTAIN	Mirabeau	£3.50	
EVELINE	Anonymous	£2.99	
MORE EVELINE	Anonymous	£3.99	
FESTIVAL OF VENUS	Anonymous	£4.50	1992
'FRANK' & I	Anonymous	£2.99	
GARDENS OF DESIRE	Roger Rougiere	£4.50	1992
OH, WICKED COUNTRY	Anonymous	£3.50	
LASCIVIOUS SCENES	Anonymous	£4.50	1992
THE LASCIVIOUS MONK	Anonymous	£2.99	
LAURA MIDDLETON	Anonymous	£3.99	
A MAN WITH A MAID 1	Anonymous	£3.50	
A MAN WITH A MAID 2	Anonymous	£3.50	
A MAN WITH A MAID 3	Anonymous	£3.50	
MAUDIE	Anonymous	£2.99	
THE MEMOIRS OF DOLLY MORTON	Anonymous	£3.99	

A NIGHT IN A MOORISH HAREM	Anonymous	£3.99	
PARISIAN FROLICS	Anonymous	£2.99	
PLEASURE BOUND	Anonymous	£3.99	
THE PLEASURES OF LOLOTTE	Andrea de Nerciat	£3.99	
THE PRIMA DONNA	Anonymous	£2.99	
RANDIANA	Anonymous	£4.50	
REGINE	E.K.	£2.99	
THE ROMANCE OF LUST 1	Anonymous	£3.99	
THE ROMANCE OF LUST 2	Anonymous	£2.99	
ROSA FIELDING	Anonymous	£2.99	
SUBURBAN SOULS 1	Anonymous	£2.99	
SUBURBAN SOULS 2	Anonymous	£2.50	
THREE TIMES A WOMAN	Anonymous	£2.99	
THE TWO SISTERS	Anonymous	£3.99	
VIOLETTE	Anonymous	£2.99	

"THE JAZZ AGE"

ALTAR OF VENUS	Anonymous	£2.99	
THE SECRET GARDEN ROOM	Georgette de la Tour	£3.50	
BEHIND THE BEADED CURTAIN	Georgette de la Tour	£3.50	
BLANCHE	Anonymous	£3.99	
BLUE ANGEL NIGHTS	Margarete von Falkensee	£2.99	
BLUE ANGEL DAYS	Margarete von Falkensee	£3.99	
BLUE ANGEL SECRETS	Margarete von Falkensee	£2.99	
CAROUSEL	Anonymous	£3.99	
CONFESSIONS OF AN ENGLISH MAID	Anonymous	£3.99	
FLOSSIE	Anonymous	£2.50	
SABINE	Anonymous	£3.99	
PLAISIR D'AMOUR	Anne-Marie Villefranche	£2.99	
FOLIES D'AMOUR	Anne-Marie Villefranche	£2.99	
JOIE D'AMOUR	Anne-Marie Villefranche	£3.99	
MYSTERE D'AMOUR	Anne-Marie Villefranche	£3.99	
SECRETS D'AMOUR	Anne-Marie Villefranche	£3.50	
SOUVENIR D'AMOUR	Anne-Marie Villefranche	£3.99	
SPIES IN SILK	Piers Falconer	£4.50	1992

CONTEMPORARY EROTICA

AMAZONS	Erin Caine	£3.99	1992
COCKTAILS	Stanley Carten	£3.99	
CITY OF ONE-NIGHT STANDS	Stanley Carten	£4.50	1992
CONTOURS OF DARKNESS	Marco Vassi	£3.50	
THE GENTLE DEGENERATES	Marco Vassi	£3.99	

MIND BLOWER	Marco Vassi	£3.50	
THE SALINE SOLUTION	Marco Vassi	£2.99	
DARK FANTASIES	Nigel Anthony	£3.99	
THE DAYS AND NIGHTS OF MIGUMI	P.M.	£3.99	
THE LATIN LOVER	P.M.	£3.99	
THE DEVIL'S ADVOCATE	Anonymous	£3.99	
DIPLOMATIC SECRETS	Antoine Lelouche	£3.50	
DIPLOMATIC PLEASURES	Antoine Lelouche	£3.50	
DIPLOMATIC DIVERSIONS	Antoine Lelouche	£3.99	1992
ENGINE OF DESIRE	Alexis Arven	£3.99	
DIRTY WORK	Alexis Arven	£3.99	
DREAMS OF FAIR WOMEN	Celeste Arden	£2.99	
THE FANTASY HUNTERS	Celeste Arden	£3.99	
A GALLERY OF NUDES	Anthony Grey	£4.50	
THE GIRL FROM PAGE 3	Mike Angelo	£3.99	
THE INSTITUTE	Maria del Rey	£3.99	1992
LAURE-ANNE	Laure-Anne	£2.99	
LAURE-ANNE ENCORE	Laure-Anne	£2.99	
LAURE-ANNE TOUJOURS	Laure-Anne	£3.50	
Ms DEEDES AT HOME	Carole Andrews	£4.50	1992
MY SEX MY SOUL	Amelia Greene	£2.99	
ONE WEEK IN THE PRIVATE HOUSE	Esme Ombreux	£3.99	
PALACE OF SWEETHEARTS	Delver Maddingley	£4.50	1992
THE SECRET WEB	Jane-Anne Roberts	£3.50	
STEPHANIE	Susanna Hughes	£3.99	
STEPHANIE'S CASTLE	Susanna Hughes	£4.50	1992
THE DOMINO TATTOO	Cyrian Amberlake	£3.99	
THE DOMINA ENIGMA	Cyrian Amberlake	£3.99	
THE DOMINO QUEEN	Cyrian Amberlake	£3.99	

EROTIC SCIENCE FICTION

PLEASUREHOUSE 13	Agnetha Anders	£3.99	
THE LAST DAYS OF THE PLEASUREHOUSE	Agnetha Anders	£4.50	1992
WICKED	Andrea Arven	£3.99	
WILD	Andrea Arven	£4.50	1992

ANCIENT & FANTASY SETTINGS

CHAMPIONS OF LOVE	Anonymous	£3.99	
CHAMPIONS OF DESIRE	Anonymous	£3.50	
CHAMPIONS OF PLEASURE	Anonymous	£3.50	
THE SLAVE OF LIDIR	Aran Ashe	£3.99	
THE DUNGEONS OF LIDIR	Aran Ashe	£3.99	

THE FOREST OF BONDAGE	Aran Ashe	£3.99	
PLEASURE ISLAND	Aran Ashe	£4.50	1992
ROMAN ORGY	Marcus van Heller	£4.50	1992

CONTEMPORARY FRENCH EROTICA (translated into English)

EXPLOITS OF A YOUNG DON JUAN	Anonymous	£2.99	
INDISCREET MEMOIRS	Alain Dorval	£2.99	
INSTRUMENT OF PLEASURE	Celeste Piano	£3.99	
JOY	Joy Laurey	£2.99	
JOY AND JOAN	Joy Laurey	£2.99	
JOY IN LOVE	Joy Laurey	£2.75	
LILIANE	Paul Verguin	£3.50	
MANDOLINE	Anonymous	£3.99	
LUST IN PARIS	Antoine S.	£2.99	
NYMPH IN PARIS	Galia S.	£2.99	
SCARLET NIGHTS	Juan Muntaner	£3.99	
SENSUAL LIAISONS	Anonymous	£3.50	
SENSUAL SECRETS	Anonymous	£3.99	
THE NEW STORY OF O	Anonymous	£3.50	
THE IMAGE	Jean de Berg	£3.99	1992
VIRGINIE	Nathalie Perreau	£4.50	1992
THE PAPER WOMAN	Francoise Rey	£4.50	1992

SAMPLERS & COLLECTIONS

EROTICON	ed. J-P Spencer	£3.99	
EROTICON 2	ed. J-P Spencer	£3.99	
EROTICON 3	ed. J-P Spencer	£2.99	
EROTICON 4	ed. J-P Spencer	£3.99	
THE FIESTA LETTERS	ed. Chris Lloyd	£2.99	
THE PLEASURES OF LOVING	ed. Maren Sell	£2.99	

NON-FICTION

HOW TO DRIVE YOUR MAN WILD IN BED	Graham Masterton	£3.99	
HOW TO DRIVE YOUR WOMAN WILD IN BED	Graham Masterton	£3.99	
HOW TO BE THE PERFECT LOVER	Graham Masterton	£2.99	
FEMALE SEXUAL AWARENESS	Barry & Emily McCarthy	£4.99	
WHAT MEN WANT	Susan Crain Bakos	£3.99	
YOUR SEXUAL SECRETS	Marty Klein	£3.99	

Please send me the books I have ticked above.

Name   ....

Address ....

        ....

        ....Post code ....

Send to: **Nexus Books Cash Sales, PO Box 11, Falmouth, Cornwall, TR10 9EN**

Please enclose a cheque or postal order, made payable to **Nexus Books**, to the value of the books you have ordered plus postage and packing costs as follows:

UK and BFPO – £1.00 for the first book, 50p for the second book, and 30p for each subsequent book to a maximum of £3.00;

Overseas (including Republic of Ireland) – £2.00 for the first book, £1.00 for the second book, and 50p for each subsequent book.

If you would prefer to pay by VISA or ACCESS/MASTERCARD, please write your card number here:

— — — —   — — — —   — — — —   — — — —

Signature: _____